A SECOND CHANCE AT LOVE

"I don't want to be just friends. I can't do it," Yost said. He stood up and paced back and forth in front of her. "Be honest with me, Martha Sue. Do you truly want nothing more than a friendship between us?"

He looked at her with such intensity that she couldn't look away. She certainly couldn't lie to him. "If your son, Jonah, loved me, I would marry you tomorrow."

His whole face lit up like a bonfire, and he sat next to her again. "*Ach*, Martha Sue, that is all I need to hear."

"But Jonah doesn't love me, and I won't be the reason his world crumbles around his ears."

"Can we try again?" he said breathlessly. "Please tell me it's not too late. Will you still consider marrying me?"

"I don't know what to say, Yost."

"With Gotte, all things are possible," he said.

She smiled in spite of herself. "Would you quit quoting scripture? It makes me think you know something I don't."

"I have a scripture for every occasion."

"For sure and certain you do." She sighed and gazed into his eyes. She saw so much love there, she couldn't bear to disappoint him. Couldn't bear to give up on him just yet. "I think I'm going to regret this, but it's not too late, even for you."

Second Chances on Huckleberry Hill

JENNIFER BECKSTRAND

ZEBRA BOOKS
Kensington Publishing Corp.
www.kensingtonbooks.com

ZEBRA BOOKS are published by

Kensington Publishing Corp.
119 West 40th Street
New York, NY 10018

All Kensington titles, imprints, and distributed lines are available at special quantity discounts for bulk purchases for sales promotion, premiums, fund-raising, and educational or institutional use.

Special book excerpts or customized printings can also be created to fit specific needs. For details, write or phone the office of the Kensington Sales Manager: Kensington Publishing Corp., 119 West 40th Street, New York, NY 10018. Attn. Sales Department. Phone: 1-800-221-2647.

Zebra and the Z logo Reg. U.S. Pat. & TM Off.
Bouquet Reg. U.S. Pat. & TM Off.

First Printing: June 2023
ISBN-13: 978-1-4201-5528-0
ISBN-13: 978-1-4201-5529-7 (eBook)

10 9 8 7 6 5 4 3 2 1

Printed in the United States of America

Chapter 1

Martha Sue Helmuth stomped down the cellar stairs wondering just how she'd gotten herself into this mess.

She loved Christmas. She *adored* Christmas. Usually by December first every year she had a silly grin on her face that didn't leave until well into January. Christmas celebrations, school Christmas programs, and Christmas goodies made her wildly happy. But this year, every smidgen of Christmas cheer had completely abandoned her. She didn't want to sing Christmas carols or hear her relatives wish each other "*Frehlicher Grischtdaag*." She did not want to decorate the house with pine boughs or light candles or go on a sleigh ride.

She wanted to put on her pajamas, sit next to Mammi's woodstove, and read a book—something depressing like *Martyr's Mirror* or *Tongue Screws and Testimonies*. But she couldn't even do that because it was Christmas Eve, and at least a dozen cousins and assorted aunts and uncles congregated in Mammi and Dawdi's great room for the family's traditional Christmas Eve dinner and carol singing.

Martha Sue had volunteered to fetch Mammi Helmuth's famous—or infamous—huckleberry raisin jelly just so she could be alone with her unpleasant thoughts for two minutes instead of having to put on a *gute* face for her merry, filled-with-the-Christmas-spirit relatives. Huckleberry raisin jelly didn't sound half bad, but Mammi meant for the jelly to go on her famous—or infamous—cheesy jalapeno bread at tonight's Christmas Eve party. It didn't seem a very appetizing combination, but Mammi was famous—or infamous—for her out-of-the-ordinary recipes and stomach-churning food creations.

If she didn't want to starve, Martha Sue was going to have to take over the cooking while she stayed here with Mammi and Dawdi.

Martha Sue had arrived at Mammi and Dawdi's house three days ago, and she wasn't here just for the Christmas holiday. She'd be staying with Mammi and Dawdi all winter and into the spring. Maybe longer. Martha Sue wasn't exactly sure whose idea it had been for her to come to stay with her grandparents. Mamm had wanted her to get out and see the world. And by "get out and see the world," Mamm had meant getting out of Ohio and going to Wisconsin.

Dat said Martha Sue's visit was a *gute* way for someone in the family to keep a close eye on Mammi and Dawdi. They weren't getting any younger—Dawdi was eighty-seven—and Dat thought they might need some help. Mammi and Dawdi were old, but they seemed perfectly capable of taking care of themselves and their farm. Mammi was healthy enough to knit a dozen pot holders each week, cook three simply awful meals a day, and gather eggs every morning, rain or shine. Dawdi mucked out the barn and hitched up the horse like a forty-year-old. They didn't need Martha Sue's help.

Martha Sue had been so eager to get out of Charm, Ohio, that she hadn't paused to consider why Dat or Mamm or Mammi really wanted her here in Bonduel, Wisconsin. And then, three days ago when she'd stepped off the bus and had seen Mammi's beaming face, Martha Sue had suddenly known why she was here. She'd been tricked into coming so Mammi and Dawdi could find her a husband.

Why hadn't she realized it before she had made the long trip to Bonduel? Mammi and Dawdi were famous— or infamous—in the family for being persistent and successful matchmakers to many of their grandchildren, and Martha Sue was the next victim on the list. She was thirty years old, and there were no prospects in Charm. *Ach*, *vell*, no prospects she hadn't already rejected, and she certainly wasn't going to give Yost Beiler a sideways glance ever again. Lord willing, her moving to Wisconsin would be the final nail in the coffin of that relationship.

Yost was the real reason Martha Sue had agreed to come to Bonduel, no matter what Mamm's or Mammi's reasons were.

Martha Sue wiped a foolish tear from her cheek. She didn't want to think about Yost Beiler or any other man from Charm or any other man from anywhere else, for that matter. She didn't want Mammi and Dawdi to find her a husband, because at this point it would be an old bachelor who was sick of cooking for himself or someone with very bad eyesight who was willing to settle for a plain Amish *maedel*. It didn't matter that Mammi and Dawdi had found suitable matches for more than a dozen of their grandchildren. They wouldn't find anyone Martha Sue wanted to marry, and no one who would want to marry her.

And that was that.

Mammi was the dearest soul in the world, and she was going to be very disappointed that Martha Sue didn't want her help finding a husband. But it would be best to let Mammi down sooner than later, before she invited half the single Amish men in Bonduel to dinner.

Martha Sue found a pint of deep purple huckleberry raisin jelly on the shelf next to a row of bottles labeled "Pickled Kitchen Scraps." She didn't even want to know what that was. Huckleberry raisin jelly on cheesy jalapeno bread was bad enough.

Upstairs, someone knocked on the front door, and there were muted Christmas greetings and laughter. The family was still gathering. Now would be the perfect time to mention to her grandparents that she didn't want a husband and to please not try to set her up with anybody. Mammi would be too distracted to be upset, Dawdi wouldn't care, and then maybe Martha Sue could enjoy the party.

She hurried up the stairs and into the great room. At least another dozen relatives had arrived since she'd been downstairs. Cousin Titus and his wife, Katie Rose, knelt next to Dawdi's easy chair having a conversation with Dawdi while their two little girls ran around the great room with some cousins. Several of Martha Sue's cousins and aunts busied themselves in the kitchen with dinner preparations. Mammi didn't fix Christmas Eve dinner anymore. Her daughters had taken over the meal several years ago with the excuse of easing Mammi's burden with the added benefit that the Christmas Eve dinner was actually something everyone enjoyed eating.

Mammi sat in her rocker holding the hand of little Isaac, Moses and Lia's youngest, listening intently as he told her something that looked to be very important to a three-year-old. Mary Anne and Jethro were there with their twins, as well as Martha Sue's sister Mandy and Mandy's family. Even Cassie and Zach Reynolds had come. Cassie had jumped the fence a few years ago and married Zach, who was a very important doctor in Chicago. Cassie hadn't been baptized, so she hadn't been shunned, and everyone loved having them at get-togethers because Zach told the most interesting medical stories and didn't mind giving piggyback rides to all the great-grandchildren. Zach also gave free medical advice, and he was always cornered at these gatherings by anxious mothers wanting him to look in their children's ears or curious adults wanting him to diagnose a rash or a weird mole.

Martha Sue handed her sister Mandy the jelly. Mandy grimaced when she read the label, then took it into the kitchen to add to the goodies piling up on the counter. Martha Sue sat on the sofa next to Mammi's rocker and waited for Isaac to finish his story about almost getting stepped on by a cow. Mammi listened and nodded at all the right moments and kissed Isaac's finger, which had been injured in a separate incident with a wringer washer.

Isaac skipped off to play with his cousins, and Martha Sue found her opportunity. She leaned closer to Mammi. "Mammi, *denki* for letting me stay here with you for a few months."

Mammi's eyes sparkled. "It's my pleasure." She patted Martha Sue's cheek. "You look so much like your mother. Just as pretty as a picture. I know some boys who will be very interested to meet you."

"Well, Mammi, I want to talk to you about that."

"Oh? About what?"

"Mammi," Martha Sue said, taking her *mammi*'s hand. "I love you very much."

"And I love you. I'm shocked that some nice boy hasn't snatched you up already."

Martha Sue cleared her throat. "That's what I want to talk to you about. I know that you invited me here so you could find me a husband."

Mammi's eyes widened in surprise, and then she grinned. "*Ach*, *vell*, I guess the cat is out of the bag. Who told you? Was it Felty? He's usually so *gute* at keeping secrets."

"*Nae*. I figured it out on my own. But I'm not here to meet boys. I'm here to spend time with you and Dawdi."

Mammi blew a puff of air from between her lips. "*Ach*, why would you want to spend time with us? We're old and boring. You need to be with people your own age. You're so happy and bubbly all the time, people are naturally drawn to you, and you are naturally drawn to other people."

Martha Sue was going to have to be more blunt. "I'm old too, Mammi. Nobody wants to marry me. It would be an awful chore for you to have to find me a husband."

Mammi patted Martha Sue's hand. "But, my dear, it's not a chore. I love helping my grandchildren find spouses." She gestured around the room. "Your *dawdi* and I have helped at least a dozen people in this very room to *gute* marriages. It would be our pleasure to do the same for you. No thanks necessary."

"But I don't want a husband."

She must have said that louder than she thought because the adult chatter in the room went silent. *Die kinner* still made a commotion, but the noise level in the room dropped considerably. Twenty pairs of eyes stared at her. She felt her face get warm. This was definitely the worst Christmas ever.

"*Ach*," Mammi said. "You don't mean that. Everybody wants to get married."

"Not everybody," Martha Sue said, because there really was nothing to do but stand her ground. "No one wants to marry me." That wasn't precisely true, but Martha Sue wasn't about to try to explain Yost Beiler.

Dawdi patted the arm of his easy chair. "That's just what your *mammi* thought when she was a girl. She didn't believe anyone wanted to marry her, but every boy in Bonduel was secretly in love with her."

Mammi blushed from her neck to the top of her forehead. "*Ach*, Felty, no one was in love with me but you.

And maybe not even you. Maybe you only married me for my cooking."

Dawdi laughed. "For sure and certain I love your cooking, Annie-banannie, but I was so in love with you, I wouldn't have cared if you served cardboard every night for dinner. I would marry you all over again a thousand times."

Martha Sue wasn't sure if it was a deliberate attempt to distract her, but Mammi and Dawdi completely forgot about Martha Sue as they told everyone the story of how they fell in love. It was a lovely story with Red Hot cinnamon rolls, Christmas caroling, and plenty of knitted scarves to go around.

After Dawdi and Mammi finished their story, Mammi gave Martha Sue a grandmotherly smile. "You see, dear, you may not know it yet, but you definitely want a husband."

Martha Sue's heart sank to her toes. "I don't think it will work for me the way it worked for you."

"Of course not. It will be your own beautiful love story." Mammi's smile faltered. "The truth is, I've already found you a husband. He's coming after dinner to meet you."

Most of Martha Sue's relatives laughed. Some, like Mandy, looked as if they felt sorry for her. Martha Sue felt sorry for herself.

Someone knocked on the door, and Martha Sue nearly jumped out of her skin.

Mammi drew her brows together. "I don't like tardiness, but I dislike earliness even more."

Martha Sue's cousin Moses grinned at her. "You might as well answer the door. Apparently it's for you."

Martha Sue trudged to the door as if she were going toward her doom. It didn't help that every eye in the room was focused on her. She opened the door and lost the ability to breathe. Yost Beiler stood on Mammi's porch bundled up like a snowman.

Chapter 2

"*Hallo*, Martha Sue. *Vie gehts?*" A doubtful smile played at Yost's mouth.

Yost Beiler? Mammi had brought Martha Sue to Huckleberry Hill to match her up with Yost Beiler from Charm, Ohio?

Mammi stood and clapped her hands, obviously willing to overlook the transgression of early arrival. "Invite him in, Martha. I'd like everybody to meet him."

Martha Sue stepped back so Yost could come into the house, but as soon as he crossed the threshold, Mammi's smile stiffened. "You're not Vernon Schmucker."

Puzzled, Yost looked behind him and turned back to Mammi. "Um, *nae*, I'm not. I just came to take Martha Sue back to Charm."

Martha Sue folded her arms. "You're not taking me anywhere."

Yost frowned. "I'm sorry. Poor choice of words." He looked at Mammi. "I came to beg Martha Sue to come back."

Martha Sue's heart beat an irregular rhythm. This was one of the things she most adored about Yost but also made her the most aggravated. Yost was always willing to lay his heart out for everyone to see. She would have to be equally as blunt, and she hated hurting him. "I'm not going back," she said.

"Of course you're not going back," Mammi said. "You haven't met Vernon Schmucker yet."

Yost's expression fell. "Who . . . who is Vernon Schmucker?"

Mammi's look of confusion faded, and she gave Yost a genuine smile. "This isn't your fault, young man. How could you have known what I had planned for Martha Sue? We'd love it if you stayed for dinner, but I would be wonderful grateful if you would leave before seven. It would be quite awkward if Vernon showed up and Martha Sue's boyfriend was here."

"He's not my boyfriend," Martha Sue said, but she said it gently, almost regretfully, because she just couldn't be harsh with Yost, not after everything that had gone on between them. He'd made a lot of effort to come all this way.

Mammi seemed unruffled. "*Ach*, Felty, this is more exciting than I could have hoped. A love triangle."

Yost glanced at Martha Sue, seeking her approval, which he wasn't going to get. "I'd love to stay for dinner."

Mammi shook Yost's hand. "Well, then, welcome, and *Frehlicher Grischtdaag*."

"Merry Christmas to you too," Yost said.

Mammi took Yost's coat, hat, and scarf and led him to the sofa. "Now Martha Sue will have two men to choose from." Martha Sue pressed her lips together as Mammi showed Yost her latest knitting project and gave him a pot holder to take home, even though he wasn't Vernon Schmucker.

There was nothing Martha Sue could do but ignore Yost completely and help the others get Christmas dinner on the table. She barely paid attention as Titus and Moses engaged Yost in a conversation about farming and what crops Yost was going to plant this year. She didn't even notice when Yost told her cousins about his son, Jonah, and about how his first wife had died nine years ago. She couldn't have cared less when Yost recounted his bus ride to Bonduel in the heavy snowstorm and how he had hired a driver to bring him here to Huckleberry Hill.

Yost helped Moses and Zach carry the sofa into the back hall, and they quickly set up two folding tables for *die kinner* in the great room. The adults used the big table that Dawdi had built for Mammi when they were first married. That table had seen thirteen children come and go, plus too many relatives and friends to count.

Because Mammi and Dawdi had taken so long to tell the story of how they met, dinner was almost an hour late, which meant they had fifteen minutes to eat before Vernon Schmucker arrived. Martha Sue's dread grew like poison ivy. She did not want to eat Christmas Eve dinner while Yost stared at her with those piercing blue eyes. She didn't want to think about how far Yost had come only to be rejected. Again. She didn't want to be reminded about how much she loved him while trying to gag down Mammi's cheesy jalapeno bread. She most certainly didn't want to have second thoughts about her decision. What was done was done, and it was best if

Yost moved on with his life. Martha Sue would never move on with hers.

What made it worse was that Mammi had already found a potential husband for Martha Sue, and Martha Sue didn't want to meet him. She most certainly didn't want Yost to meet him. Yost would be hurt at the thought of Martha Sue marrying someone else, and he didn't deserve even one more ounce of heartache. She just wanted him to be happy—wildly, perfectly happy—without Martha Sue in his life. Was that too much to ask?

Maybe the cousins and aunts and uncles thought they were being kind or maybe they were teasing her, but when they all sat down to eat, they arranged themselves so that Martha Sue and Yost were forced to sit next to each other. Martha Sue profoundly felt the awkwardness of the moment. Her face got warm, and her ears started ringing. *Ach*, to be anywhere but here! Was it too cold to spend Christmas Eve in the barn with the cow? She kept her head down and tried to make herself invisible. If no one noticed her, she might be able to get through dinner without being sick.

After silent prayer, Mammi passed her cheesy jalapeno bread around the table. "Now, Yost," she said, "I hope you don't think I'm being rude, but I don't want Martha Sue making any final decisions about marriage until she meets Vernon."

Yost nodded in his solemn, stoic fashion. "Even though I want Martha Sue to pick me, I want her to be certain of her choice."

A few uncomfortable seconds of silence followed when Martha Sue was sure every eye at the table was on her. They no doubt wondered why she was so cruel to a man who was clearly in love with her. Zach Reynolds must have noticed Martha Sue's distress, because he started in on a wonderful, horrible story about a leg amputation he'd performed last week. Zach almost never talked about medical procedures during dinner, but he must have recognized that this was an emergency. Martha Sue was deeply grateful.

Soon, all the family but Martha Sue and Yost were eating and visiting and laughing. Martha Sue nibbled on a piece of corn, and Yost had taken three sips of water. He leaned closer to her and whispered, "Who is Vernon Schmucker?" Yost was unfailingly kind. There wasn't an ounce of censure in his voice.

Martha Sue nearly choked on a kernel of corn. She took a drink of water. "I . . . I don't know him."

"But you came all this way to meet him?"

"I didn't come all this way to meet anybody. Mammi invited me, and you know very well why I had to leave."

"You didn't have to leave," he said. His voice was raw with pain, even as his expression was unreadable. He was obviously trying to keep his emotions in check for the relatives' benefit. His eyes searched her face. She had to look away. "Please won't you come back? I've missed you. I've missed your smile and your laugh. It seems like you used to laugh almost as often as you took a breath."

She swallowed hard and tamped down the regret that threatened to bubble out of her throat. She couldn't indulge in regret. Regret would lead to uncertainty, and uncertainty would lead to giving in. She had to be strong for both Yost and herself. "Where is Jonah?" she said, because changing the subject was easier than talking about things that couldn't be changed.

He winced as if she'd poked him with a pin. "Spending Christmas with my *mamm* and *dat*."

"And he doesn't mind that you're here?"

Yost looked stricken. He closed his eyes and lowered his head. "You know very well that he does."

She shouldn't have asked that. It only hurt Yost to be reminded. But maybe he needed the reminder. His coming here meant he had forgotten why they couldn't be married.

Dawdi piled a heaping helping of mashed potatoes on his plate. "So, Yost, tell us about yourself. All we know is that you like our granddaughter enough to take the twelve-hour trip to Bonduel in a snowstorm." He stroked his beard. "And that you're married or were once married." Married Amish men grew beards. Unmarried Amish men were clean-shaven. Widowers usually kept their beards, and Yost had a nice beard without a speck of gray. "Since you like my granddaughter, Lord willing, you're a widower."

Mammi threw up her hands in dismay and sent her fork flying into the kitchen behind her. "Felty, what a shocking thing to say." She stood, maneuvered around the table, and pulled another fork from the drawer.

"What did I say?" asked Dawdi.

"You said you hope he's a widower. It's a terrible thing to *hope* that someone's wife is dead."

Dawdi frowned. "*Ach*, I suppose you're right, Annie.

I'm just concerned that a married man is pursuing our granddaughter."

"You're very sensible, as always, Felty." Mammi sat back down, propped her fork on the table like a staff, and leaned toward Yost. "You're not married, are you?"

Yost leaned forward as well. "Let me put your mind at ease, Anna. I'm not married."

"*Ach, vell,* that is *gute* news." She frowned to herself. "But not *gute* news that you are a widower. Or *are* you a widower? Some single men grow beards. If you aren't a widower, I take back my condolences."

Yost had been devastated by his wife's death, but time had a way of smoothing out the sharp edges, softening the pain, and sweetening the memories. He smiled kindly at Mammi. "My wife died nine years ago. Cancer. It was very hard."

"We're very sorry to hear that," Zach said.

"But *froh* you're not married," Mammi said. She drew her brows together and fell silent, obviously unsure if it was more appropriate to be glad or sad.

"Do you have children?" Aendi Esther asked.

Yost's gaze flicked in Martha Sue's direction. "*Jah.* I have one son. Jonah. He is thirteen years old."

"*Ach,* I love that age," Mammi said. "They're so full of life. Everything is an adventure." She beamed at Martha Sue. "Don't you just adore him?"

Martha Sue stared at her plate, struck mute by the question. She couldn't have yelled "Fire!" if the house was burning.

Yost nodded. "He certainly knows how to get himself into mischief."

"So sad to grow up without a *mater,*" Mammi said.

"But I'm glad he still has a *fater*." The wrinkles deepened around her eyes, and she went quiet. She was obviously torn, once again, between being sad and glad.

Yost picked up his fork. "He was young enough that he doesn't even remember his *mater*. It's both sad and a blessing. We've always been very close. We do everything together because we've always only had each other." He glanced at Martha Sue and laid his fork on the table as if he'd just lost his appetite.

"*Ach*, that's *wunderbarr*," Mammi said. "Both Felty and I were very close to our *faters*. I lost my *mater* when I was nine, and my *dat* raised me. He is the one who taught me how to cook."

Martha Sue felt an inkling of a smile for the first time since she'd sat down at the table. They had Grossdawdi Yoder to blame for Mammi's bad cooking.

Any amusement Martha Sue might have felt fled the minute someone knocked on the door. Cousin Katie was closest to the door so she stood and opened it. A wall of frigid air blew in, along with hundreds of snowflakes. "*Cum reu*," Katie said, stepping back to let the newcomer in.

Whoever it was looked very much like a real snowman. He was covered in snow from head to toe, and his belly was as round and large as any well-built snowman. He wore a black coat, a straw hat, and a blue scarf on his head that came down around his ears and was knotted around his chin. Katie closed the door, and the stranger stomped his boots on the mat and took off his hat and scarf.

"Vernon," Mammi exclaimed. "You're here." She jumped from her seat at the table, bustled to Vernon's side, and brushed some of the snow off Vernon's coat. "Did you have a hard time making it up the hill?"

Breathing heavily, Vernon took off his coat and handed it to Katie. "I had to walk the horse up the hill pulling the sleigh without me in it." He looked around the table until his gaze landed on Martha Sue. He waggled his eyebrows up and down. "I kept going because you promised there would be pie. And a pretty girl."

Martha Sue strangled the napkin in her hands. Vernon had a pasty complexion, a missing tooth, and unruly eyebrows that floated over his face like two hairy caterpillars. Martha Sue's heart fell to her toes. This was the man Mammi wanted her to marry? Just how desperate did she think Martha Sue was?

Martha Sue took a deep breath and silently scolded herself. She of all people shouldn't be so quick to judge a book by its cover. She certainly wasn't pretty enough to have high expectations. But even if Vernon was the nicest, handsomest man in the world, it didn't matter to Martha Sue. She had decided to never marry.

Mammi seemed pleased that Vernon had noticed Martha Sue first thing. "Something unexpected has happened, Vernon," she said, gushing with excitement and anticipation. "I didn't know when I invited you, but there is more than one person interested in Martha Sue." She motioned to Yost. "This is Martha Sue's boyfriend, Yost."

If Martha Sue hadn't been so mortified, the look of horror on Vernon's face would have made her laugh out loud. Cousin Moses cleared his throat. Zach Reynolds looked as if he was trying very hard not to laugh. Mandy's eyes were as round as buggy wheels. The discomfort and embarrassment in the room could only have been cut with a very sharp knife.

Martha Sue had never liked uncomfortable situations, especially uncomfortable situations where she was the reason for the discomfort. She considered throwing a napkin over her head and running from the room. Unfortunately she wouldn't get very far because *die kinner* were packed in the great room like sardines, the back hall was blocked by a sofa, and she wasn't a very *gute* jumper. She could crawl under the table, but she'd surely get kicked in the face, and then she'd have a swollen nose and wounded pride. She could start laughing hysterically, as if Mammi had told a hilarious joke, but she'd be the only one laughing. *Ach*, *vell*, Zach Reynolds might join in because he was on the verge of laughter already, but she couldn't hope that anyone else would.

The only sensible thing to do was stare faithfully into her water glass and pretend Mammi hadn't just ruined every shred of dignity she had left.

"Join us for dinner," Mammi said. She furrowed her brow. "Unless you've already eaten. I don't want you to feel overstuffed for your first date with my granddaughter."

Now it was a date? Even Martha Sue's water glass started to sweat.

"Do you have brown gravy or turkey gravy for those mashed potatoes?" Vernon asked.

Martha Sue's heart did a backflip when Yost stood up, strode to Vernon, and vigorously shook his hand. "It is wonderful *gute* to meet you, Vernon. *Cum*, sit down." Vernon looked mildly suspicious as Yost grabbed one of the extra folding chairs leaning against the wall. "Moses, Zach, could you make room?" Everyone on Martha Sue's side of the table scooted around to make room for another chair. Martha Sue's throat tightened as Yost planted Vernon's chair next to his own so Yost would be between Vernon and Martha Sue.

Mammi fished a plate out of the cupboard and got Vernon a glass and some silverware. "I'm afraid the rolls are gone." She beamed from ear to ear. "But there is still some cheesy jalapeno bread." Everyone had taken a slice of Mammi's cheesy jalapeno bread just to make Mammi happy, but there was plenty left. Mammi had made three loaves.

Mandy's smile faltered as she handed Vernon the basket of sliced cheesy jalapeno bread. Mammi slid the jar of huckleberry raisin jelly in his direction.

Vernon took one look at Mammi's bread and made a face. "*Nae, denki.*"

Mammi's face fell.

Vernon picked up his fork. "Pass the mashed potatoes and gravy. And the corn." He glanced at Katie. "That Jell-O salad doesn't look too bad."

Katie passed down Martha Sue's festive Jell-O salad, and all Martha Sue could hope for was that Vernon wouldn't find out she had made it. It was beautiful and delicious, and she didn't want Vernon to have one positive feeling about her by the time he left. Vernon piled his plate high with food, seemingly unaware that everyone was staring at him.

Yost reached past Vernon, grabbed the basket of cheesy jalapeno bread, and put three slices on his plate. He took a hearty bite of the top slice and closed his eyes as if enjoying it. "Mmm. You're missing out, Vernon. This is *appeditlich*. Who made this *wunderbarr* bread?"

Mammi's smile returned in all its brilliance. "I did. It's a recipe I've been making ever since Felty and I got married."

Dawdi nodded. "And it just gets better every time she makes it."

Yost used his spoon to scoop a huge glob of huckleberry raisin jelly from the jar and smear it all over the other two slices of bread. He ate one slice in four bites and started in on the other slice. He was going to be sick for days, but Mammi's smile grew wider and wider the more he ate. Most of the cousins smiled too. Less cheesy jalapeno bread they would have to eat.

Martha Sue both loved and resented Yost for his kindness. He would be so much easier to forget if he was more like Vernon. But if he were like Vernon, she wouldn't have fallen in love with him in the first place.

Yost wiped his hands on his napkin. "Vernon, I don't know you, but you seem like a nice fellow. Do you live here in Bonduel?"

Vernon paused shoveling food into his mouth. "*Jah*. With my *mamm* and *dat*. I like fishing. Mostly fly-fishing." He chewed quickly and leaned forward so he could look Martha Sue in the eye. "Come to my house, and I'll show you my collection of flies. I'll even teach you how to tie a fly. I'm very *gute* at it. Anna says you're a *gute* cook. Do you know how to make raisin pie?"

Yost leaned forward, blocking Vernon's view of Martha Sue. "What flies do you like the best? I'm partial to the Yellow Zonker for trout."

"You know fly-fishing?" Vernon said.

"My son and I like to go fly-fishing in the summer months."

Vernon smacked his lips. "The Yellow Zonker is *gute*. I like the Muddler Minnow too. I once caught a three-foot trout on the Kickapoo River, but I usually stay closer to home because my *mamm* gets worried." He leaned back so he could see Martha Sue behind Yost's back. "Do you know how to make *yummasetti*? Why don't you bring a casserole when you come to watch me tie flies? I'd like to sample your cooking."

"Martha Sue is a wonderful *gute* cook," Moses said, and Martha Sue wanted to kick him under the table. Vernon did not need any more encouragement.

"Have you fished in Ohio?" Yost asked, leaning back in his chair, effectively blocking Martha Sue from Vernon's view again.

Onkel Titus was excessively interested in fly-fishing, along with Yost, but the rest of the relatives began talking about other things. Lia and Mandy got up and tended to *die kinner* at the other tables. Martha Sue was no longer the center of attention. The rest of them waited until Vernon had finished eating, then the women popped up and started clearing the table. Martha Sue immediately stood and filled the sink with water. Vernon was unlikely to come near her if she was on dishwashing duty. Happy chatter filled the kitchen as all the women, Cousin Moses, and Zach Reynolds helped with dishes. The *onkels* and male cousins moved chairs, took the two heavy leaves out of the table, and generally straightened up the room for Christmas singing and games.

Yost stayed glued to Vernon's side, and while Martha Sue couldn't hear much of the conversation, she could tell it revolved around fishing and Vernon's love of fly-tying. She didn't know why Yost was spending so much time with Vernon, but she knew he was doing it for her. Her heart felt as if it would burst even as she was on the verge of disintegrating into tears. Why was Yost torturing her like this? Why was he torturing himself?

When the kitchen was sparkling clean, everyone gathered in the great room. Martha Sue sat in a corner on a folding chair where she would be least likely to be noticed by anyone. It worked on Vernon. He was so engrossed in telling Yost and Onkel Titus about his new fishing rod that he didn't even glance at her. Yost, on the other hand, rarely let his gaze stray from her face, even though he was supposed to be conversing with Vernon. It made Martha Sue feel warm and squishy on the inside. How long had she dreamed of having a man look at her like that? But now it was too late.

Dawdi told the Christmas story while *die kinner* acted it out. Then Aendi Sally Mae was the *Vorsinger* and led them in several Christmas carols. Vernon was forced to quit talking during the singing, but he apparently liked singing just as much as fishing. He had a nice bass voice, and if he sang a little too loudly, nobody mentioned it to him. Martha Sue moved her lips without singing. She wanted to savor the silky smoothness of Yost's tenor voice one last time. For sure and certain she would miss it when he went back to Charm.

When the singing was over, the *aendis* handed out pie to everyone. Vernon was disappointed when he found out that Martha Sue hadn't made any of the pies, but he cheered up considerably when Aendi Diana gave him a slice of each of four kinds of pie. He glanced at Martha Sue. "Do you know how to make raisin pie? It's the most important thing."

Did he mean that raisin pie was the most important thing to know how to make or the most important thing he was looking for in a *fraa*? She didn't really want to find out.

After pie and more fish talk, Yost stood, yawned, and stretched his arms over his head. "*Cum*, Vernon, I will help you find your coat." Yost reached out his hand, and Vernon instinctively took it and let Yost help him from the sofa. It was no small task. Vernon had sunk deep into the sofa, and he wasn't exactly skinny. Yost, however, was full of muscle and had broad shoulders. He didn't seem to have much trouble pulling Vernon from the sofa.

Yost helped Vernon on with his coat, handed him his straw hat, and even tied Vernon's scarf around his head for him, as he would have done with a child. It all happened so fast that Vernon looked like he couldn't quite figure out what was going on.

"Vernon is leaving now," Yost called to the room.

"*Bis widder*, Vernon," three or four of the cousins called.

Mammi snapped her head up from the game of checkers she was playing with Crist, Moses and Lia's oldest. "Leaving so soon, Vernon? What a shame."

Vernon collected himself just in time to remember why he'd come in the first place. "*Bis widder*, Martha

Sue. Come next week and bring a casserole, and I'll teach you how to tie flies."

Martha Sue couldn't think of much more to do than send him a weak wave. She most certainly didn't want to give him any encouragement. Yost quickly shoved a cookie into Vernon's gloved hand, ushered Vernon out onto the porch, and shut the door. Martha Sue couldn't contain a smile. Vernon had been dismissed.

Yost didn't waste another minute. He marched straight to Martha Sue and sat down next to her. She didn't want him here. She hadn't asked him to come. But she'd be very ungrateful if she didn't thank him for saving her from a night of misery. She sighed in resignation. "*Denki*, Yost."

His eyes twinkled with amusement. "For what?"

"You know very well for what," she scolded. "For keeping Vernon occupied so I didn't have to talk to him. I think I would have locked myself in the cellar after five minutes of fly-fishing stories."

"It was purely selfish. I don't want you to fall in love with him."

Martha couldn't help that her eyebrow arched skeptically. "I'm not going to fall in love with him."

Yost let out a long breath. "I'm *froh* to hear it, but he's definitely going to fall in love with you."

She waved her hand to dismiss that thought. "I just need to make him a bad-tasting raisin pie, and I'll never see his face again."

Yost scooted his chair closer to hers. "I don't want to talk about Vernon Sensenig."

"It's Schmucker."

"I don't want to talk about him either." His gaze pierced right through her skull. "We need to talk about us."

Martha Sue almost wished for Vernon's return. He would keep Yost occupied until Martha Sue had a chance to lock herself in the cellar. "There's nothing more to say."

He took her hand as if reaching for a lifeline. "I'm determined, Martha Sue. I'm going to be a better *fater*. A better disciplinarian. Jonah will treat you with respect or he will not be welcome in our home. He can go live with his grandparents."

Martha Sue snatched her hand from his grasp. "*Nae, nae, nae*, Yost, that's not what I want at all. I will not come between you and your son. You will eventually come to resent me because of it. Your first responsibility is to him, not to me. I could never love a man who would abandon his son because of a woman. It's not right. You know it's not right."

A fire flared to life behind Yost's eyes. "But I can't agree that losing you or losing Jonah are the only two choices. He's misbehaving for the very purpose of getting rid of you, and if I were a better *fater*, he wouldn't misbehave."

"You're a *wunderbarr fater*, Yost. Jonah adores you. He thinks I'm trying to steal you away from him, and he hates me for it. You might be able to make him behave, but my presence will only drive a wedge between the two of you. His world will fall apart."

Yost scrubbed his fingers through his hair. "You have never driven a wedge between us. You've been patient and kind and persuasive. You've made him cookies and pizza. You've tried everything to win him over. He's the one who's being unreasonable and selfish."

Martha slumped her shoulders. "He's a thirteen-year-old boy, Yost. That is the definition of unreasonable and selfish."

Dawdi was suddenly standing in front of Martha Sue with a kind and slightly amused smile on his face. "It appears that there is a whole library of stories between the two of you."

Martha Sue felt her face get warm, and she looked away from Dawdi. "Maybe there is."

"No need to be embarrassed, *heartzley*. After tonight, it's not a secret." Dawdi pulled up a chair and sat knees to knees with Yost and Martha Sue. "When a man comes all the way from Ohio to see you, there's no *maybe* about it." He grinned, folded his arms, and leaned back in his chair. Dawdi still looked amazingly fit for a man in his eighties. "I'm impressed with you, young man," he said, nodding to Yost. "It only took you two hours to get rid of Vernon. Last time Annie invited him, he ate supper and lingered until dinner. He only left when Anna insisted he eat one of her Red Hot cinnamon rolls."

Martha Sue wrung her hands. "Dawdi, I don't want to seem ungrateful, but I don't want to marry Vernon, and I don't want Mammi inviting every man in the neighborhood older than thirty over for dinner."

Dawdi stroked his beard. "She's also looking at the twenty-five to twenty-nine age group."

Martha Sue grimaced. "Help me."

Dawdi chuckled. "Annie-banannie isn't one to sit in her rocker all day and watch the world go by. She likes to make things happen. She likes to get the wheels turning, even if they're on the wrong road and going in the wrong direction."

Martha Sue crossed her arms over her chest. "Well, I don't like it, and she's trying to turn the wheels of my life."

"Your *mammi* loves her grandchildren too much to let well enough alone. It's one of the things I adore most about her. She wants all her relatives to be as happy as she is." Dawdi slapped his hand against his knee as if they'd just solved all Martha Sue's problems and the conversation was over. "Yost, you have a place to stay tonight?"

Yost shook his head. "I didn't really think past getting here and seeing Martha Sue."

That wasn't like Yost. He usually had a plan for everything. He was so organized, he alphabetized the canned food in his cellar.

"When were you planning on going back?" Dawdi said.

Yost looked longingly at Martha Sue. "I had hoped to be going back tomorrow with Martha Sue. I will probably go back tomorrow anyway."

Dawdi nodded, deep in thought. "You can't stay in the house because Martha Sue and seven grandchildren are staying overnight. But you're welcome to sleep in the barn."

"*Ach*, Dawdi, he'll freeze out there."

Yost's look of affection was impossible to ignore. "I'm *froh* you care."

Martha Sue's heart thudded painfully in her chest. "Of course I care." It would be easier if she didn't care.

"We've got extra blankets, and there's a propane space heater for when people need to sleep out there."

Martha Sue raised her eyebrows. "Do people sleep out there often?"

Dawdi shrugged. "When they do, we have a space heater for them."

"That will work," Yost said. His whole body seemed to sag. "Since it's only for one night."

She wanted to scold him and tell him that he shouldn't have dreamed of being away from Jonah on Christmas, but she didn't have the heart to scold him for loving her, even though his coming to Wisconsin was bound to make Jonah resent Martha Sue even more. But Jonah's resentment didn't really matter. Martha Sue was out of his life for good. If that didn't satisfy Jonah, then nothing would.

"*Cum*," Dawdi said, patting Yost on the shoulder. "Let's get you some blankets."

Yost and Dawdi disappeared down the hall toward the bedrooms. Martha Sue marched into the kitchen where Mandy had brewed a pot of *kaffee*. Thank Derr Herr for Mandy. Martha Sue found a Thermos in the cupboard and filled it with *kaffee*. Yost would not freeze to death if she had anything to say about it. She also cut a generous slice of apple pie and put it on a napkin. A midnight snack in case he got hungry.

Yost came down the hall carrying a thick stack of blankets. He set the blankets on the table and put on his boots, coat, and hat. He smiled sadly at Martha Sue and picked up his blankets. "I should be as snug as a bug in a rug."

Martha Sue set the Thermos and the piece of pie on top of his stack. "If you get cold, don't be proud. Come in the house."

His eyes were alight with affection. "If you get too lonely, don't be proud. Come back to Charm."

Chapter 3

"*Ach, du lieva*," Mammi said, gazing out the kitchen window. "He certainly is dedicated."

Martha Sue's heart leaped as she swiped the dish towel across the wet plate. "Who is dedicated?"

"Noah Mishler. I didn't think he'd be able to get his wagon up the hill in this snow."

"Oh," Martha Sue said. It was only her *bruder*-in-law. She took a deep breath and chastised herself for even thinking that Mammi had been talking about somebody else. But to be fair, her reaction wasn't completely her fault. She'd heard nothing from Mammi but Yost and Vernon, Vernon and Yost since Christmas Eve two weeks ago. Who could blame her if she was a little jumpy?

Mammi was still peering out the window. "He's put on runners in place of the wheels, and he's got four horses pulling the thing. That Noah is such a *gute* boy, and I never saw it coming between him and Mandy. Derr Herr works in mysterious ways."

Martha Sue smiled to herself. A few years ago, Mammi had invited Mandy to Huckleberry Hill to find her a husband. She had introduced Mandy to just about every boy in Bonduel *but* Noah, because she hadn't seen quiet, brooding Noah as a *gute* prospect. But Mandy had recognized Noah's sensitive spirit and big heart, and she'd fallen madly in love with him. Mammi had been quite surprised.

Martha Sue set down the plate and dish towel and joined Mammi at the window. A light snow fell, with no breeze to impede its downward progress. Noah, bundled from head to toe against the cold, sat atop the wagon with his Polish hound dog, Chester, at his side. A huge stack of lumber and Sheetrock rested in Noah's wagon. No wonder he needed four horses. "Why is he hauling all that wood up here?"

Mammi sighed in resignation. "*Ach*, he's working on the same project we all are, even though he and Felty are going about it the wrong way. I suppose that finding you a husband is more important than *who* the husband is."

Martha Sue felt as if she'd been smacked in the face with one of Noah's two-by-fours. "The project you're all working on is me?"

Mammi smiled as if she hadn't done anything wrong, as if she wasn't a conniving grandmother trying to ruin Martha Sue's life. "Of course, Martha Sue. We told you that from the very beginning. I want you to be happy. I want you to find someone to love, just like Felty and I found each other. I'll admit that Vernon Schmucker doesn't make the best first impression, but it wonders me if he won't grow on you."

"Like mold?" Martha Sue said.

"*Jah*, dear." Mammi obviously hadn't heard the

panic in Martha Sue's voice. "Felty and Noah think Yost is the one. So do Mandy, Titus, Sally Mae . . ." Mammi counted on her fingers. "Esther, Moses . . ." She threw up her hands. "*Ach*, just about everybody else really. But I feel sorry for Vernon. I've tried to match him with three of my granddaughters, and the poor boy has always taken second place."

Martha Sue couldn't imagine that Vernon would place any higher than tenth with any of her cousins. "So you're all plotting against me?"

Mammi looked hurt. "Not plotting against you, dear. Trying to help you. Only trying to help."

That was the problem. Mammi never dreamed that all her meddling could hurt anyone. Unfortunately, Mammi had been so "successful" in finding matches for her grandchildren that she believed she was always right. Martha Sue wasn't going to talk Mammi out of anything. "What does Noah's hauling wood have to do with finding me a husband?" She was so afraid of the answer that the question almost strangled her.

Mammi frowned. "It's a very expensive, inconvenient plan. Noah is building a cozy room and bathroom up against the far wall of the barn. There will be a shower, a toilet, a solar water heater, a woodstove, and a window, because Felty thinks Jonah needs a window."

Martha Sue suddenly got very dizzy. "Jonah? Yost's Jonah?"

"*Jah*. He's moving up here as soon as Noah finishes the room."

"I . . . don't understand. Jonah is coming up here to live?" She had to brace her hand on the table to avoid falling over. "Yost is sending him away? Sending him to *me*?" Martha Sue couldn't think of a worse situation.

Mammi's lips curled into the smile that said, *I love you, but I feel sorry that you don't know very much.* "Of course not, dear. Yost is coming too. He and Jonah are going to live here until either you agree to marry him or he gives up. But he doesn't seem like a quitter. He might be here a long time." She drew her brows together. "I suppose there is a third option. He'd probably leave if you married Vernon."

Martha Sue shuddered. Option number three was even less appealing than the first two. "Mammi, I'm trying to be a *gute* granddaughter, but I'm starting to get annoyed."

Mammi's look of concern was tempered by her smile. "Poor girl. We've pushed you to the edge of patience." She pulled two chairs out from the table and motioned for Martha Sue to sit. Martha Sue slumped her shoulders and slinked into the chair. She was tired of being lectured to, but it would be best to let Mammi have her say and be done with it.

Mammi grabbed the cookie jar from the counter and set it on the table. "Have a gingersnap. My gingersnaps are famous for making people feel better."

Martha Sue obediently pulled a golf-ball-size brown cookie from the cookie jar. Mammi's famous—or infamous—gingersnaps were as hard as rocks. They couldn't be eaten as much as licked to death.

Mammi shuffled to the great room, retrieved something from the end table, and sat down next to Martha Sue. "Here," she said, handing Martha Sue a hot pink pot holder. "I usually save these to give to boys who want to marry my granddaughters, but you need one worse than anybody."

Martha Sue fingered the bright pink yarn. A pot holder was a token of Mammi's deep affection. Martha Sue had forgotten how blessed she was to have so many people who cared about her, even if those same people were wildly irritating. "*Denki*, Mammi." She took a lick of her cookie, just to make Mammi happy.

"Felty and Yost are trying to get you to do something you don't want to do."

Martha Sue didn't want to be rude, but Mammi needed the truth. "You are too, Mammi."

Mammi heaved a sigh. "*Ach, vell*, all right. I try to find my grandchildren matches—sometimes against their will—but no one has complained yet. I think they were all secretly happy that someone was trying."

"Really, Mammi? No one has ever complained before? I know for a fact that Moses and Ben and Gideon and—"

Mammi giggled. "Okay. I suppose I've had a few complaints." She placed her hand over Martha Sue's. "I'm sorry if anything I've done has made you unhappy, but I always try to act with the end in mind. You have to break a few eggs to make a cake."

"What does that mean?"

"You have to go through hard things and hard times if you want to find something beautiful on the other side. We often run away from the very experiences that help us grow. We can't learn happiness if we haven't learned to fight for it."

Martha Sue took another lick of her cookie. "I refuse to fight a teenage boy for the right to marry his *fater*."

The wrinkles on Mammi's forehead piled on top of each other. "So that's what this all comes down to? Jonah doesn't want you to marry Yost?"

"And he's made it a contest of me against him. Jonah will always see me as the enemy."

"I can understand that. He doesn't want a stepmother." Mammi frowned. "Wicked stepmothers do have a bad reputation."

"Jonah and Yost are inseparable. They do everything together. Yost and I started seeing each other, and Jonah suddenly wasn't the center of attention. Can you blame him for considering me an intruder? Someone who wants to ruin his perfect life? He started . . . misbehaving."

"Oh, dear," Mammi said. "What did he do?"

"At first it was little things. He refused to come to the table if I was there for dinner. He stopped talking to me. If I asked him a question, he would pretend he hadn't heard me. He threw eggs at my parents' home, though I suppose I don't know for sure if that was him. The night we told him we were getting married, he threw a lantern and broke it. Then he yelled at me for five minutes."

Mammi gasped.

"Yost and I decided that Yost needed to spend more time with Jonah. We didn't see each other for a whole month. But when Yost started visiting me again, things got worse. Jonah threw a smoke bomb into my buggy. One morning I came out of my house, and he had rigged a bucket of water to fall on my head."

Mammi bunched her lips together. "He sounds like he's too smart for his britches."

"*Ach*, he is. The water soaked me and then the bucket fell and conked me in the forehead." Martha Sue slid her finger along the little scar just above her right eyebrow.

Mammi's mouth fell open. "The little monster!" She clapped her hand over her mouth. "*Ach*, that was very unChristianlike of me to say."

"I started feeling guilty because I couldn't forgive an innocent child."

"Not so innocent," Mammi protested. She took a cookie from the jar and pounded it against the table in irritation. "My *bruder* Isaac was much like that, though maybe not quite so spiteful."

Martha Sue widened her eyes. "Onkel Isaac?" Kind, sweet Onkel Isaac? The man who once let a homeless family stay with him for a whole year? The *onkel* who rescued horses and spent summers building houses in Mexico?

Mammi nodded. "I thought he was hopeless. He jumped the fence, joined the army, got put in jail, and finally came to his senses. I suppose there's hope for Jonah too."

"I suppose there is," Martha Sue said. "But in the meantime, I refuse to be abused, no matter how much I love Yost."

"Of course not. Everyone deserves to be treated with kindness. You should never volunteer for such a thing. What does Yost say? Has he given Jonah just punishment?"

Martha Sue shrugged. "What is just punishment? Yost has a tender heart, and I can't step in or I look like an angry, jealous woman. Jonah is Yost's problem, not mine."

In her indignation on Martha Sue's behalf, Mammi thumped her cookie on the table so hard it broke in half. "It sounds like Yost needs to learn how to discipline his son. No child should be allowed to get away with treating someone like that."

"I agree to a point. Yost hasn't ever really had to discipline Jonah because it's always been so easy between them. It's just the two of them, and up until Yost met me, Jonah was always a compliant child."

"Or maybe a spoiled child is more accurate." Mammi frowned. "My first impression of Yost was wrong. Felty would never let one of our children or grandchildren treat me like Jonah has treated you. Your cousin Reuben got snippy with me, and Felty made him sleep in the barn." She nibbled on one of the broken halves of her cookie.

"I'm in an impossible situation, Mammi. If I insist that Yost discipline Jonah, I look spiteful and bitter. Yost thinks he has to choose between the two of us, and I won't come between him and his son. It's not right."

Mammi nodded. "For sure and certain, that's exactly what Yost thinks. It's also what Jonah is afraid of—that his *dat* will choose you instead of him. No wonder his behavior is monstrous. Jonah doesn't understand that the more love you spread around, the more it multiplies." She heaved a sigh. "You're usually such a cheerful, happy person. I've never known you without a song on your lips and a smile on your face. Love should make you happy, not miserable. I think it's best to forget

Yost and look for greener pastures. Vernon is eager to get to know you."

Martha Sue groaned. "Mammi, I'm sorry to offend you, but I think I'd rather eat horse manure every day for the rest of my life."

"Is it because you don't want me to find you a husband or you don't want Vernon?"

"Both." Mammi looked so disappointed that Martha Sue pulled her in for a one-armed hug. "I'm sorry, Mammi. There is no future for me and Vernon."

Mammi's eyes filled with concern. "Poor Vernon."

"He'll be fine," Martha Sue said. "And it's not your responsibility to find Vernon a wife."

"That's true. I am quite busy finding matches for my own relatives." She frowned at Martha Sue. "But if I match you with Vernon, I can kill two birds with one stone. Not that I'd ever compare marrying Vernon to getting hit with a rock."

"*Nae*, Mammi. I'm never going to marry."

Mammi studied Martha Sue's face, and the wrinkles deepened around her mouth. "I can't talk you into Vernon, but I don't think Yost is quite right for you. You'd have to be Jonah's stepmother."

"And Jonah won't stand for it. It's impossible for me to be with Yost."

Mammi was so deep in thought, she took a few seconds to respond. "*Ach*, dear, you're wrong. With Gotte, nothing is impossible yet."

"All right then. I've *chosen* to give Yost up. I'm not willing to come between him and Jonah, and I'm not willing to suffer more abuse at Jonah's hand. Can you imagine if Yost and I married? Jonah would find ways to terrorize me every day."

"I don't blame you for running away. Under those conditions, I probably would too." She gently tapped her cookie against the table. "You love Yost, Jonah is a trial, and you won't give Vernon a chance. The question is: What are we going to do about it?"

Martha Sue wiped her eyes with a napkin. "Option four looks appealing."

"I don't think we talked about an option four."

"I could move back to Ohio."

Mammi always tried to be kind and encouraging, but she grimaced as if Martha Sue had just had the worst idea in the history of ideas. "You know Yost will just follow you back there."

"Although Vernon probably wouldn't."

Mammi smiled eagerly. "Do you want Vernon to follow you there? I could probably arrange it, though I'd have to knit him something bigger than a pot holder."

Mammi was persistent about Vernon, but she was right about Yost following her back to Charm. "I don't want Yost or Vernon to follow me there."

Mammi's eyebrows loomed over her face. "I don't want you to go back to Charm, especially when there are two perfectly *gute* single men right here in Bonduel, one of whom will be living in our barn."

Martha Sue slumped in her chair. "He's going to get his hopes up."

Mammi nodded, though she didn't seem convinced. "He's persistent. I like that about him, but it can also be quite irritating."

Mammi had no idea that she was also talking about herself. There was no one more persistent than Mammi Anna.

"It's very irritating and very painful. I feel so cruel every time I reject Yost. Why won't he just accept my answer and move on with his life?"

Mammi's concern seemed to double. "Do you really want him to move on with his life? Do you want him to marry someone else?"

It seemed Mammi wouldn't let Martha Sue get away with pretending the truth didn't exist. A lump lodged at the base of her throat. "*Nae*," she said softly. "I couldn't stand to see him marry anyone else, but letting him go means he might find another *fraa*. Maybe she'll have better luck with Jonah. Maybe it's me Jonah doesn't like."

Mammi waved away that suggestion. "*Nae*, he doesn't like the idea of being replaced." Mammi fell silent. She was obviously thinking deep thoughts. "All right then. If you're determined to marry Yost, we know what we need to do."

Martha Sue sighed in exasperation. "I'm determined *not* to marry Yost."

"Stuff and nonsense. You deserve to be happy and so does Yost. Jonah's happiness should not come at the expense of yours."

"Neither should my happiness come at the expense of Jonah's. He's just a boy."

"He's just a boy who doesn't know anything about true love or real life. Do you truly want someone that ignorant telling you and Yost what you can and cannot do? You broke up with Yost because Jonah wanted you to. Do you want to give a thirteen-year-old boy that much control over your life?"

It didn't matter what Martha Sue wanted, not when it came to Yost and Jonah.

"I gave birth to thirteen children. They'll try to get away with what you'll let them."

Martha Sue smiled in spite of herself. "Mammi, do you even like children?"

"*Ach*, I adore them, but you don't let a puppy pee on the rug no matter how cute he is. That's always been my motto." Sparky, Mammi's white, fluffy dog, lifted her head from the rug and peered at Mammi.

Martha Sue giggled. It might have always been Mammi's motto, but Martha Sue had never heard her say it before.

Mammi was quiet for a few seconds. "It will be a complete waste of time if you leave Bonduel without a husband. This would all be so much easier if you were in love with Vernon, but I won't be discouraged. I'll find a way. It wonders me if I should talk to Onkel Isaac."

"Not a complete waste of time," Martha Sue said, suddenly feeling a little bit better. Mammi might have invited Martha Sue to Huckleberry Hill to find a husband, but that was not why Martha Sue had come. She had come to put some distance between her and Yost, but she had also come to be with her aging, adorable grandparents who weren't going to be around forever. She wouldn't let Yost, Jonah, Vernon, or even Mammi distract her or spoil her time here. She grabbed Mammi's hand. "I came to see you and Dawdi."

Mammi patted Martha Sue's hand. "Of course you

did, dear. And we're glad you're here." Martha Sue couldn't hope that would be the end of it. "But we might as well kill two birds with one stone. Leave it to me. I'm going to make this right if it's the last thing I do."

"I hope it's not the last thing you do. I hope it's not the first thing you do. Don't try to find me a husband, Mammi. Let's just enjoy the time we have together."

"You make it sound as if I already have one foot in the grave." Mammi huffed out an indignant breath. "Eighty-five is the new seventy, you know."

"Lord willing you'll be around for another forty years, Mammi. I still want to enjoy our time together without worrying about husbands or teenage boys or Vernon Schmucker's favorite kind of pie."

"It's pecan," Mammi said. "Or maybe raisin. Lately, all he can talk about is raisin pie and fishing." She smiled her kindly, deceptively innocent smile at Martha Sue. "I don't want you to worry about a thing. Just enjoy your time here on Huckleberry Hill. I'll take care of everything else."

Martha Sue didn't really want to know what *everything else* was, but it was better to be prepared. "What are you going to do?"

Mammi's eyes seemed to light up from the inside. "We need Vernon Schmucker."

Chapter 4

Yost Beiler was a desperate man—desperate enough to lease out his land to an *Englischer*. Desperate enough to drag his son all the way to Bonduel, Wisconsin. Desperate enough to move into a barn to be close to the woman he loved.

He could not live without Martha Sue Helmuth. She was his air. He just had to convince Jonah of that.

Jonah picked up the quilt that was folded at the foot of his new bed. "Here, Jonah, let me help you with that," Yost said. Jonah handed Yost a corner of the quilt, and together they spread it over the bed. "It's pretty," Yost said, not expecting an answer. Jonah hadn't spoken a word since they'd arrived in Bonduel half an hour ago. Jonah was very *gute* at the silent treatment, and even better at pouting. Yost was determined to be strong, but who would break first, Yost or Jonah?

Yost smoothed down the quilt. He loved Martha Sue. He had to be stronger than a thirteen-year-old boy. He watched out of the corner of his eye as Jonah sat on his bed and folded his arms across his chest. He'd been forced to come to Bonduel, but he was obviously determined to hate every minute of it and to make Yost as miserable as he was.

The sight of Jonah sitting as stiff as a board with that unforgiving look on his face pulled at Yost's heartstrings. Jonah had lost his *mater* so early that he barely even remembered her. Yost felt extraordinarily sorry for him and had tried to make up for Jonah's loss by being a *fater* and a *mater* to him. Yost and Jonah had been practically inseparable since Dinah died. Yost took Jonah fishing almost every Saturday, read him stories before bed, made him pancakes and eggs every morning for breakfast, and played games with him in the evening. They shot baskets at the park, went camping every summer, and made special doughnuts. Yost even took Jonah to school in the buggy though they only lived a mile from the schoolhouse.

For sure and certain, Jonah resented Martha Sue. She was an intruder. Yost would just have to prove to Jonah that Martha Sue would double the love and attention in Jonah's life, not halve it.

It seemed an impossible task. Jonah was already convinced otherwise.

Yost frowned to himself and spread a quilt on his own bed, making sure the sheets were tucked in with hospital corners. Maybe Martha Sue was right. Maybe he should give her up and focus on his son. But whenever he thought of not being with Martha Sue, a gaping wound opened up in his heart and the world turned dark. He couldn't do it. He couldn't let Martha Sue go.

"It's cold in here," Jonah mumbled, wrapping his arms around himself.

Yost tried not to show how happy he was that Jonah had spoken. "You're talking to me again?"

"Either that or freeze to death."

Yost looked around the room Noah and Felty had built. It was small but plenty big for the two of them, and Yost wouldn't have complained if it were half as big. Felty and Anna had agreed to let him stay there even though they barely knew him. He'd never be able to repay their kindness.

A short potbelly stove sat in the corner. "I'll start a fire. It will be toasty warm by the time we get back."

"Back? Where are we going?"

"Anna and Felty have invited us to eat with them while we stay here."

"Will *she* be there?"

Yost pretended not to hear the bitterness in Jonah's voice, though it stung like a wasp. *Don't coddle him. He can suffer the consequences of his own choices.* "She will. If you'd rather not come to dinner, you can stay here, but you'll probably get wonderful hungry. We'll be eating with Martha Sue and her grandparents for as long as we stay here."

Jonah seemed to wilt like a daisy in the heat. He blinked several times, but Yost could still see tears pooling in his eyes. "You don't love me anymore."

Yost had never been able to withstand Jonah's tears. He sat next to Jonah on the bed and put his arm around his shoulders. "Of course I love you."

"*Nae*, you don't. You love *her* and not me."

How many times would he have to reassure Jonah before he believed it? "Love isn't like a cake that you divide out among your friends. Love only grows the more you share it. I have enough love for both you and Martha Sue. It just keeps growing. Can't you understand that?"

"I don't like cake." That wasn't true. Jonah adored cake, at least until Martha Sue had started baking cakes for Jonah to try to win him over.

Trying to make a thirteen-year-old see reason was just about as constructive as clipping his toenails with a chain saw. Yost took a deep breath and started in on the lecture he'd given Jonah four times since leaving Ohio. "You will be polite to Anna and Felty and Martha Sue. You will not play any tricks on Martha Sue."

Jonah didn't seem impressed, but it was Yost's fault that his son didn't show him proper respect. Yost had always been a lenient *fater*, mostly because he felt sorry for Jonah but also because Jonah had always been an obedient child, so eager to please. The two of them had been best friends. Until Yost had met Martha Sue. Yost barely recognized this Jonah, the Jonah who got surly when it was time to do chores, the Jonah who played tricks on the woman Yost loved. Some *faters* ruled their children with fear, but Yost would never strike his son or raise his voice. Persuasion had always seemed like a better way to get Jonah to behave, but persuasion hadn't worked for a long time, and Yost was reaching the end of his rope and his patience. His love for Martha Sue was like a raging fire. He wouldn't let Jonah drive Martha Sue away again.

Yost gave Jonah a stern look. "Will you behave, or would you rather go without dinner?"

"It just proves you don't love me when you'd rather let me die of starvation."

"Jonah." Yost put a threatening edge in his voice.

Jonah heaved a sigh, as though he was suffering a serious bout of constipation. "I'll come. But I won't like it."

"As long as you're polite, you can be as irritated as you want."

Chapter 5

Jonah was mad. Mad and irritated and feeling very picked on. He'd done his very best to get rid of Martha Sue Helmuth, or the Interloper, as he called her. He'd found that word in his thesaurus. Jonah had given Dat the silent treatment, thrown dishes at the wall, and played some wonderful *gute* tricks on Martha Sue, and what had that gotten him? A trip to Wisconsin and a bed in a barn. Dat thought he was so clever. He thought that if he moved Jonah away from all his friends, he'd get Jonah to give in and accept Martha Sue into the family. Dat didn't even care about Jonah's feelings, didn't understand how horrible it would be if Martha Sue was his *stepmother*.

Getting a new *mater* wasn't like getting a new cat. A new *mater* would want to be in charge. A new *mater* would take all of Dat's attention. A new *mater* would make Dat forget he even had a son. Jonah wouldn't allow that to happen. He'd get rid of Martha Sue for sure and certain, but he'd wait until after dinner. He couldn't think straight on an empty stomach.

They walked up the porch steps, and Dat gave

Jonah a warning look before knocking. A *mammi* with wrinkles all over her face opened the door. She was kind of puny, but her blue eyes twinkled as if she didn't mind being old and short.

She burst into a smile, threw up her hands, and squealed as if there was a real live bunny on her porch. She put her arms around Jonah and pulled him in for a hug like he was her real grandson. Her hug was warm and soft, and she smelled like cinnamon, but he wouldn't be fooled. This was Martha Sue's *mammi*. She probably hated his guts. "You must be Jonah," she said, pulling away and holding him at arm's length. "I think you're taller than I am. You must take after your *dat*."

"I guess." Jonah shrugged. "But most people say I take after my *mamm*. You know, the one who died." He emphasized *died* in case Dat had forgotten that he had a lot of hardship in his life.

Anna didn't seem to care that his *mamm* was dead. She just kept smiling and twinkling as she led them into the house. The kitchen was on Jonah's right, and it opened into a great room where a fluffy white dog slept on a rug. Jonah caught himself before he smiled. Who cared about a stupid dog?

The whole room smelled delicious, like Thanksgiving dinner or Denny's restaurant. His stomach growled. In all his anger, Jonah had forgotten how hungry he was.

The kitchen table was close to the door, and a long counter, stacked with dirty pots and pans, stood between the table and the rest of the kitchen. Martha Sue was at the stove tending to a steaming pot. She turned and smiled at him, looking too cheerful for someone who was trying to ruin his life. "*Hallo*, Jonah, Yost. *Vie gehts?*"

Martha Sue always faked being nice, even though Jonah knew that as soon as she married Dat, she'd turn on him, probably make him eat broccoli for breakfast, and not allow him to go fishing with his *dat*. Dat nudged Jonah with his elbow. Jonah gave him the stink eye. "*Hallo*, Martha Sue," he mumbled.

Martha Sue seemed pleased that Jonah had spoken to her. Well, if it made her happy, he wouldn't do it again. Those were the last three words he'd say to her all night.

Dat's expression got all mushy. "*Hallo*, Martha Sue. It's *gute* to see you."

How could Martha Sue look sad even when she was smiling? "It's *gute* to see you too."

An old man, for sure and certain Martha Sue's *dawdi*, came down the hall and into the great room. His beard was white, and he wore glasses, and he was the tallest old person Jonah had ever seen, not stooped over at all. "*Vell*, who is this fine-looking young man?"

Jonah wasn't fooled. This was the Interloper's *dawdi*. He probably hated Jonah's guts too. Another elbow from Dat. Jonah gave Dat another dirty look. "I'm Jonah. Nice to meet you."

"Nice to meet you. I'm Felty. How old are you, Jonah? I'm eighty-seven years old. I always think it's fair to tell people my age before I ask theirs."

Jonah appreciated that Felty didn't talk to him like he was a little kid. He talked to Jonah like he was a normal person. It was how Dat talked to him and how Martha Sue treated him, now that he thought about it. "I'm thirteen."

Felty tilted his head to one side as if to get a better

look at Jonah. "I'll bet you're not happy about being in Wisconsin."

The comment surprised him. Most adults didn't care how Jonah felt about anything. His *dat* certainly didn't. And even if they cared, they didn't like to talk about stuff that made them feel uncomfortable. Jonah didn't know what to say. If he were honest, his *dat* would probably send him to bed without any dinner. But if he wasn't honest, then no one would understand how persecuted he was. *Persecuted* was another word from the thesaurus. It meant that his *dat* wanted to ruin his life. He took a deep breath and steeled himself against Felty's reaction. "I hate it here."

"That's rude, Jonah. Apologize to Felty," Dat said, giving him that stern look he saved for when Jonah made him really mad. It was about the only look Jonah saw these days.

Felty held up his hand. "*Nae, nae,* Yost. I brought it up. I appreciate an honest answer."

Jonah pressed his lips together to keep his mouth from falling open. Maybe he would have one friend amidst all these enemies. *Amidst* meant surrounded by. He must always be ready to defend himself or attack.

Felty smiled at Jonah, and it wasn't a fake smile either. "I'll bet you miss your friends."

"Nobody likes me here."

Dat placed a hand on Jonah's shoulder. "I like you. Felty and Anna like you. Martha Sue likes you. You have four friends already."

Jonah didn't miss the hesitation in Dat's voice when he said, "Martha Sue likes you." Of course the Interloper didn't like him. She was trying to ruin his life.

Felty didn't even pretend to agree with Dat. Jonah liked him better and better. "I'm wonderful sorry, Jonah. It is very lonely without friends. A boy needs lots of friends. Lord willing, you'll make new friends at school. I've already talked to the teacher, and she is looking forward to having you at the school."

Jonah frowned so hard, his forehead started to hurt. "I don't want to go to a new school. I won't make any friends."

Martha Sue's *mammi* slid next to Felty, her face bright like a propane lantern. "That's already been taken care of. My *bruder* Isaac has a granddaughter just your age, and we have assigned her to be your friend."

Jonah couldn't help it. He rolled his eyes. "I don't want someone assigned to me."

Anna nodded. "My single grandchildren often feel the same way, but I've got an uncanny sense about these things."

Jonah didn't know what *uncanny* meant. He'd have to look it up in his thesaurus.

"You'll like spring on Huckleberry Hill," Felty said. "Anna used to climb that big pine tree next to the barn and hide up there. There's streams and rabbits, and we've seen a bear or two, but they don't bother us because they're afraid of Sparky." He pointed to a ball of white fur lounging on the rug that didn't look like it could scare a bunny rabbit.

One side of Jonah's mouth curled upward. He couldn't help it. He liked dogs, even dogs that lived in the house of his enemies. "I'd like to see a bear."

Felty winked at him. "If you spread honey all over your head, you're sure to attract one."

Anna let out a cheerful groan. "Now, Felty, that's no way to attract bears, and your head gets sticky."

Felty chuckled. "It might work."

"Dinner is ready," the Interloper called from the kitchen.

Jonah frowned. He'd almost forgotten how mad he was at Dat and Martha Sue and the whole world. But he did remember how hungry he was.

Felty motioned toward the table. "You two can sit down wherever you want."

The only thing Jonah wanted to know was where the Interloper was sitting, because he was going to sit as far away from her as possible. He sat down at the side of the table closest to the window where Martha Sue was least likely to sit. It also put him close to the counter that cut the kitchen in half. Dat went into the kitchen and picked up the bowl of corn, but he wasn't trying to be helpful. He wanted to be close to the Interloper.

"Did you get my letters?" Dat asked Martha Sue, quietly so Jonah wouldn't hear. He didn't know that Jonah had excellent hearing.

Martha Sue backed away from Dat and rested her hands on the counter behind her. "I did. One every week for the last twelve weeks."

Dat sounded sad and pleading both at the same time. "I'm sorry to put you in this awkward position. I know you don't want me here."

Martha Sue lowered her head. "You're just going to make it harder in the end, Yost."

"I know, but I can't bear my life without you. Won't you give us another chance?"

Jonah balled his hands into fists. Dat couldn't bear

his life without Martha Sue? Until Martha Sue had come along, Dat and Jonah had a wonderful *gute* life. Suddenly Dat's life was unbearable? This was why Jonah hated Martha Sue. She had made Dat forget all the *gute* times they had ever spent together. Dat didn't care if Jonah lived or died. All he cared about was marrying Martha Sue. Jonah pressed his hand over the aching spot in his chest.

Anna sat on one side of Jonah and Felty sat on the other. He was saved from having to sit next to the Interloper. "Do you like the napkins?" Anna asked. "They were so cheery that I had to buy them. Only a dollar at Walmart."

Jonah didn't especially care about the yellow napkins with pink flowers. He was more interested in hearing why Dat didn't love him anymore.

Martha Sue put on two oven mitts and pulled a roaster pan out of the oven. "It won't change anything, Yost, but it is your choice to be here. I'm going to enjoy my time with Mammi and Dawdi. What you and Jonah do is none of my business."

Dat cupped his hand around Martha Sue's elbow. "It is your business. There's no place I can go where I don't long for you. You hold my entire life in your hands."

Martha Sue looked like she was going to cry. "I can't talk about this now. Please, let's just eat."

Dat let go of Martha Sue as if her elbow was on fire. "Okay. I'm sorry."

He brought the corn and a basket of rolls to the table. Jonah's stomach growled again. *Ach*, he was hungry, and those rolls smelled *appeditlich*.

Anna slid a jar of jelly toward Jonah. "Martha Sue

made everything on this table except for this huckleberry raisin jelly. It is wonderful *gute* on the rolls."

Jonah hesitated. He didn't want to eat anything Martha Sue had cooked, but a spoonful of jelly for dinner wasn't going to do much to satisfy his hunger, and he hated raisins. He'd have to eat Martha Sue's cooking, but he wouldn't have to like it. They bowed their heads in silent prayer then passed the food around. There was pot roast with potatoes and carrots, buttered corn, rolls, and green beans with bacon. Felty piled the food high on Jonah's plate, and Jonah thought he'd died and gone to heaven. He took one bite of pot roast and tried to pretend he didn't like it much, but it was better than anything Dat cooked for them at home.

Jonah completely ignored the Interloper, who was sitting straight across from him. He could almost enjoy his meal if he forgot Martha Sue existed. He about jumped out of his skin when Martha Sue talked to him. "Jonah, did you ever finish that birdhouse you were building?"

As a matter of fact, he hadn't been able to finish the birdhouse because Dat had dragged him away from Charm to live in a barn. That news would probably make Martha Sue feel wonderful guilty. Unfortunately, he'd promised himself he wouldn't say another word to Martha Sue, so he stuffed half a roll into his mouth and refused to answer. A half a minute of silence passed while he chewed slowly. Surely someone would take the hint and talk about something else.

Instead, Dat glared at him. "Martha Sue asked you a question, Jonah."

Jonah shoveled corn into his mouth and looked at the ceiling.

Anna peered at him with amusement dancing in her eyes. Felty put down his knife and fork and propped his chin on his elbow, as if waiting to see what Jonah would do. Martha Sue gazed at Dat, but she looked more curious than angry.

Dat's face grew dark like a gathering storm. "Jonah," he said, "answer Martha Sue's question."

Jonah was *gute* at digging in his heels, and he wasn't about to let the Interloper win. "I'm not talking to her." He shoved a potato into his mouth.

Anna put her hand over her mouth, as if trying to stop a laugh from escaping. Felty smiled, though Jonah couldn't see anything funny about a boy trying to salvage his family. *Salvage* meant he had to rescue his *dat* from the Interloper.

"It doesn't matter, Yost," Martha Sue said.

Dat glanced at Martha Sue. "It matters very much to me." He looked at Jonah, and his face turned a dark shade of red. "I'll give you ten seconds to change your mind."

Jonah stared right back at his *dat*, not blinking, not giving an inch. "I'm not changing my mind, Dat. She is the cause of all the problems in my life. She's the reason we're living in a barn. I refuse to let her hear the sound of my voice." *Ach, vell*, Martha Sue *could* hear the sound of his voice, but maybe no one would notice. "It's her fault you don't love me anymore."

Whenever Jonah accused Dat of not loving him, Dat usually felt guilty, forgot all his anger, and tried to cheer Jonah up. Not this time. Dat slammed his fork on the table, that storm cloud on his face getting darker by the minute. "You will apologize, or you will leave the table and go to the barn."

The barn. Dat couldn't send him to his room because he had no room. Just a barn, a stinky, cold, musty barn. And it was all Martha Sue's fault.

Jonah glanced at his plate. How badly did he want the rest of that delicious, tender pot roast? His mouth watered. His stomach rumbled. But then he thought about how much he loved his *dat* and how much he loved fishing and how terrible it would be if Martha Sue was his stepmother, and he found his courage. He wouldn't apologize in a hundred years, not even if he starved to death and Dat dumped him on the side of the road to die. He picked up one kernel of corn between his fingers, popped it into his mouth, and scooted his chair out from under the table. Without a word, he stood up, put on his coat, and marched out into the cold, unforgiving night.

Before he shut the door, he heard Anna sigh. "Such a nice boy."

"A very fine young man," Felty said.

Jonah lit the lamp, lay down on his bed, and pressed his fists into his eyes. He wasn't even going to stoke the fire. Dat had all but admitted that he didn't love Jonah anymore, and he didn't deserve any better than a freezing cold room when he finally decided to come back. *If* he decided to come back. He'd probably leave Jonah in the barn and sleep on Anna and Felty's sofa so he could be closer to the Interloper.

Interloper: intruder, invader, stranger.

He'd memorized all the words.

The thesaurus had been Mamm's. In first grade, Jonah had stumbled across the book in a box of some of Mamm's old things that Dat kept under his bed. Jonah had been fascinated with the big words he could barely read, and he'd asked Dat if he could keep the book as his own. Jonah loved words—how they rolled off his tongue, how some words weighed more than others in his mouth, how some were so filled with meaning that saying one word was like reciting a whole poem. Mamm had obviously loved words too. She had written little notes in the margins and drawn hearts and flowers in the corners of some of the pages. The book was Jonah's most prized possession, something that connected him to his *mamm* even though she wasn't here anymore. On days when he felt most lonely, he lay on his bed and hugged the thesaurus to him, thinking of his *mamm* and all he had lost from her death.

Jonah pulled his thesaurus from under his bed and opened it to his favorite word: *betray.* Because that's what Dat had done to him, and Jonah's eyes leaked just thinking about it. On the night Dat had gone to visit Martha Sue for the first time, he'd come home and forgotten to tuck Jonah into bed. Dat had put off more than one fishing trip to be with Martha Sue, and on Jonah's thirteenth birthday, instead of spending the day together like they had always done on his birthday, Dat had invited Martha Sue, and she had made him a carrot cake to celebrate. A carrot cake! Who put vegetables in cake?

Dat had started spending less and less time with Jonah and more and more time with Martha Sue until

Jonah started feeling like a visitor in his own house. Now he was truly a visitor, a stranger, living in a barn and going hungry. Anna and Felty were in on the joke. Jonah was all alone, fighting a battle for his *dat* that he feared he might lose. He thumbed through the thesaurus, looking up *anger*, *pain*, *sadness*, and *grief*. He felt every one of those emotions deep in his bones, and Dat didn't care.

After about twenty minutes, there was a soft knock on the door. "Jonah?"

It sounded like the Interloper. What did she want?

Another knock. "Jonah? It's Martha Sue."

Jonah thought of ignoring her, but she'd probably keep knocking. Besides, he was kind of curious. What was she doing here? Did she want to scold him? He'd like to see her try. He'd make her cry in ten minutes flat. *Ach*, *vell*, maybe not cry. He'd never been able to make her cry.

Her muffled voice got louder and more eager. "I've got pie."

Jonah's stomach leaped into his throat. Pie? Was she tricking him just to get him to answer the door? Jonah eyed the doorknob. She didn't need tricks. There wasn't a lock. She could have just walked in without asking. His noisy stomach finally won out. He could always start starving to death tomorrow. He jumped to his feet, wiped his eyes, and smoothed down his hair. "You can come in, I guess."

Martha Sue tiptoed into the room as if she didn't want to wake a sleeping bear. She did indeed carry a whole pie, and it smelled like cinnamon and butter and melted sugar. She smiled, pulled a fork from her apron pocket, and handed it to Jonah. "Do you like schnitz pie?"

Jonah loved schnitz pie, but he didn't want Martha Sue to see one speck of happiness on his face. He shrugged.

"You can eat the whole thing if you want. It's hard to go without dinner." She set it down on his bed with a pot holder under it then sat on Dat's bed facing him. "Be careful. It's hot." Jonah picked up the pie using the pot holder so he wouldn't burn his hand and sat down on his bed purposefully facing away from Martha Sue. He stuck his fork right in the middle of the pie and scooped up a thick, golden brown, steaming bite. He popped it into his mouth. It was hot, and he opened his mouth and panted to keep his tongue from burning.

Martha Sue didn't mention the fact that he wasn't even looking at her. "Do you like it?"

"It's not bad." He scooped up another huge glob, blew on it, and stuffed it into his mouth.

"What's that book?" Martha Sue asked. Jonah glanced at his thesaurus sitting on the bed open to the page with *betray* on it. "Don't touch it!" he growled. The Interloper wasn't going to get her grimy hands on Mamm's book.

A few seconds of silence. "I promise I won't touch it. I was just curious. It's a very thick book for a boy your age."

Jonah ignored the insult that Martha Sue didn't think he was smart enough to read a big book. He turned his head slightly so he could see her out of the corner of his eye. "It's my thesaurus. You look up a word, and it tells you all the other words that have the same meaning."

"*Ach*, like a dictionary, but easier to understand. I can

tell that book means a lot to you. It looks well used and well loved."

Jonah set down the pie, scooped up his thesaurus, and stuffed it under his bed. He didn't even want Martha Sue looking at it. Hurt traveled across her face, but he didn't care. Martha Sue was out to destroy his family, and he wasn't about to let her. Whatever she wanted from him, she wasn't going to get it. "Being nice to me won't make me like you."

"I don't care if you like me."

He narrowed his eyes. "Because you're going to marry my *dat* no matter what?"

"*Nae.* I'm not going to marry your *dat.*"

That was probably the biggest lie Jonah had ever heard. He sat down on the side of the bed facing Martha Sue. "Then why did you bring me pie?"

She smiled that same sad smile he'd seen in the house. "Jesus said to love our enemies and do *gute* to them who despitefully use us."

"So you're only being nice because Jesus said to?"

"*Jah.*"

"Am I your enemy?" Jonah sort of liked the sound of that.

"*Ach, vell,* I don't like you very much." She smoothed the quilt on Dat's bed. "I don't really like you at all."

Jonah reared back in surprise. Of course she didn't like him, but he was shocked she'd be honest about it. "I'm telling Dat. He won't want to marry you anymore."

Martha Sue didn't seem at all upset that Dat was going to find out what a horrible person she was. "It doesn't matter if he wants to marry me, because I don't want to marry him."

Was she playing another trick? "Why not?"

She lifted both eyebrows. "Why do you think?"

"Is it because of me?"

"*Jah*." She sighed and looked as if she was going to cry. Jonah studied her face. He hadn't even been trying to make her cry.

"You don't love my *dat* anymore?"

"I don't want to come between you and your *dat*. You are very close."

Jonah stirred his fork around in the hole he'd made in the center of the pie. "He stopped loving me when he started loving you."

"He loves you more than anything in the world. He wants you to be happy. Don't you want your *dat* to be happy, Jonah?"

Jonah lifted his chin. "He is happy. We were both wonderful happy until he met you."

"I'm sure you were. That's why I'm not going to bother you anymore."

Jonah swallowed his mouthful of pie, and it made its way slowly down his throat. When it finally settled in his stomach, he remembered that he should probably be happy about his victory. He squared his shoulders. *Jah*. He was wonderful happy that he had defeated Martha Sue. His *dat* was safe. Jonah wouldn't be replaced in Dat's love by a stranger who didn't even know how to fish. "I won," he said, smiling half-heartedly.

"I suppose you did."

Jonah took another bite of pie, but it didn't taste as *gute* as the first three bites. He wished she'd stop looking at him like that, as if all the problems in the world were his fault. "Why did Dat bring us here? Why can't we just go home?"

"You'll have to ask your *dat* those questions, but while you're here on Huckleberry Hill, I would appreciate if you didn't play any of your tricks. There's no need, now that you know I'm not going to marry your *dat*."

Jonah couldn't feel entirely comfortable. "He still wants to marry you. That's why we came to Wisconsin."

"I am not the boss of your *dat*. He makes his own choices. He'll have to work that out for himself. I came to Wisconsin because I want to spend time with my *mammi* and *dawdi*. I don't want to find honey in my apron pocket or get a bucket to the head when I walk out the door in the morning."

Jonah poked several holes in the pie with his fork. The bucket trick had been mean, very mean, and the guilt nearly choked him. "I had to do it. I wanted you to stay away from my *dat*."

"You didn't *have* to do anything, but what's done is done."

"How do I know this isn't just a trick to get me to behave?"

"I hope you'll behave anyway just because your *fater* has taught you better than that. You honor your *fater* when you do *gute* works instead of playing tricks on people. It only upsets your *dat* when you refuse to talk to me or throw a tantrum. It doesn't upset me. I don't like you. I don't care if you talk to me or not."

Jonah frowned. He should have been *froh* that Martha Sue didn't like him, but she was so honest about it, it kind of hurt his feelings. He also thought about what she said about honoring his *fater*. What if Dat really did want to leave Jonah by the side of the road?

Martha Sue folded her arms. "This is not a trick. You've accomplished what you set out to do. I'm not going to marry your *dat*. I hope you'll be satisfied with that."

"I guess so." Jonah wasn't sure why he didn't feel like jumping for joy, except that maybe the guilt at giving Martha Sue a scar was eating at him. Or the guilt at not honoring his *fater*. He hated doubting himself. He squared his shoulders. He'd done the right thing, and he wouldn't let himself feel bad about it.

Her smile didn't reach her eyes. "I sneaked that pie out while your *dat* was washing dishes. You'd better eat what you can before he comes back." She patted the bed as if telling it goodbye, stood up, and walked out the door.

Jonah took another bite of pie before setting it down, picking up his thesaurus, and looking up *satisfied*.

Pleased, happy, proud.

Martha Sue said she hoped he'd be satisfied, but he didn't feel pleased, happy, or proud. Despite having eaten a third of the pie, there was still a gaping hole in his stomach.

Not ten minutes later, Jonah nearly jumped out of his skin when someone else knocked on the door. Why suddenly all these visitors? He hid his pie and thesaurus under the bed and opened the door, too curious to be surly. *Surly* meant grumpy, and being grumpy took too much energy this late at night. Anna stood there holding a plate with what looked like three clods of dirt on it.

She smiled that twinkly smile of hers. "I brought you a snack, since you didn't get dinner."

Jonah did his best to look happy about what was on Anna's plate. "Um, *vell*, *denki*, I guess."

"They are my famous bran and roughage muffins. There were three left over this morning after breakfast."

Jonah didn't know what roughage meant. He'd have to look that one up later, but if the color of those muffins were any clue, *roughage* meant *disgusting*. He unenthusiastically took the plate from Anna.

She enthusiastically nudged her way into the room without being invited. She clapped her hands. "*Ach*, it looks so sweet with my quilts on the beds. Martha Sue and her *schwester* Mandy helped me make both of them. I'm *froh* you could put them to *gute* use." She wrapped her arms around herself and rubbed her hands up and down over them. "*Ach*, *du lieva*, it's cold in here. Is the stove not working?" She opened it up. A few dying embers glowed inside. "We should put in more wood so you'll be toasty warm. We can't have you freezing to death on your first night in Wisconsin." She picked up two small logs from the pile next to the woodstove.

Jonah thought about what Martha Sue had said about honoring his *fater*. Even though he'd purposely not stoked the fire, he couldn't let an old *mammi* do it while he stood and watched. He was young and strong, and she would probably hurt her back if she bent over too far. He set the roughage muffins on the bed and took the logs from her. "I can do it."

She gazed at him as if he'd just saved her life. "*Ach*,

you're such a fine boy. I told Martha Sue just tonight what a fine boy you are."

Jonah grunted. Martha Sue's brutal honesty still stung. "Martha Sue doesn't like me."

"Of course she doesn't like you. You've been very naughty." He was surprised that Anna hadn't tried to make him feel better. Wasn't that what *mammis* were supposed to do?

Ach, vell, Mammi Magdalena in Charm mostly didn't talk to him. She was grumpy and surly and not really nice to anybody. Was Jonah just like her? Because he didn't ever want to be like Mammi Magdalena. He drew his brows together and finished loading the woodstove.

Anna sat down on the bed and sort of bounced up and down as if she were testing it out. "My *bruder* Isaac let us borrow the beds. He always has extras." She patted the space next to her. "Sit down, Jonah. We need to talk."

Jonah wanted to honor his *fater*, he truly did, but if he sat right next to Anna, she might pull him into a tight hug and suffocate him, either on purpose or on accident. He opted to sit on Dat's bed and look at Anna straight on.

She didn't seem to notice that he hadn't done as she'd asked. She clasped her hands together. "I have a favor to ask you, Jonah."

"Okay?"

"Martha Sue isn't getting any younger. She needs a husband."

Jonah's heart clawed its way up his throat. "She's not marrying my *dat*."

"Absolutely not. I won't allow it."

"You . . . you won't let her marry my *dat*?"

Anna's expression softened. "I suppose she'd go ahead and do it even if I disapproved, but as I said, you've been very naughty, and we agreed that it would be better for her to find someone else. One scar in the name of love is quite enough."

Jonah turned his head and stared out the window. "I had to save my family," he mumbled. Why was everybody picking on him?

She reached out and patted his leg as if she was on his side. "Of course you did."

Of course you did? Did she agree with what he'd done, and was this just another way to try to soften him up? He didn't know, but he'd be wise to keep his guard up. "What favor do you need?"

"I have someone very special in mind for Martha Sue. His name is Vernon Schmucker. I need you to help Vernon and Martha Sue fall in love. If Martha Sue and Vernon get married, then for sure and certain your *dat* will move you back to Ohio."

Jonah's heart beat faster. "Do you think it will work?"

"I think it's worth a try." Anna picked up the plate of muffins and handed it to him. "Have a muffin. They keep you regular."

Jonah wasn't sure what she meant, but she had come up with a plan to get back to Ohio, so he felt like he should be polite and eat one of the dirt clods on the plate. He picked up a muffin. It was unexpectedly heavy and dense. He faked a smile and took a bite. It tasted like sawdust and cardboard mixed with sugar and raisins. He did his best to smile through the pain. He swallowed, and the roughage muffin slid down his throat like cold tar.

Anna seemed pleased. "Okay then. Please remember what I said about Vernon Schmucker. If you want to move back to Ohio, you're going to need to help me."

Jonah nodded. His tongue seemed to be stuck to the roof of his mouth. What had Anna put in those muffins?

She brushed some crumbs off the bed. "I've got to get back. I sneaked out of the house while your *dat* was drying dishes, so eat them before he comes back." She patted him on the cheek. "Such a nice young man. I told Felty first thing. Jonah is such a nice young man."

Jonah could only nod. He needed a drink and a toothbrush.

As soon as she left, the rest of the roughage muffins were going into the fire. Lord willing, they wouldn't stink up the room.

Chapter 6

Martha Sue strolled to the chicken coop with her basket, not feeling any better this morning than she had last night. But she'd made up her mind to be happy, so maybe just deciding was *gute* enough for now. As she'd told Jonah last night, what was done was done. She'd made the best decision she knew how to make, and she didn't want to look back. Didn't want to be miserable anymore. Could she be happy in the life Gotte had given her? It was easier to make up her mind to be happy than it was to actually be happy, but when she set her mind to something, she could be quite stubborn.

Martha Sue filled the pan and spread the feed around the yard for the chickens. Then she scattered the potato and carrot peelings Mammi had been collecting. The chickens seemed ecstatic, pecking at the feed and peelings as if they hadn't eaten in a week. Martha Sue sidled toward the coop, thinking about eggs and the other ingredients she would need to make quiche. She'd found a new recipe in one of Mammi's many recipe books and was eager to try it. Would Jonah like quiche? He wasn't a picky eater, and he loved eggs and cheese. Maybe she should make French toast for dinner as well in case Jonah wasn't fond of the quiche.

Martha Sue had inherited her love for trying new recipes from Mammi, even if Martha Sue's experiments usually turned out better than Mammi's did. In Charm, Mamm left most of the cooking to Martha Sue now, even though she was always exasperated at the mess Martha Sue made in the kitchen. Martha Sue loved to cook, and part of the joy of cooking was making a mess. Messy or not, her dinner rolls were always the first to disappear at any fellowship supper, and her herb sausage stuffing was the most popular dish every Thanksgiving. Martha Sue sighed. It was probably pure pride to take pleasure in watching family and friends enjoy her cooking, but Mammi felt the same way. It was why everybody ate whatever Mammi put in front of them. It gave her so much joy to feed her family, even if the family didn't find much joy in eating it.

Martha Sue shooed the chickens away from the roost and quickly gathered the eggs, glad she could do this chore for Mammi. It was getting harder and harder for Mammi to bend over, and the hens sometimes pecked at your hands when you reached in to take their eggs. Of course, Mammi and Dawdi didn't have to manage completely alone up here, even when they didn't have a grandchild staying with them. Cousin Moses and his son Crist came up twice a day to milk the cow, Noah hauled hay, and Titus shoveled snow and pruned the fruit trees. Every fall, the entire family would meet on Huckleberry Hill to pick huckleberries, and all the cousins near Bonduel would help with the maple trees when the sap started flowing in late winter.

Huckleberry Hill had always been a second home to Martha Sue. It was a place where cousins and aunts and uncles gathered, where the food was plentiful if not tasty, and where everyone felt completely loved, no matter who they were.

Martha Sue finished gathering the eggs. She'd have enough to make quiche, French toast, and a cake if she wanted to, though Jonah had stopped eating any cake she made. She turned to go back to the house just as Yost was coming from the barn. Her heart betrayed her, leaping like a skittish horse when she saw him. He was so handsome, and she would mourn his loss for a very long time.

He gave her a tentative smile, and she responded with a wide one of her own. She'd made a decision, and she was determined to see it through.

"*Vie gehts?*" he said.

"*Vie gehts?* Did you get Jonah off to school yet?"

He turned and walked with her toward the house. "*Jah.* He didn't want to go, but he could see it was better than sitting here all day watching me frown at him."

"You know you don't have to force him to go to a new school," she said. "All his friends are in Ohio. Everything he knows is there."

A shadow fell over his face. "He needs to learn that there are consequences when he mistreats people."

"We need to talk, Yost."

His frown sank deep into his face. "We don't need to talk. We need to get married."

She set her eggs on the porch and pulled him to sit

down next to her on the steps. "I sneaked a pie out to Jonah last night."

"I know. The room smelled heavenly all night. I could barely sleep thinking about your *gute* heart even after how Jonah has treated you."

"I told him I'm not going to marry you."

Yost fell silent for a few seconds. "I was hoping I could convince you otherwise. That's why I moved up here."

"I know." She took his hand. It felt so *gute* in hers. She knew the calluses like she knew old friends. "What about your farm? If you don't plant, you won't be able to pay the mortgage. You can't pay your bills if you're up here wasting your time with me."

His expression softened. "It's never a waste of time when I'm with you. It's the only *gute* part of my life." He leaned forward. "Don't worry about my farm. I've leased it to an *Englischer* for the season. Your cousin Moses says I can work at his cheese factory while I'm here. I've always wanted to learn how to make cheese."

At least Martha Sue wouldn't have to feel guilty for Yost's financial ruin. She sighed. "I love you, Yost. I love your goodness and your loyalty. I love that your hair doesn't lie flat unless you're wearing a hat. I love how your tools at home are always clean and meticulously organized. I love your bright blue eyes and the scar on the back of your hand. I love what a *gute fater* you are. But if you lost your son because of me, I would never forgive myself. And you would come to resent me."

"I am not going to lose my son. He will get used to you, to us. He's young. He needs time."

Martha Sue nodded. "He is young, but he is also as smart as a whip, and he is determined to hate me. He's even more stubborn than I am."

Yost cracked a smile at that. He had told her that stubbornness was one of her best qualities. He probably didn't appreciate it now.

"He swore to me that if we got married, he would run away from home. He said he'd jump the fence and never speak to either of us again."

"He told you that last night?" Yost asked.

"*Nae.* Right before I left Charm."

Yost took off his hat and ran his fingers through his hair. "That crafty, devious, conniving . . ."

"He's doing what he thinks he needs to do to keep his world from falling apart."

"There's no reason." He stopped short and went silent for a few minutes. "He keeps telling me I don't love him. I thought he was being dramatic, but maybe he believes it."

"Of course he believes it."

He took both of her hands in his and rubbed his thumb across her knuckles. "Do you know how much I love you?"

"It doesn't matter."

His eyes flashed with anger and pain. "Just listen, Martha Sue. When Dinah died, I thought I would never be able to breathe normally again. But when I met you, it was like this anvil I'd been carrying around my neck for nine years finally fell off. Not only that, but I felt lighter than air, like I could float off the ground if a breeze came up. You have made me so happy." She opened her mouth to protest, but he stopped her. "I think maybe I have been so caught up in loving you that I have neglected my son, and he has felt it like a knife."

"The two of you are everything to each other."

"I forgot his birthday," he whispered.

"You didn't forget it. I made a cake. Jonah hated it."

He narrowed his eyes. "Every year on his birthday, I would let him stay home from school, and we'd spend the day together. We'd go wherever he wanted to go. One year I hired a driver to take us to Wisconsin Dells. Sometimes we went fishing or camping. This year I couldn't bear to be away from you, so I told him we were staying home. I haven't been fishing with him for months. He wanted a new fishing pole last year. We haven't even shopped for one."

"He's terrified of losing you, and you're right, you haven't paid enough attention to him. No wonder he tried to get rid of me." She frowned. "He didn't try. He *did* get rid of me. Your coming here was the worst thing you could have done. He thinks you love me more than you love him. You've got to go back, Yost."

He shook his head. "I'm not leaving."

The adamant set of his jaw and the hard line of his mouth made her both angry and relieved. She silently chastised herself. She shouldn't be relieved that he refused to leave, but whether she should or not, she still felt it to her bones. "Nothing will get better if you stay here."

"Nothing will be right if I'm not near you." His look melted her heart and made her want to weep. "I can't bear the thought of a life without you."

Martha Sue didn't know what to say. Anything she tried would only make both of them feel worse.

"I know you don't want to come between me and Jonah, but if I lose you, who do you think I'll resent for that? It will be Jonah, not you."

"Maybe you should be grateful."

"I can't see anything about your leaving to be glad about."

"What if I do turn out to be a wicked stepmother?" It felt as if an invisible hand clamped around her throat, but maybe if he knew what was really in her heart, he'd give up trying to talk her into marriage. "Do you know what Mayne King said to me?"

He drew his brows together. "What does Mayne King have to do with anything?"

Mayne King had been a widow for three years when she married Tim, who had six children. "We were both at the market the day after Jonah refused to talk to me, and she asked me about you. I was trying to be cheerful, but I suppose my unhappiness showed on my face. I told her my worries about getting Jonah to accept me. Out of the blue, she grabbed me by the arms, yanked me close to her, and whispered in my ear, 'Run.'"

Yost's eyes flashed with resentment. "She shouldn't have said that."

"She was being honest."

"She frightened you."

Martha Sue looked away. "*Jah*."

"I'm sorry," he said softly. "Heartache, pain, sorrow. They follow us wherever we go, even if we try to run away from them. 'In the world ye *shall* have tribulation,' Jesus said. Not *might* had tribulation but *shall*. You can't run from it, Martha Sue. No matter how much you want to." He squeezed her hand. "I can't promise you marriage to me will be all pies and cakes. Dinah and I had some loud disagreements and our fair share of conflict. Jonah almost died as a baby. Dinah got cancer. It was hard, but nothing important is ever easy. I wouldn't trade anything for the life we shared together, *gute* and bad."

A lump lodged in Martha Sue's throat. Was that what she was doing? Running away?

"Maybe Mayne would have made different choices. Maybe she wishes she hadn't married Tim, but I beg you not to reject me just because Mayne King is unhappy in her life. We are all given our own set of trials, and I choose to be happy." He smoothed his finger down her cheek. "I'm surprised Mayne's advice bothered you. You've always been someone who chooses to be happy."

Martha Sue shook her head. "I choose to be practical. It's the same thing. I'd rather laugh than cry because crying gives me a headache. I smile because it seems ungrateful to be gloomy when Gotte has done so much for me."

"Then you understand how impractical it is to try to control things to avoid pain. Jesus will always walk with us, but so will pain. Will the pain of loneliness be any easier to bear than the pain of Jonah?"

She cracked a smile. Jonah would be quite offended to hear his *dat* talk about him that way. "You might be right, but I'm so afraid of what might happen."

He wrapped his arm around her and pulled her close. "There is no fear in love. I'm right here. I will support you and protect you from anything Jonah can think to do."

"Which brings us right back to where we started. I won't come between you and your son."

"You sound like Jonah. That's what he's afraid of, but I can love both of you at the same time. And I do."

Martha Sue drew her brows together. "*Ach*, the truth is, I'm not very fond of Jonah."

Yost's expression didn't change, even though Martha Sue had just revealed a very ugly part of herself. His temper was as even as a lake on a clear summer day. "You don't have to beat yourself up about it," he said, as if he already knew. "He's been wonderful mean to you. And even before that, I never expected you to love him instantly. Love grows with time. It's not like an electric light switch you can turn on and off, especially since Jonah is a rude, unruly boy who is determined to not like you."

"But what if I never learn to love him? I'd feel fake and dishonest being his mother."

"Could we cross that bridge when we come to it? I can only work on one problem at a time."

"What problem do you want to work on first?"

He smiled tentatively at her. "The problem of convincing you to marry me."

"I told you, Yost. We should just be friends. Friendship is a blessed relationship too."

His eyebrows loomed over his face. "I don't want to be just friends. I can't do it." He stood up and paced back and forth in front of her. "Be honest with me, Martha Sue. Do you truly want nothing more than a friendship between us?"

He looked at her with such intensity that she couldn't

look away. She certainly couldn't lie to him. "If Jonah loved me, I would marry you tomorrow."

His whole face lit up like a bonfire, and he sat next to her again. "*Ach*, Martha Sue, that is all I need to hear."

"But Jonah doesn't love me, and I won't be the reason his world crumbles around his ears."

"Can we try again?" he said breathlessly. "Please tell me it's not too late. Will you still consider marrying me?"

"I don't know what to say, Yost."

"'With Gotte, all things are possible,'" he said.

She smiled in spite of herself. "Would you quit quoting scripture? It makes me think you know something I don't."

He pumped his eyebrows up and down. "I have a scripture for every occasion."

"For sure and certain you do." She sighed and gazed into his eyes. She saw so much love there, she couldn't bear to disappoint him. Couldn't bear to give up on him just yet. "I think I'm going to regret this, but it's not too late, even for you."

"*Denki*. That means everything to me." He paused and wiped some moisture from his eyes.

"I told Jonah I'm not going to marry you."

"And I told him I am going to marry you. One of us will be a liar no matter what." His look was still warm and affectionate, but his smile became more subdued, more thoughtful. "Now that you've given me new hope, Jonah is the one I need to convince. I'm going to work on him."

"Work on him how?"

He scrubbed his hand down the side of his face. "I need to show him that he can be sure of my love. I need to make him the center of my attention and my life." He glanced at her. "I hate the thought of neglecting you, but I'm afraid I'm going to have to concentrate on Jonah until he is sure of me."

His expression made Martha Sue smile. "As you should."

His eyes flashed with mischief. "I've got a plan. I'm going to smother him."

"Smother him?"

"Smother him with love. Smother him with attention. He'll be so sick of me, he'll beg you to take me off his hands. Don't be offended when I ignore you. You'll be in my thoughts constantly."

Martha Sue's heart swelled at the thought of having the love of such a *gute* man. "That plan could backfire. Mammi won't give up on her dream of Vernon Schmucker. He's bound to shower me with attention, especially when he tastes my pecan pie. Like as not, he'll be lurking around here more often."

"Then, after I've convinced Jonah, I'll just have to steal you back from Vernon Schmucker."

Martha Sue laughed. "It won't be a very hard job."

He nodded, the amusement barely perceptible on his face. "I'll keep my eye on Vernon Schmucker, but unfortunately, there will be others. I'll have to be vigilant."

"I think you'll have to worry more about Mammi than anyone else. When she sets her mind to something, she can be very stubborn."

"So can I." He said it with such eagerness that she had to laugh.

"What if Jonah finds out you're trying to trick him?"

"I won't be trying to trick him. I truly do need to

spend more time with him." He rubbed his hands together as if he were planning something devious. "Then I'll smother him."

Despite her doubts, Martha Sue hadn't felt this light-hearted in over three months. "I don't know if this will work out or not, but just knowing that Yost Beiler once loved me will be enough warmth to last a lifetime."

He growled, leaned closer, and laid a swift kiss on her lips. "I'm offended that your expectations of me are so low."

The unexpected kiss made her breathless. "*Ach*, *vell*, someone has to be realistic."

His eyes glowed with affection. "My realistic, stubborn sweetheart. I find you very irritating." A smile grew slowly on his lips. "I wouldn't want you any other way."

Chapter 7

Jonah zipped up his coat and picked up his lunchbox. His first day at the new school hadn't been the worst day of his life, but it hadn't been the best day either. There was only one other boy in the seventh grade, Ben Stoltzfus, and he hadn't said one word to Jonah the whole day. But then at recess, the boys in the upper grades had invited him to play kickball, and Jonah had made a couple of acquaintances who seemed nice. *Acquaintances* were people who didn't really care about you but needed one more player on their team. Jonah had kicked a ball way out into the field, and he'd gotten to third base. After that he'd made more acquaintances at second recess because everybody wanted him on their team.

Jonah missed his two best friends, Tyler and LaWayne, something wonderful, but school in Wisconsin wasn't so bad. Jonah had always liked school. He probably liked it because he was *gute* at it. He could add and multiply numbers faster than most teachers, and he could read big words that not even the eighth graders knew. Mapleview School was a smaller building than his school in Charm, but there were two teachers, and after singing time, one teacher pulled a curtain down the center of the room, dividing the older kids from the younger ones. It was nice not to have to sit through the lessons for the little kids.

Sarabeth, the older kids' teacher, was pleased when she saw what a *gute* speller Jonah was. She asked him to write the spelling words on the board for the rest of the class. He felt strange being up at the front of the class when he didn't know anybody, and after he'd raised his hand for the fifth time, the teacher said, "*Cum*, Jonah. Let's give someone else a chance."

His face had gotten warm, and he'd slumped in his chair, vowing not to say another word the rest of the day. Was it his fault that he was the only one who knew the answers to all the questions? Teachers shouldn't humiliate their students like that.

But then the eighth-grade girl who sat right in front of him had turned around and smiled. "You're wonderful smart," she had said, and Sarabeth was forgiven.

Jonah sighed. He wanted to be in Ohio with his friends. He didn't want to have to make new friends. But it didn't matter how hard he begged Dat to take them back to Charm, Dat wouldn't listen. Dat said Jonah had to live with the consequences of his actions, but Dat didn't realize that Jonah had to live with the consequences of Dat's actions, and Dat was ruining his life.

What was he supposed to do? He'd thought about running away, taking a bus back to Charm, and living with Mammi and Dawdi, but he didn't have any money, and it would have been wasted, because Mammi would have sent him right back to Wisconsin without another thought. Besides, Mammi Magdalena was grumpy, and Jonah didn't want to live with her. What should he do?

His lips twitched upward. Anna could help him. She wanted Martha Sue to marry someone named Vernon Schmucker, and she needed Jonah's help. He'd be on the lookout for this Vernon Schmucker. Then he'd see what he could do to make Martha Sue fall in love with him. It wouldn't be easy, but the alternative was letting Dat talk Martha Sue into marrying him. That couldn't happen.

Jonah trudged down the stairs and out the door of the school, then scanned the road for his *dat*. Dat had been forced to borrow Felty's buggy this morning to drive Jonah to school, and he was going to pick Jonah up the first day. After that, Dat said Jonah would have to walk until school got out for the summer or until they moved back to Charm, whichever came first. Who ever heard of that? A kid having to walk home from school uphill? Dat was so in love with Martha Sue, he couldn't be bothered to pick up his own son from school. It was another reason Jonah didn't like her.

Jonah lumbered up the incline to the road to wait for Dat, fully expecting Dat to forget to pick him up, just like he'd forgotten that Jonah needed a new fishing pole or that he hated carrot cake.

"Jonah Beiler?"

Jonah turned around to see one of the girls in his class coming toward him. She was skinny and short with hair so bright yellow, he had to squint against the sun to look at her face. She held out her hand. Jonah didn't especially want to touch a girl's hand, but it would be rude to just let her stand there waiting for a handshake. He shook her hand. She pursed her lips and drew her eyebrows together. "I'm Lily Yoder. I don't know if I'm going to like you or not."

Jonah took a step backward and away from Lily. "So what if you don't like me? Girls are annoying." *Annoying* was one of his favorite thesaurus words, because he could insult his classmates without hurting their feelings. Most kids didn't know what *annoying* meant.

Apparently Lily did. She puckered her lips as if she'd eaten a lemon. "Boys are more annoying than girls."

Jonah made a face as if he'd eaten a whole bag of broccoli. "They are not. If I'm so annoying, why did you shake my hand?"

She sniffed in the air and looked him up and down as if she suspected he hadn't taken a bath in a whole year. "My *dawdi* Isaac is paying me a dollar a week to be nice to you."

"I don't want you to be nice to me."

"I'm going to earn my money whether you want me to or not."

Jonah scowled. Someone had hired a sixth-grade girl to be nice to him? It was so embarrassing, he thought about putting his coat over his head and running down the road as fast as he could. "Who is Dawdi Isaac?"

"He's Anna Helmuth's *bruder*, and he's my *dawdi*. He's paying me a dollar a week."

Jah. Jonah had already heard that. Embarrassing. "I don't care how much he's paying you. Stay away from me."

She acted as if he'd shoved her to the ground. "I can't do that. It wouldn't be honest to take his money without doing my job."

"Then don't take his money."

She gave him another sour look, as if he was the dumbest boy in Bonduel. "I need that money. I'm saving up for a set of dishes for my hope chest."

"I don't care."

She huffed out a breath. "You've got to do your part, or I'll never get my money."

"*Nae*, I don't," Jonah said. "I don't want to be friends with a girl."

"And I don't want to be friends with a boy. Boys are *dumm*. You think you're so smart, but you're a boy so you're *dumm*."

Jonah's cheeks burned. "I do not think I'm so smart." What was wrong with thinking you were smart?

"You raised your hand on every question and finished your math problems ten minutes before anyone else. We're supposed to let the fifth graders answer sometimes."

"They can't answer if they don't know it."

"Well, maybe you should have thought how you could help them instead of making them feel even dumber."

Jonah glanced down the road toward Huckleberry Hill. Where was Dat? He was sick of talking to this Lily girl. She was the *dumm* one, and he wasn't going to help her earn her money by trying to be nice.

She folded her arms. "My *dawdi* says you're living in a barn."

How hot could his cheeks get? He wouldn't have a chance making friends if anybody else found out he was living in a barn. "Don't tell anybody."

To his surprise, she nodded. "I know how to keep a secret. My *mamm* says I talk too much, but I never tell secrets, even when my *dat* sneaks ice cream from the freezer before dinner." Her eyes went wide, and she clapped her hand over her mouth. "Don't tell my *mamm*."

"I won't tell if you won't tell about the barn."

She scratched her chin. "Why are you living in a barn?"

"It's my *dat*'s fault."

Lily gazed at him sympathetically. "Parents do the funniest things. One time my *mamm* chopped the rooster's head off because she was sick of his crowing. We had chicken for dinner, but I had to pluck the feathers. Have you ever plucked a chicken? It is not fun." She scrunched her lips together. "Why is it your *dat*'s fault?"

"We were doing fine in Charm, and then he fell in love with someone. He wants to marry her. She came up to Wisconsin, and Dat made us follow her."

Lily pushed some dirt around with her toe. "Is your mother dead?"

"*Jah*. Since I was four."

"I'm sorry about that."

Jonah didn't want a sixth grader to feel sorry for him. "I don't remember her."

"I'm still sorry. It must be lonely without a *mater*." She caught her breath as if he'd scared her. "If your *dat* marries that lady, you'll have a new *mater*. That would be nice. When are they getting married?"

"She wouldn't be my new *mater*," Jonah said, the resentment nearly choking him. "She'd be my stepmother, and I don't want a stepmother."

Lily's lips formed into an O. "Is she mean?"

Jonah hesitated. He couldn't exactly say yes to that question. "I just don't want a stepmother. She'd kick me out of the house and make me go live with my grandparents so she could have Dat all to herself."

Lily's eyes widened. "That sounds mean."

"My *dat* only pays attention to her, not me."

Lily thought about that for a minute. "I still think it would be nice if you got a new *mater*. She would bake cookies and fix holes in your trousers."

Jonah didn't care about holes in his trousers, but he did like cookies. "Martha Sue makes *gute* cookies. My *dat* doesn't know how."

"My *mamm* makes the best bread pudding. She doesn't even put raisins in it." She studied his face. "Aren't you glad my *dawdi* is paying me a dollar a week to be nice to you? You're going to need friends if you get a stepmother."

Jonah frowned. "I'm not getting a stepmother. I've made sure of that."

"How have you done that?"

Jonah gazed down the road, not quite proud enough of what he'd done to look Lily in the eye. "I made for sure and certain she wouldn't want to marry my *dat*. That's why she moved to Wisconsin. I put honey in her pocket and a smoke bomb in her buggy. She knows if she marries my *dat*, she'll get more of that."

Lily's face turned red, even her freckles. "That's just plain mean."

"Sometimes you have to be mean in an emergency. They were going to get married. I had to do something."

"There's never any call to be mean to people." She tilted her head to one side as if to get a better look at him. "This is going to be harder than I thought. I'm going to ask my *dawdi* for two dollars a week."

Jonah stuck his tongue out at her. "You would have done the same thing."

"I would not have. I have manners, and I'm not mean to people. Ever."

"It was an emergency."

Thank Derr Herr, Dat pulled up in his buggy just then. He was ten minutes late, but at least he'd gotten here before Jonah was forced to talk to Lily one more second. Dat reined in the horse and got out of the buggy. His smile was a mile wide as he came around to Jonah's side. "Well, *hallo* there. Who is your friend, Jonah?"

"She isn't my friend," Jonah mumbled. He wished he'd been smart enough to run down the road when he had the chance.

Lily shook Dat's hand. "My name is Lily Yoder. My *dawdi* Isaac is paying me one dollar a week to be nice to Jonah."

Dat chuckled as if that was the funniest thing he'd ever heard. "It's nice to meet you, Lily Yoder. I'm glad you're being nice to Jonah, no matter the reason. Two are better than one because they have *gute* reward for their labor."

"*Ach*," Lily said, "everybody was nice to Jonah today. He's already the best kickball player in the school, and

Teacher let him write the spelling words on the board. We all like him."

Jonah eyed Lily as if she'd just sprouted antlers. That was news to him.

"I'm *froh* to hear it," Dat said.

Lily didn't even pause to breathe. "Jonah says you're living in a barn, but I won't tell anybody." She motioned toward the buggy. "My *mamm* says I can come home with you for dinner as long as I eat all my vegetables and help do the dishes, but you'll have to drive me home before bedtime."

Jonah raised his eyebrows. "Tonight?"

She nodded. "*Jah.* I have to earn my dollar."

"I suppose you do." Dat chuckled again, though Jonah couldn't see what was so funny. Dat slid the buggy door open for Lily, and she climbed in.

Jonah climbed in after her, and they all sat in the front seat, Lily in the middle. Jonah plastered himself against the door. Lily chatted all the way to Huckleberry Hill, and by the time they got there, Jonah had chewed three of his fingernails down to nubs.

Dat pulled the buggy into the barn. "*Vell,* Lily, it's two hours to dinner yet. I was going to have Jonah help me with some repairs, but if you two would rather play, I'll do it myself."

Play? What was Dat thinking? Jonah was thirteen years old. He didn't play anymore. "I want to help you, Dat," he said.

Dat smiled, as if Jonah's answer pleased him. "Okay. Do you want to help too, Lily?"

Jonah would have to put his foot down or Dat was going to keep embarrassing himself. "Dat, girls don't know how to repair stuff. Maybe she can go in the kitchen and help with dinner." *Jah*. That was a *gute* idea. Jonah could be alone with Dat, and Lily would be out of his hair.

Lily squared her shoulders and folded her arms across her chest. "I can fix stuff. My *dat* taught me how to use a screwdriver and a hammer."

Dat seemed on the verge of laughing again, but he swiped his hand across his mouth and cleared his throat. "Okay, then, Lily. You can help me and Jonah. We need to tighten some loose boards and oil the barn door hinges. There's also a latch that needs to be replaced on one of the doors."

"Sounds fun," Lily said.

Jonah groaned softly. Lily was going to make a pest of herself. If he had any money, he'd pay her a dollar a week to stay away.

Martha Sue plopped the butter into the noodles and stirred them together until all the butter melted. Buttered noodles were still one of her favorite dishes, a staple at many Amish meals. She poured the noodles into a bowl and set the bowl on the table. Her lips twitched when she thought of Yost's kiss this morning. He wasn't one to spread his kisses around freely. He only kissed her, as he said, "when it is absolutely necessary."

Martha Sue couldn't resist that kiss if she tried. And she'd tried. Was there really a future for her and Yost? His kiss could make her believe almost anything, even persuade her to hold on to a sliver of hope, no matter how small. A movement out the window caught her eye. Yost, Jonah, and a young girl walked up the porch steps together, no doubt coming in for dinner.

"Mammi," Martha Sue said, "do you know who that is?"

Mammi set her stack of plates on the table and glanced out the window. "That is Onkel Isaac's granddaughter Lily. She's the one we've assigned to be friends with Jonah."

Martha Sue gazed out the window. "She looks young."

"Don't let her size fool you. She's just a year behind Jonah in school, and she's smarter than a pistol. Jonah will either run for the hills or make her his best friend."

Martha Sue laughed. "Which do you want him to do?"

Mammi shrugged and grinned. "I can work either reaction into my plan, but I hope they'll become great friends. Jonah needs friends."

Martha Sue nodded. "Everyone needs *gute* friends."

The trio came in the door in their stocking feet. Springtime on Huckleberry Hill was muddy, and the boots and shoes got left outside on the porch. The three of them took off their coats and hung them on the hooks by the door.

Lily marched right over to Martha Sue, smiled wide, and held out her hand. "I'm Lily Yoder. I'm eleven years old. I hope it's okay that I stay for dinner. Dawdi said I should just invite myself." Lily had white-blond hair and a smattering of freckles across her nose. She was small boned and thin but carried herself with the confidence of a much older girl. Her eyes were wide and intelligent, as if she were observing everything and taking mental notes. Martha Sue liked her instantly.

"*Hallo*, Lily. I'm Martha Sue."

Lily peered at Martha Sue as if giving her an inspection. "You don't look mean. I think you're pretty, but Jonah says you're mean."

Martha Sue didn't want Jonah's opinion to hurt, but like it or not, the judgment sent a shard of glass through her heart. Jonah seemed to shrink into the corner behind the door. Before this morning Yost would have sent Jonah to bed without dinner for such a comment or at the very least would have demanded Jonah apologize. This time, he pretended he hadn't even heard. Martha Sue wanted to kiss him. This was just what Jonah needed.

Martha Sue forced a smile. "*Ach*, *vell*, I'll guess you'll have to decide for yourself once you get to know me."

Lily waved her hand as if she were swatting a fly. "*Ach*, I already decided. Jonah doesn't know anything, and you seem wonderful nice. Jonah says you make *gute* cookies. Mean people do not make cookies."

"*Vell*, *denki*, Lily. That's a very nice thing to say." Martha Sue's heart swelled to twice its size. She had made cookies just this afternoon. Peanut Butter Blossoms. Jonah's favorite. She motioned to the counter where the batch of cookies was sitting on the cooling rack. "I made cookies earlier. You'll have to try one."

Lily nodded eagerly. "Oh, I will. This is even better than a dollar."

Martha Sue wasn't quite sure what she meant by that, but she didn't have time to ask because someone knocked on the door. Mammi lit up like a lantern and clapped her hands, seemingly the only person in the room not curious about who was there. Martha Sue's heart sank. That could only mean one thing.

Mammi hurried to answer the door. "Vernon Schmucker! What a nice surprise."

Vernon frowned in confusion. "You told me to be here at five."

Mammi blushed, giggled, and gave Martha Sue a guilty look. "I meant, it's a surprise that you're here early. I love promptness."

Martha Sue wasn't even irritated. She'd expected as much from Mammi, Jonah hadn't glared at her once, and Yost had kissed her this morning. All was right with the world.

Vernon took off his hat and coat and smiled hungrily at Martha Sue. "You said there'd be cookies."

Jonah took a cookie from the cooling rack and handed it to Vernon. Martha Sue's eyebrows inched up her forehead. "You should try one. Martha Sue makes the best cookies."

Martha Sue's eyebrows went higher. It might have been the first compliment she'd ever heard from Jonah, and why did he care if Vernon got a cookie?

Vernon smiled as if he wasn't especially fond of children but was glad to get a cookie. "That's why Anna invited me to dinner, so I could try the food. The girl I marry has to be a *gute* cook."

Yost coughed as if he'd swallowed wrong. The cough sounded suspiciously like laughter in disguise. Martha Sue's gaze flew to his face. His eyes danced with amusement. Vernon didn't seem to notice.

Martha Sue's face felt like a hot stove on a cold morning. She would have to put her foot down. She was not going to cook for Vernon every night, and she certainly didn't want to waste any of her precious cookies winning Vernon's approval.

Lily held out her hand to Jonah. "I want one."

Jonah folded his arms, planted his feet, and stood steadfastly between Lily and the cookies, as if guarding a pile of money. "It will ruin your dinner."

Lily's mouth fell open in indignation. "You gave one to him."

Jonah was unimpressed. "He's a special guest. You invited yourself to dinner."

"Dawdi said I could invite myself as long as I helped with the dishes."

"Well, you don't get a cookie." Jonah wasn't in charge of the cookies, but Martha Sue wasn't about to argue with him. Waiting until after dinner to have dessert was just *gute* manners.

"Num," Vernon said, smacking his lips. "This is *gute*, but you should have used more peanut butter."

Another loud cough from Yost. He seemed to be thoroughly enjoying himself. Martha Sue resisted the urge to roll her eyes at him.

Dawdi came down the hall from the back bedrooms. "Well, goodness me, it's Lily Yoder and Vernon Schmucker. We get double the blessings tonight."

Lily ran into Felty's arms, and Felty twirled her around as if he wasn't eighty-seven years old. He set her down and patted the top of her head. "I think you've grown taller, Lily girl."

"I have," Lily said. "One inch since my birthday."

"One inch! That is something." Dawdi took Lily's hand and led her to the table while Lily told Felty that Jonah wouldn't let her have a cookie and launched into the story of how her *mamm* had made her a pink cake for her birthday, and her *bruder* Raymond had eaten so much he was sick all over the floor, and her *mamm* had made Raymond clean it up because, "for goodness' sake, son, you're seventeen years old. You can get yourself to the bathroom."

"I love buttered noodles," Vernon interjected. Martha Sue gave him a weak smile, because she didn't want to be rude and ignore him, but neither did she want to encourage him. She frowned. No matter what Mammi wanted, Martha Sue would have to speak with Vernon. It wasn't fair of Mammi to keep inviting him over when Martha Sue had no intention of encouraging a relationship.

Jonah stood guard near the cookies, his arms folded, staring impatiently at Lily. Martha Sue didn't especially want to talk to Jonah, but things would only seem natural between them if she made it natural. She handed Jonah half the plates to set around the table and leaned in to whisper to him. "Lily is a wonderful nice girl."

Jonah grimaced. "I guess, but we should just start eating. If we wait for her to stop talking, we'll be here until next Christmas."

Martha Sue cracked a smile. Lily was going to keep Jonah on his toes. "She's loquacious, for sure and certain."

Jonah's eyes widened. "What does that mean?"

She winked at him. "You'll have to look it up in your thesaurus."

He seemed pleased that she mentioned the thesaurus. "I will. Does it have a *Q* in it?"

"*Jah*. And a *C*." Martha Sue set the rest of the plates on the table. Yost grabbed silverware, and Martha Sue started placing napkins. She and Yost passed each other, and his hand brushed against hers, sending a spark of electricity up her arm. Her gaze flew to his face. His expression was flat, but his eyes flashed, and he gave her a small wink. He'd brushed her hand on purpose! Could she work her way around to the other side of the table and get him to do it again?

He'd have to stop sneaking touches and winks, or Jonah would get suspicious. Jonah was no doubt already completely on edge. One amorous look between Martha Sue and Yost might throw him into a temper tantrum.

Mammi finished slicing a loaf of her banana raisin olive bread and set it on the table. "*Cum*, everybody. Let's eat." She smiled innocently at Martha Sue. "Martha Sue, sit next to Vernon and tell him all about your *yummasetti* recipe." She turned her gaze to Vernon. "Martha Sue makes it with two whole pounds of cheddar cheese. Most cooks only use one."

Vernon scooted close to the table and picked up his napkin. "I don't like it when girls are stingy with the cheese."

Mammi nodded eagerly. "Martha Sue uses so much cheese, the cows are jealous."

Vernon seemed quite impressed with jealous cows. He eyed Martha Sue. "Can you make it for me? My *mamm* doesn't make *yummasetti* anymore because she says it's fattening."

"But she still makes you a pecan pie every week?" Yost said, amusement playing at his lips.

Vernon picked up his fork. "She says nuts are heart healthy."

Yost had assured Martha Sue that he was going to ignore her for Jonah's sake, but he had no such obligation when it came to Vernon. He sat next to Vernon and immediately asked him about fishing. Martha Sue felt his kindness all the way to her heart.

After the silent prayer, Anna passed around her bread first, followed by the noodles, the corn, and the baked chicken. Vernon took more than his fair share of everything.

Lily sat on the other side of Martha Sue, and Martha Sue helped her fill her plate, just in case she felt shy about taking food. But Martha Sue needn't have worried about that. Lily seemed completely unembarrassed about everything. She pointed to the noodles. "I want some of those, but just a small piece of chicken. And is it okay if I don't have any corn? I don't like it." Martha Sue was impressed when she took a slice of Mammi's banana raisin olive bread and didn't seem to bat an eye. That girl had been trained well.

Vernon, on the other hand, again refused a slice of Mammi's bread. He wasn't winning any points with Martha Sue. Although, what did it matter? Even if he earned a thousand points, Martha Sue wasn't interested. The trouble was, it seemed that he was winning points with Mammi without even trying.

Lily asked for the butter and slathered a fourth of the cube on her bread. She was a very smart girl. Everything tasted better with butter. If you had to eat banana raisin olive bread, you might as well hide the flavor with a mouthful of butter. Lily took a hearty bite and chewed vigorously, as if trying to get it over with as quickly as possible. She eyed Martha Sue. "Are you going to make Jonah move out of the house when you get married?"

Martha Sue's heart lodged in her throat. Was that truly what Jonah expected if she married Yost? Of course it was. That was why he'd been trying so hard to get rid of Martha Sue. "I . . . uh . . . what makes you think I would ever do such a thing?"

Lily glanced at Jonah, but to her credit, she didn't put the blame on him. "Sometimes stepmothers get rid of their children, like in *Hansel and Gretel*."

Martha Sue was shocked that Lily had read a fairy story and hurt that Lily or Jonah would even think her capable of such a thing. She swallowed hard and reminded herself that Lily was eleven years old, precocious, and apt to say whatever came into her head. Jonah, on the other hand, was determined to paint Martha Sue in the worst light possible.

Vernon stuffed a forkful of noodles into his mouth. "There was a house made out of candy in that book."

Jonah stared at Martha Sue, his expression a mixture of embarrassment, defiance, and curiosity. The emotions on Yost's face were equally unsettling. He looked angry yet defeated, as if he didn't quite know what to do about his son.

Martha Sue dearly wanted to take Yost's hand and

reassure him everything would be all right, but she couldn't even convince herself of that. At the same time, she wanted to chastise Jonah for making his *fater* miserable and hug him for trying to keep his family together the only way he knew how. She wanted to scold her *mammi* for inviting Vernon to dinner and lecture Vernon about chewing with his mouth open. *Ach*, if only she could fix what was broken with a stern look and a few sharp words. Or even a few soft words. She had neither.

She wiped her fingers on her napkin and smiled her warmest smile. "*Ach*, Lily, what an imagination you have! But Jonah doesn't need to worry about that. I would never throw a child out of my house. I love children."

Lily nodded, as if she'd known it all along. "I can tell." She sighed. "Boys are so *dumm*."

Mammi patted Jonah on the arm and smiled at him as if they shared a secret. "She still might marry someone else."

Vernon looked like he wanted to say something, but his mouth was so full, it was all he could do to chew carefully.

"I can't see that I will ever marry," Martha Sue said, even though she knew it would hurt Yost. But like it or not, they had agreed that Yost needed to work on Jonah first.

"I think you should marry Vernon," Jonah blurted out, as if he'd been holding it in for a long time.

Mammi raised her eyebrows, pursed her lips as if trying not to smile, and nodded at Jonah. Martha Sue pressed her fingers to her forehead. Oh, *sis yuscht*! Mammi and Jonah were conspiring to get her married to Vernon Schmucker.

Vernon dabbed his mouth with his napkin. "*Ach, vell*, I don't know yet," he said, as if he were deciding what shirt to wear to church. "I suppose I can overlook the fact that she doesn't like to fish. But I won't make any commitments until I taste her *yummasetti*."

Martha Sue would have liked to take that arrogant, oblivious confidence down a notch or two, but she refused to be rude to a guest in Mammi's home. Besides, being rude to Vernon would hurt Mammi's feelings. Vernon probably wouldn't even notice.

"It wonders me why you aren't already married, Vernon," Yost said, trying not to smile and obviously having a very hard time of it.

A ribbon of warm chocolate trickled down Martha Sue's spine. Yost's earlier distress was gone, replaced with something more tender and subdued on his face. He and Martha Sue shared a secret smile while Vernon launched into an explanation for why none of the girls in Bonduel could make a *gute* pecan pie and how his *mamm* wouldn't let him drink Diet Coke because she was afraid it would give him an ulcer.

Vernon ate seven cookies after dinner, again proclaiming that they needed more peanut butter. Jonah tried to hide the fact that he ate three cookies, because, of course, he didn't want Martha Sue to think he enjoyed anything she made. For some reason, his stubbornness made Martha Sue smile. For sure and certain he resented her, but he hadn't refused to eat her cooking, which meant his resentment didn't go stomach deep. It was a start. They said that the way to a man's heart was through his stomach. Could she touch Jonah's heart with food, and could she do it without attracting Vernon at the same time?

Yost cleared his plate and smiled at Lily. "We need to get you home before your *mamm* starts to worry."

"*Ach*, she won't worry. She knows I want to earn my dollar."

"*Cum*, Jonah," Yost said. "Help me hitch up the buggy, and we'll take Lily home."

Jonah made a face, but he put on his coat and followed Yost outside. Vernon stayed firmly planted at the table, eating his last cookie and telling Anna about how he'd been asked to be the *Vorsinger* on the Christmas hayride. "I have a *gute* bass voice. I'm really the only one who can carry the part."

Lily held out her hand to Martha Sue. She obviously liked shaking hands. She smiled, glanced in Vernon's direction, and leaned in to whisper, "No matter what Jonah says, don't marry Vernon. Jonah's *dat* is much nicer, and he smiles at you all the time."

Martha Sue had obviously been starved for a word if the encouragement of an eleven-year-old brought tears to her eyes. "*Denki*, Lily. I'll keep that in mind."

Lily put on her coat. "Jonah doesn't know anything about wicked stepmothers. Don't let him hurt your feelings. Boys are just *dumm* sometimes."

Martha Sue tried to swallow past the lump in her throat. It was *gute* advice.

There were five cookies left on the cooling rack. Martha Sue quickly piled them on a plate and stretched plastic wrap over the top. She slid on her sweater and followed Lily out the door. Yost and Jonah pulled in front of the house in the buggy. Martha Sue slid open the door, and Lily jumped inside. Jonah immediately slid as close to his *dat* as he could get. Martha Sue held out the plate to Jonah. "Here are the rest of the cookies, just in case you get hungry tonight."

Jonah nodded and acted as if he were reluctant to take the cookies, even though Martha Sue knew better. *Ach*, *vell*, his heart wasn't going to soften in a day.

"Is that the leftover cookies?"

Martha Sue turned and flinched. Vernon stood right behind her. She'd left him sitting at the kitchen table not thirty seconds ago, and now there he was, eyeing her cookies like a wolf. She had no idea he could move so fast. "*Jah*," she said. "This is the rest of the cookies."

Before she knew what was happening, Vernon snatched the plate from her hand. "I'll take them. I want my *mamm* to try them."

"Actually I was going to give them to Jonah."

Vernon peered inside the buggy. "You don't care if I take them, do you, Jonah? They weren't that *gute*."

The battle of emotions on Jonah's face was almost comical. His gaze flicked from the plate to Vernon and back again. "I don't care if you take them," he finally said through gritted teeth. "I don't wonder but Martha Sue made them especially for you."

Martha Sue didn't know whether to be annoyed that Vernon got her cookies or amused that Jonah was stuck between a rock and a hard place. When she saw Jonah eye the plate with regret, she had to swallow her laughter.

For sure and certain, he and Mammi were plotting to get Martha Sue and Vernon to fall in love.

Martha Sue stifled a smile. There were consequences to conspiring with Mammi. Jonah was going to miss out on a lot of cookies.

Chapter 8

Jonah took off his hat and tapped it against his thigh while watching for Dat. The day after Dat had told Jonah that he would have to walk home from school for the rest of the year, Dat had changed his mind. Now Dat went to the dairy very early in the morning, and Jonah walked to school, but Dat picked him up every afternoon after school without fail.

Jonah still didn't like being in Bonduel, away from his real friends, but it was April, and the weather was getting warmer. He and Dat went fishing twice a week, and Martha Sue was making him his own triple-layer chocolate cake because Jonah had helped her prune the peach trees last week.

Martha Sue was much nicer to be around now that she wasn't trying to steal Dat. She practically ignored Dat and never talked about him when he wasn't around. While they pruned trees last week, they'd talked about school, Lily Yoder, and Jonah's favorite ice cream. Martha Sue had told him the story of the time she was bitten by a dog and had to get rabies shots and about when she almost drowned at the lake. Jonah liked the drowning story because he was kind of afraid of water and Martha Sue understood.

Jonah didn't mind Martha Sue so much, but Dat had started acting weird. He never scolded Jonah about anything, even when Jonah wore his shoes on the bed or left his wet towel on the floor. He never made Jonah eat everything on his plate, and he always let him have dessert, even if Jonah hadn't eaten anything at dinner. But that wasn't the worst of it. If Lily came over, Dat had to be with them every second, like an annoying little *bruder* who tagged along even when he wasn't wanted. Lily and Jonah had taken to running into the woods on Huckleberry Hill when Dat wasn't looking. Dat read Jonah bedtime stories as if Jonah was a little kid and had even started singing Jonah lullabies before they went to sleep. Jonah frowned. No one must ever find out about the lullabies.

Dat wouldn't let Jonah go to friends' houses because he said, "I want to spend time with my son. Friends come and go, but family is forever." The forever family part was true, but that didn't mean Jonah had to spend every waking hour with his *dat*. A boy needed friends like Lily and Ben Stoltzfus and Gideon who sat by him at school, played with him at recess, and invited him over to their houses to eat. Dat just couldn't understand that Jonah needed his own friends and his own private time. Poor Dat needed some friends of his own. Maybe then he'd leave Jonah alone.

Someone ran up behind Jonah and grabbed his arm.

It was Lily. "Jonah, some of *die kinner* want to play softball at Wengerds' house. Do you want to come?"

Jonah's heart jumped like a rabbit. For sure and certain Dat would let him go play softball. Dat always said exercise was *gute* for him. "Right now?"

Lily clapped her hands. "We're going to walk over there. Come on."

Jonah turned and peered down the road. "Can you wait? I have to tell my *dat* when he comes." Surely Dat would say yes if Lily was standing right there looking cute and innocent like she always did.

Lily rolled her eyes. "If your *dat* didn't pick you up every day, you and I could walk home together, and you could come over and see my goats."

"I've seen your goats."

"*Jah*, but you haven't really played with them. You need to feed them and cuddle them and give them some love. That's what my *dawdi* says. He pays me three dollars a week to take care of them."

"Three dollars a week? He's only paying you a dollar a week for me."

Lily shrugged. "I know. But goats poop on the floor, so I guess it's harder."

Jonah smiled about that. It sounded as if Lily liked being his friend. He hoped so because even though he would never say it out loud, he was sort of starting to like Lily, even though she was being paid to be his friend. Her curls were the color of that hairy stuff from an ear of corn, and when she smiled, her nose crinkled really cute. She had turned twelve last week, and Lily's *mamm* had invited Jonah over for a piece of cake. Dat had let him go but insisted on coming too. "It will be fun to eat cake together."

To get away from Dat, Jonah and Lily had explored every inch of Huckleberry Hill looking for bears and huckleberries and wild beehives. They'd found hundreds of huckleberry bushes with no huckleberries on them and hardly any leaves either. They'd never seen a bear or a wild beehive. They liked to pretend they were hunters searching for wild game using long sticks as rifles and the binoculars from Lily's *dat*'s hunting gear box. Lily was as fun to play with as a boy. She liked to climb and jump and run as much as Jonah did, and she never cried when she got hurt. Last week she'd tripped over a branch and cut her leg, and there was blood everywhere, but she just kept walking and didn't complain once.

"Why don't you come to our house for dinner tonight?" Lily said. "After softball."

"I'll ask," Jonah said. If Dat didn't say yes, he'd give him a whiny speech about how a boy needed his own time, and *dats* needed to stay out of the way.

Lily glanced behind her. "*Vell*, ask quick. They're leaving."

Dat finally came down the road. He hadn't even come to a full stop when Jonah opened the buggy door. "Dat, I'm going to play softball at Wengerds'. And then Lily invited me over for dinner."

Dat smiled that weird smile he wore a lot lately. "I love softball. Let's go together."

Jonah's heart all but stopped. Lullabies were one thing, Dat showing up to a softball game was quite another. "Um, no, Dat. It's just for *die kinner*."

"Who made that rule?"

"It's not a rule. It's just how it is."

Dat looked unhappy. "But I want to spend time with you."

"We spend plenty of time together."

"*Nae*," Dat said. "We don't. You can't play softball today. We have to go home and finish that birdhouse."

Jonah was desperate enough to distract his *dat* by being surly. "What home? I live in a barn."

"I'm sorry," Dat said, not looking sorry at all with that smile plastered on his face. *Plastered* meant fake and weird. "I feel wonderful bad for making you sleep in a barn, but it doesn't matter where we live, as long as we're together. Anywhere I'm with you is home."

Ach, Jonah shouldn't have said anything about the barn. Dat was going to turn into a bowl of frosting if he got any sweeter.

Dat may have been talking all sickly sweet, but apparently, he wasn't going to budge about the birdhouse. "We need to finish that birdhouse so we can start on the wooden baskets. I can show you how to cut one using a single piece of wood."

Lily leaned into Dat's line of vision and waved. "*Hallo*, Yost."

"*Hallo*, Lily. Do you want to come to our barn and help us finish the birdhouse?"

Lily looked at Jonah as if it was a lost cause. "I want to play softball. So does Jonah. Can't he come?"

"Of course he can come. I already told him I'd go with him."

"You can't come, Dat."

Dat pinned Jonah with a look that said, *I love you in an annoying sort of way, but I'm not going to bend.* "We need to finish that birdhouse, and I want to spend as much time with Jonah as I can. Fathers and sons together forever. Right, Jonah?"

What could Jonah say to that? He didn't want to make Dat feel bad, not when Jonah was his only friend and the only person in the whole world who loved him. But it sure was irritating. "*Jah.* Together forever," he said, with as much enthusiasm as he could muster, which wasn't much. He really wanted to play softball.

He climbed in the buggy as if he were going to the dentist. Lily gave him a sour look before reaching out and closing the door behind him.

Dat didn't seem to notice Jonah's resentment. "We've got to get that birdhouse done so a bird family can move in. It's spring, you know."

It was spring, but the bird families had already built nests. That birdhouse wasn't going to do any *gute* for anybody until next spring. Jonah sighed. "Dat, I like making birdhouses, but . . ."

"I'm *froh* you do. I feel really bad about bringing you up here, and I really want to make amends."

"You don't have to do that. We could just move back to Ohio." Jonah drew his brows together, not sure if he wanted to move back to Ohio just yet. He was making friends, Lily Yoder paid attention to him, and Martha Sue's cooking was much better than Dat's had ever been.

"We can't move back yet," Dat said.

"Martha Sue said she's not going to marry you, Dat." At least that was settled. One less thing for Jonah to worry about.

"We can't move back because I've already leased out the land to Blaine Porter. I've got a job here at the cheese factory that will tide us over until we can go back and take over the farm."

Jonah didn't let the relief show on his face. He missed his friends back in Ohio, but he also had friends here, most especially Lily Yoder. He wouldn't mind spending the whole summer playing softball and running around Huckleberry Hill with her.

Dat jiggled the reins to get the horse going faster. "I'm thinking of taking a break from work over the summer. We're not paying anything for food or rent so I think I'd be able to afford it." He turned and plastered that smile on his face. "You and I would never have to be apart. We can go fishing and camping every week. We can make a dozen birdhouses and baskets. Of course we'll help Anna and Felty with their garden and their trees. We can even take over milking the cow and picking huckleberries. Just you and me together the whole summer. What do you say to that?"

Dat looked at Jonah as if expecting him to jump up and down for joy, which would have been hard to do in a buggy even if he had felt like doing it. But Jonah didn't feel like jumping or leaping or even hopping. He would not give up his summer with Lily and the others just because Dat felt guilty. He understood that Dat loved him deeply, but love didn't mean you had to spend every minute of every day with someone. Jonah had to put a stop to this as gently as possible. "Dat, I know you feel bad for moving us up here to Wisconsin, but it's okay. You don't have to quit your job. I'll find things to keep me busy this summer without your help.

And I promise I won't be mad at you for moving us up to Wisconsin. There's no use crying over spilled milk."

"I guess that's true, but I still want to take the summer off and spend it with you. I know how lonely and unhappy you are here, and it's all my fault. I wouldn't be a *gute fater* if I didn't at least try to make the best of it for you, to repair the damage I've done. It's not about crying over spilled milk. It's about making restitution for hurting my son."

Jonah would have to look up *restitution*, but he understood Dat's meaning.

His summer was ruined.

Jonah pressed his lips together. He'd never been one to give up easily. He had found a way to get rid of Martha Sue. He'd find a way to save his summer too.

By the time they finished the stupid birdhouse, it was dinnertime. *Ach, vell*, it wasn't a stupid birdhouse. It was extra-large with a steep roof and a small round hole for the birds to get in and out. Tomorrow they were going to fasten it to a pole and see if any birds would move in. It was a hopeless cause, because all the birds had already found homes, but it made Dat feel *gute*, and Dat needed all the *gute* feelings he could get.

Jonah and Dat washed up and went to the house for dinner. Jonah had been looking forward to his cake all day. He had decided to like cake again, and he loved triple-chocolate layer cake. Martha Sue always sprinkled little shavings of white and dark chocolate over the top. The shavings were Jonah's favorite part.

His cake sat in the center of the table like the centerpiece at a wedding alongside a bowl of something white and lumpy. The cake was no bigger than two cupcakes stacked on top of each other. The sides and top were covered with smooth chocolate frosting, and Martha Sue had indeed sprinkled shavings of white and dark chocolate over the top. She'd also made a little scalloped design with frosting around the cake. It looked prettier than anything Jonah had ever seen in a bakery.

Anna greeted Jonah at the door with a hug as if she was truly happy to see him. It made him feel warm and mushy inside. "*Ach*, Jonah, Martha Sue made you your very own cake. I made rice pudding for the rest of us so we don't feel left out. Vernon loves dessert."

Jonah tried to hide a grimace. Vernon was coming to dinner? *Ach*, didn't he have anything better to do than bother people?

Anna pulled him close and whispered in his ear, "I think our plan to match Martha Sue and Vernon is working. *Denki* for being so nice to him."

Jonah couldn't remember being nice to Vernon, except maybe when he let Vernon have the last of the Peanut Butter Blossom cookies. *Jah*, he'd been very nice about the cookies because watching Vernon walk away with the cookies that should have been his had been very painful.

Jonah sort of faked a smile. "You're welcome. I want to help you." But he wasn't giving Vernon any more of his food, not even for Anna's sake.

Martha Sue was at her normal place by the stove. She turned and smiled at Jonah and his *dat*. "What do you think of the cake?"

Jonah didn't want her to think he liked her just because of a cake, but he'd be ungrateful if he didn't say something. "It looks *appeditlich*."

"It's just your size. You don't have to share it with anyone."

"*Denki*," Jonah said. He liked not having to share his special cake, even though Dat always said it was nice to share. Sometimes it was okay to be a little selfish.

"*Nae*," Martha Sue said. "Thank *you* for helping with the pruning. It's a hard job."

Martha Sue was smiling a lot more than she used to, and she looked happy that Jonah liked his cake. Jonah swallowed past the lump in his throat. When she and Dat had begun seeing each other, she smiled and laughed all the time. Then Jonah had started playing tricks on her, and Martha Sue had stopped smiling. He kind of felt bad about it, but he didn't feel too bad. He had saved his family, and that was the most important thing. It didn't matter now anyway because Martha Sue seemed happy again. No harm done.

Felty sat on the sofa fiddling with something on the coffee table. "Jonah, Yost, come and see this new gadget."

Jonah and his *dat* strolled into the great room, and Martha Sue and Anna followed. Anna sat on the sofa next to Felty. "*Ach*, my grandson-in-law Noah is so clever. He made this bubble gum dispenser for *die kinner*. He and Mandy came for a visit earlier today."

A round glass container full of colorful gumballs sat atop a wooden box. Felty pulled a lever on the side of the box, and a gumball rolled out of a hole at the bottom. Jonah smiled. The birdhouse was fun, but making this would take a little bit more creativity. But he wouldn't tell his *dat*. Dat would have them making gumball machines and birdhouses all day, and Jonah's summer was already in danger.

They took turns getting gumballs from the dispenser. Dat and Felty talked about how Noah might have fashioned the lever, and Anna commented on what flavors the gumballs were.

Suddenly, Martha Sue gasped. "Vernon, what are you doing?"

Jonah hadn't heard him come in, but Vernon was standing next to the table, fork in hand, with a smear of chocolate frosting on his lips. Jonah's gaze flew to his special cake. It looked as if it had fallen to the enemy in an attack. Every last chocolate shaving, white and dark, had been scraped off the top, and Vernon's fork had demolished one whole side of the cake, leaving the inside layers visible to the whole world.

The way everyone was looking at him, Vernon seemed to know he'd done something wrong. He smacked his lips and frowned. "I'm wonderful hungry, and life is short. You should always eat dessert first."

Did Vernon really think he'd die before he got a chance to eat dessert tonight?

"Vernon," Martha Sue moaned. "I made that cake especially for Jonah."

"How was I to know? I assumed you made the cake especially for me." He pumped his enormous eyebrows up and down. "I know you want to impress me."

Martha Sue glanced at Jonah, and he thought he might have heard a growl from deep in her throat.

"It's a little dry," Vernon said. "But it's chocolatey, and I like the shavings on top."

Jonah nearly choked on his anger. How dare Vernon eat his special cake, especially when there was a perfectly *gute* rice pudding sitting right next to it?

Anna cleared her throat loudly and gave Jonah a significant look, like he was in on her secret. He pretended not to know what she meant. He didn't care that they were trying to get Vernon and Martha Sue married to each other. Vernon had eaten his cake!

Felty gave Martha Sue a half smile. "At least you know it turned out *gute*."

Anna was almost giddy. "I'm *froh* Vernon is enjoying it."

Dat placed his hand on Jonah's shoulder and smiled as if he didn't care about Jonah's loss. "You can still eat Anna's rice pudding. That's just as special as a cake."

Jonah narrowed his eyes. They were trying to be so nice. Didn't anybody care about *his* feelings?

Martha Sue marched to the kitchen, grabbed the fork from Vernon's fist, and slammed it on the table. "Vernon, that was very rude of you. You're not entitled to eat everything in this house just because Mammi invited you to dinner. You need to apologize to Jonah."

Jonah's heart played drums in his chest. He had never seen Martha Sue so indignant, not even after he'd set that water booby trap over her door. She might have been even madder than Jonah was.

Vernon took off his hat and pursed his lips as his gaze traveled between Jonah and Martha Sue. "I'm sorry for eating your special cake, Jonah. But since it's already halfway gone, it wonders me if I can eat the rest."

Martha Sue's eyes grew as round as buggy wheels. "You can't eat the rest of it. It's Jonah's."

Jonah skulked over to the table and peered at his cake. Most of the frosting was gone, and the top layer leaned precariously over the bottom layer. *Precariously* meant that it was going to collapse any second now. He looked at Martha Sue. Her eyes blazed with anger, and she was glaring at Vernon as if she'd like to skewer him with his own fork. Jonah was kind of glad that Martha Sue felt so bad about the cake. At least somebody cared about his feelings, but Jonah wasn't going to touch that cake now that it had Vernon's spit all over it. "Vernon might as well finish it."

A small smile crept onto Vernon's lips. He kept his eyes on Martha Sue as he picked up his fork, slid the cake plate closer, and took another large bite. "It's wonderful *gute* cake," Vernon said. "Some of the best I ever tasted. Even my *mamm* would approve of this cake."

Now he was just trying to make Martha Sue feel better, but if the look on her face was any sign, it wasn't working. She leaned over and whispered in Jonah's ear, "Is there a *gute* thesaurus word for how I'm feeling right now?"

"Are you mad?"

"Very."

Jonah grinned in spite of himself. "Incensed," he said.

Martha Sue nodded thoughtfully. "Incensed. I like it. It sounds like a hissing snake."

Jonah liked that about *incensed*. Cats hissed when they were mad. So did people.

Anna clapped her hands as if all the happiness in the world was in her house at this very moment. "Well, isn't that nice."

Martha Sue's lips curled upward, but it didn't look

like she was smiling. "Let's eat before the pizza gets cold."

Jonah didn't mind so much about losing his cake when Martha Sue removed two wonderful-smelling pizzas from the oven. He liked pizza almost as much as he liked cake.

Anna sat next to Jonah at her regular place at the table and patted his arm. "Thank you for sacrificing your cake," she whispered. "It was for the greater good."

Jonah didn't know what that meant. He'd have to look it up in his thesaurus.

Vernon sat in his regular place next to Martha Sue. They all watched him finish his cake before prayer. He'd probably get a stomachache for eating food that hadn't been blessed yet.

After silent prayer, Martha Sue reached over and passed the pizza to Jonah. "Here. I want to make sure you get all you want. This one is barbecue chicken, and this one is pepperoni."

"Pepperoni, please," Jonah said, taking two large slices from the pizza stone. He hesitated. Should he take three? The way Vernon was eating, there might not be any left after the pizza got to him.

Vernon took two slices of each kind of pizza. "I should bring some trout next time I come, and you can fry it. Our freezer is full of trout. I tie my own flies, and they are wonderful *gute* for catching trout." He looked at Martha Sue. "Do you know how to cook trout? Too many girls overcook it, and it turns out dry."

Martha Sue glanced at Dat and smiled. She knew how to cook trout. In Ohio, Dat and Jonah caught trout almost every week, and Martha Sue just fried it in a pan with a little lemon, onion powder, and salt. It was always *appeditlich*. Jonah frowned. Before Martha Sue had invaded their lives, Dat had cooked the trout, and he made trout just as *gute* as Martha Sue's. They certainly didn't need Martha Sue for anything.

Vernon looked at Martha Sue as if she was a chocolate doughnut with sprinkles. "You should come over on Friday and watch me tie flies. Mamm says it's like watching an artist paint a picture."

Suddenly, a *wunderbarr* idea hit Jonah right between the eyes. If he wanted to play softball on Friday, he needed to get rid of Dat. He made his eyes and his smile wide. "Dat, you like to tie flies. You should go help Vernon tie flies on Friday. You're the best fly-tyer in the whole world." Jonah turned to Vernon. "You don't mind if my *dat* goes, do you?"

Vernon narrowed his eyes. "I'm probably the best fly-tyer. It takes years of practice."

Jonah didn't believe it for a minute. Dat was better at everything than anybody, especially Vernon Schmucker. But if he wanted to get rid of Dat, Jonah needed to pretend Vernon was the best. "Since you're so *gute*, you can show my *dat* how you do it."

Vernon's frown etched itself more deeply into his face. "I don't know. I don't like to share my secrets."

Jonah nearly growled his frustration. First Vernon had wanted to show Martha Sue how he tied flies, now he didn't want anyone to see? "Then just show my *dat* how to do the easy ones."

Vernon puckered his lips. "I suppose I can do that,

but you can't talk. I need complete silence to do my work."

Dat looked at Jonah and shrugged. "That sounds fun." He didn't sound even a little excited, but as long as he went, Jonah didn't care if he had a *gute* time. "You could show Vernon some of the flies you know how to tie," Dat said.

Jonah's heart did a somersault. "Not me, Dat. Vernon doesn't want a little kid in his shop. Do you, Vernon?"

Vernon took a swig of milk. "I don't like having *kinner* there. They make too much noise, and I can't concentrate."

"Jonah isn't a little kid," Dat said. "And we do everything together. I can't go without him."

Jonah grasped at a straw. "Go without me. You won't have fun if I'm there." Jonah couldn't imagine Dat having any fun alone with Vernon anyway, but Jonah had to get Dat out of his hair for at least one afternoon.

"I have a better idea," Anna said. "Why doesn't Martha Sue go along?" She winked at Jonah, who grinned back at her. He could kill two birds with one stone. Dat would be out of his hair, and Martha Sue and Vernon could fall in love.

Anna was a genius. Jonah couldn't have planned it any better himself. "*Jah*, Martha Sue," he said eagerly. "You'd have fun learning to tie flies."

Vernon bloomed into a wide, delighted smile. "*Jah*, Martha Sue. I want you to come see my shop. Mamm says it's like watching an artist paint a picture."

Martha Sue looked at Dat. "It might be fun."

Anna beamed. "For sure and certain you'll fall in love with it. Won't she, Jonah?"

Jonah didn't like the way Martha Sue was looking at Dat. Maybe he shouldn't be encouraging them to spend more time together, even if Anna thought it would help Martha Sue fall in love with Vernon. Jonah flinched when Anna kicked him under the table. What did she want him to say? "Uh, *jah*, Martha Sue. It's fun tying flies."

Martha Sue smiled doubtfully at Jonah then glued her eyes on Dat. "I'd like it if you taught me how."

Martha Sue most definitely shouldn't go with Vernon and Dat.

Anna balled her napkin in her fist. "Jonah can teach you. He's the best fisherman in his whole family."

Jonah turned a puzzled gaze to Anna. He wasn't that *gute* at tying flies. And he'd certainly never taught someone how to do it. "I can't do that." Anna kicked him under the table again. He grunted in surprise.

"Of course you can," Anna said. "Martha Sue needs a teacher."

"It's going to be wonderful crowded in my shop," Vernon muttered, peeling a piece of pepperoni off the top of the pizza with his bare hands—not from his piece, but from the pizza sitting in the middle of the table.

"You're right about that," Anna said. "You won't have room to tie flies at all."

Jonah narrowed his eyes. What was Anna up to? Ten seconds ago, she'd wanted everyone to tie flies at Vernon's house. They didn't need to give up on the original plan, which was to get rid of Dat so Jonah could play softball. Martha Sue would have to fall in love with

Vernon another time. "Dat still wants to learn how. Let Dat go by himself."

Either Anna didn't hear him, or she didn't like his idea. "I think it would be more fun to have a picnic."

Vernon's ears perked up. "A picnic?"

"*Jah*," Anna said, her eyes alight with the excitement of her new idea. "It will be more like a snack picnic, since Yost doesn't get off work until three, and Jonah won't be out of school earlier than that."

Jonah drew his brows together. Dat, Martha Sue, and Vernon together on a picnic? It didn't sit quite right with Jonah, but he was dying to play softball. "A picnic sounds fun."

"Martha Sue could make her famous rolls and a pecan pie, and you could go to that grassy spot on the backside of the hill by the rocks. Felty built a bench there, so you don't even have to sit on the ground."

"It's a little cold for a picnic," Martha Sue said. "Maybe we should put it off until June."

Oh, no. Jonah wasn't going to miss that softball game. "You can take blankets."

"Will you bring raspberry jam?" Vernon asked.

Martha Sue gazed at Dat again. "For sure and certain."

Vernon shrugged. "I'll come if there's pecan pie and raspberry jam."

Jonah wasn't completely satisfied about the situation. He didn't trust Martha Sue and Dat to be together and not fall in love again, but he could worry about that later. At least he could go play softball.

Anna patted her mouth with her napkin. "I'll make

my gingersnaps that Jonah loves so much since he'll be going with you."

Jonah's mouth fell open. "I'm not going! I'm playing softball." He hadn't planned on telling anyone about the softball game, but he *was not* going on a picnic with Vernon, Dat, and Martha Sue. Everybody had to know that.

Anna kicked him under the table again. Thank Derr Herr she was nearly a hundred years old and didn't kick very hard. "Now, Jonah, nobody knows how to get to the picnic spot but me, Felty, and you, and Felty and I are too old to make the trek."

"I'm not too old," Felty said. Was it Jonah's imagination, or did he have a mischievous twinkle in his eye?

Anna jerked her leg, and Felty flinched and gave her a look of complete shock. Apparently, she'd just kicked him under the table too. "Felty, you have work to do in the garden. Those peas aren't going to plant themselves. Jonah knows the way. He and Lily have been all over this hill."

Jonah wasn't going to give up that easily. "Why don't they just have a picnic on the front porch? Then Vernon wouldn't have to walk all that way."

Vernon licked pizza sauce off his fingers. "I'd rather not go if it's far."

Anna's smile pushed all her wrinkles to the back of her face. She handed Vernon another piece of pizza. "Stuff and nonsense. There's a giant forsythia bush growing wild right there, and it is a sight to see in the spring. Wouldn't you like to see the brilliant forsythia bush, Vernon?"

Vernon eyed Anna suspiciously. "You've seen one forsythia bush, you've seen them all."

"Not so, Vernon. This one grows like a canopy over the bench. It's very romantic. Wouldn't you like to see that?"

Vernon glanced at Martha Sue and pumped his eyebrows up and down. "I wouldn't mind a little romance."

Anna gazed around the table as if she'd just put a very hard puzzle together. "*Gute*. It's settled. Yost can pick Jonah up from school on Friday, and then you can all go for a picnic." She gasped and covered her mouth with her hand. "I'm afraid the three of you will have to go without Yost. I forgot that Yost needs to take care of the limbs before it rains again."

Limbs? What limbs?

Jonah didn't even try to stifle a groan. "Can't he do that another day?"

Out of the corner of his eye, Jonah saw Anna move her foot in Felty's direction. Felty flinched and sat up straighter. "I've got to plant peas, so I need Yost to stack the limbs," he said. "I'm afraid the three of you will have to go alone."

Martha Sue seemed to feel the same way Jonah did. "Everybody is busy. We can do it another time."

"I wouldn't hear of it," Anna said. "You three go and have fun."

Dat stared faithfully at his plate, but the ghost of a smile played at his lips. "*Jah*, Jonah. Even though you and I can't be together, I think you'll really enjoy yourself with Vernon and Martha Sue."

Jonah felt uneasy, as if in some way, the joke was on him. But Vernon needed to marry Martha Sue, and Dat needed to help with the limbs, and Jonah didn't want to get kicked again. He said goodbye to any fun he might have had on Friday afternoon. A picnic with Martha Sue and Vernon was going to be worse than going to the dentist. He choked down his dry pizza crust, wondering how his perfect plan had gone so wrong.

Chapter 9

Jonah lifted his hat, slid on his beanie, then put his straw hat back on his head. The weather was definitely warmer this week, though it was still too cold to be out without a coat. He wouldn't have had to wear a coat if he'd been playing softball. Running around always warmed him up. Unfortunately, he wasn't playing softball, and it looked as if he wouldn't get to play softball at all this year except at recess, because Dat was determined to ruin his life.

Lily and Ben and the other kids were playing softball without him. Again. Because he was stuck at a romantic picnic spot on the rugged side of Huckleberry Hill with Vernon Schmucker, who had stolen his special cake, and Martha Sue Helmuth, who had tried to steal his *dat*. Not even Sparky the dog had been willing to come with them today. It was too cold, and nobody liked Vernon. Not even Sparky. This was all Anna's fault, and Jonah had only forgiven her because she was a *mammi* and she wanted to help Jonah get rid of Martha Sue by marrying her off to Vernon.

Jonah almost felt bad for Martha Sue. A life with

Vernon Schmucker would be very unpleasant. *Unpleasant* meant that Vernon would eat all the food, criticize Martha Sue's cooking, and chew with his mouth open.

Getting to the picnic spot hadn't been easy. Vernon couldn't walk more than a hundred feet without stopping to rest, and he'd complained the whole way that he'd rather be fishing. More than once, Jonah had wanted to tell him that he could have been playing softball instead of attending this stupid picnic, but he'd kept his mouth shut because he didn't want to say anything that might make Vernon think twice about falling in love with Martha Sue. If Martha Sue and Vernon married, it would be worth missing a hundred softball games.

So instead, Jonah had dropped hints about how romantic the grassy spot was and how much Vernon was going to enjoy sitting next to Martha Sue on the bench and eating her pecan pie. Vernon had been a little less grumpy after that.

They had to climb down a few large rocks to get to the grassy area, but the climb was just like going down three tall steps. Jonah and Martha Sue hadn't needed to hold on to anything to get down. Vernon had held tightly to a protruding tree branch to navigate the steps, but they'd all ended up safely at the picnic spot, and Vernon had stopped gasping for air five minutes ago.

The grassy spot was more mud than grass because spring was young and plants were just beginning to peek out from under the dirt. But Anna hadn't lied about the forsythia bush. Its branches stretched eight feet long and high, growing into the surrounding bushes and trees. Little yellow flowers covered the branches, and the whole area looked like a hundred yellow paint cans had exploded and left splashes of color everywhere. Jonah could appreciate a pretty bush, even though he was only thirteen. He'd have to bring Lily out here to see it.

Martha Sue had laid a small plastic tarp on the ground, which was a smarter idea than a blanket that just would have gotten wet. She'd laid a tablecloth over the tarp and pulled a bag of rolls and a jar of jam out of her tote.

Vernon sat on the bench, and Martha Sue and Jonah sat on the tarp. It was obvious that Martha Sue didn't want to sit by Vernon and Vernon didn't want to sit on the ground. He might not have been able to get up. Jonah cleared his throat. "Martha Sue, why don't you sit on the bench? The ground is wonderful cold."

Martha Sue gave Jonah a sweet smile, almost as if she felt sorry that he had missed his softball game and he was stuck out here with her and Vernon. "It's easier to reach the food if I'm sitting down here. But *denki* for being so thoughtful. *Denki* for bringing us here. It's a very pretty spot."

"I like the yellow blossoms."

"What is another *gute* word for *pretty*?" Martha Sue asked. "*Pretty* doesn't seem descriptive enough."

Jonah scratched his head beneath his beanie and hat. "I wish I had my thesaurus. I'll have to look when I get home. *Beautiful* is always nice."

"*Jah. Beautiful* is a *gute* word."

Vernon wiped the beads of sweat from his upper lip. "It's not the prettiest place I've ever seen. For sure and certain, it wasn't worth the walk it took to get here."

Martha Sue gave Jonah a secret smile, and Jonah smiled back. Vernon complained about everything.

Martha Sue cut a roll in half. "Do you want jam on your roll, Jonah?"

He nodded. "*Jah*. Raspberry is my favorite."

Her eyes flashed with something like affection. "I know. Remember last summer when we picked raspberries and made three dozen pints of jam?"

"I remember. I burned my pinky finger."

She gave him a sympathetic frown. "I felt so bad for you. For sure and certain you were a wonderful *gute* help that day. We couldn't have done it without you."

"My *mamm* makes jam and orange marmalade," Vernon said, "even though I don't especially like marmalade. Sometimes I think she makes it just to spite me." He pointed to Martha Sue. "You don't make marmalade, do you?"

Martha Sue shook her head. "I don't, but I'm thinking of learning how."

Jonah pressed his lips together to keep from laughing at the look on Vernon's face. He eyed Martha Sue as if she had just insulted his whole family.

Martha Sue spread a whole glob of jam on Jonah's roll, put the top back on, and handed it to him. "Vernon, do you want jam on your roll?"

"*Jah*. Lots please."

She fixed a roll for Vernon, but Jonah noticed how she only put about half as much jam on Vernon's as she had on Jonah's. Did that mean she liked Jonah better than she liked Vernon? Jonah tried not to think about that. He didn't want Martha Sue to like him. He wanted her to leave his family alone. He wanted her to marry

Vernon, even though she'd be miserable and Vernon would be the worst husband in the whole world.

Martha Sue spread jam on a roll for herself and took a bite. "So, Jonah," she said, "have you learned any new words from your thesaurus this week?"

He grinned. "I looked up *loquacious*."

"And do you agree that Lily is loquacious?"

"For sure and certain."

She leaned back on her hands. "I like that about her. She gets excited about things and wants to tell everybody. She certainly likes you."

Jonah felt his face get warm. "I guess. But her *dawdi* is paying her a dollar a week to be friends with me."

"That was probably why she agreed to be friends with you, but that's not why she sticks with you. She sees what a nice boy you are. Not all *die kinner* are as nice as you."

Jonah looked away. He hadn't been nice to Martha Sue. Why was she saying what she knew wasn't true? "I'm not that nice."

"Of course you are. You used to take Mrs. Unger's garbage can in from the street every week. She couldn't have done that without you. Remember when Mayne King threw up in church? You entertained little Matthew while others cleaned up the mess. You're very thoughtful like that."

Jonah took a bite of his roll. He guessed he was sort of nice, but that didn't mean he would go out of his way to be nice to Martha Sue. She shouldn't expect it. Besides, she needed to concentrate on Vernon. "I learned another word this week. It's *ardor*."

"What does that mean?" Martha Sue said.

Jonah peered at Vernon and smiled innocently. "Romance."

Vernon's expression brightened. "Mamm says girls like romance. Mamm says I should always try to do romantic things like bring girls fish and compliment their cooking."

There wasn't anything romantic about fish, and that was probably why Vernon wasn't married yet. "You should try flowers," Jonah said. "Girls like flowers."

Vernon immediately stood, pulled a forsythia blossom from the nearest branch, and handed it to Martha Sue. "Here you go."

Martha Sue's face turned red, but Jonah couldn't tell if it was from awkwardness or delight. Probably awkwardness. Vernon was as clunky as a pair of wooden shoes. "*Denki*, Vernon," she said. She placed the blossom on the tarp next to her tote bag and then acted as if he'd never given it to her. "Jonah, you like words. Have you ever done a crossword puzzle?"

"*Nae*. I don't know how."

Martha Sue brushed some crumbs from her skirt. "*Ach*, I love crossword puzzles. You're very smart. I know you'd like them. I have a whole book full. When we get back, I'll let you borrow it."

"Okay," Jonah said. Martha Sue thought he was nice *and* smart? How could that be? She didn't even like him.

They finished off the rolls, and Martha Sue pulled the pie out of her tote along with a knife, a spatula, three forks, and three paper plates. She cut three pieces of pie and gave Jonah the biggest piece.

Vernon noticed. "I think you gave Jonah my piece," he said.

Martha Sue took the plate from Vernon's hand and studied it as if it contained some sort of riddle. "*Nae*, Vernon. This is your piece. You can always have more."

Vernon frowned. "I need to get my fair share."

Martha Sue acted like she wanted to laugh. "What is your fair share?"

"*Ach, vell*," Vernon said. "I guess since this is our romantic picnic, my fair share is all of the pie."

Jonah clutched his plate closer and turned slightly away from Vernon. Vernon wasn't getting his piece, no matter what.

Martha Sue ate one small piece of pie, Jonah ate two big pieces, and Vernon had the rest. He ended up eating the last piece right out of the pie tin.

While Vernon finished up the pie, Martha Sue put the rest of the trash and dirty dishes in her bag. She handed Jonah a wet wipe to clean his fingers. "Do you want to play a game?"

"I don't like games," Vernon said, his mouth so full Jonah could barely understand him. "Why play games when you could be fishing?"

Martha Sue gave Jonah that secret smile again, as if the two of them shared a joke that Vernon didn't know about. "Why indeed." She wiped her hands. "Here is the game. I'll go first. I pick a category and a letter, and then we take turns saying a word in that category that starts with that letter. For instance, I might say, *T* and flower. Then we would have to name all the flowers that start with *T*. The winner is the last one who can think of a flower starting with that letter."

Jonah sat up straighter. "I'm good at word games."

"I don't wonder but you are."

"I don't want to play," Vernon said.

Martha Sue didn't seem disappointed about Vernon. Jonah certainly wasn't. "We'll play without you. All right, Jonah, animal starting with *S*."

"Snake!" Vernon shouted.

"*Denki*, Vernon, but you said you didn't want to play."

"I don't," Vernon mumbled.

Jonah didn't even have to think. "Seal."

"Sea lion," Martha Sue countered.

"Seahorse."

"Sheep."

"Salmon," Vernon shouted. For someone who didn't want to play the game, he sure had a lot to say.

Jonah drew his brows together. He would have said *salmon*, but Vernon stole it. "Skunk."

"Swan."

A familiar chatter in one of the trees saved Jonah from losing the game. "Squirrel."

"Spider." *Ach*. Martha Sue was quick.

"Snail."

Martha Sue hesitated, then made a face. "I can't think of another one. You win, Jonah."

Jonah grinned. "I'm *gute* at this game."

"I want to play," Vernon said, setting the empty pie tin on the bench next to him.

"Okay. It's Jonah's turn to pick a category and a letter."

They played three more rounds of Martha Sue's game. Jonah won two. Martha Sue won one. She was smarter than Jonah had realized. He didn't notice the clouds gathering in the sky until it started to lightly rain.

Martha Sue tucked her coat tighter around her neck. "*Ach*, we better go before we get soaked."

Jonah stood and pulled Martha Sue to her feet, then picked up her tote. When she tried to take it from him, he shook his head. "I can carry it."

The two of them scurried up the rock steps and headed toward the house without realizing that Vernon wasn't behind them. "Martha Sue, help. You can't just leave me here."

Jonah turned around, but he couldn't see Vernon. He and Martha Sue trudged back to the top of the rocks. Vernon stood at the bottom looking up at them like a waterlogged puppy. "I tried to get up, but the rocks are too slippery, and I can't reach the branch to pull myself up."

"Can you crawl?" Martha Sue said.

Vernon looked shocked that she would suggest such a thing. "And get my knees wet?"

Jonah was a little disgusted that Vernon couldn't climb up three medium-size rocks. "It's not that hard. Just hold on to the tree and step up."

Vernon gave Jonah the stink eye. "Don't you think I'd do that if I could? I was born with weak knees, and I've never been a *gute* climber. That's why I took up fishing."

Jonah had half a mind to give up fishing just because Vernon liked it so much. He heaved a sigh. "I guess we could pull you up."

Vernon reached out. Jonah stretched out his hand and leaned down, but his arms weren't long enough. Martha

Sue grabbed on to Jonah's other hand to give him some support, but he still couldn't reach Vernon. Even if they managed to grab Vernon's hand and Martha Sue pulled with all her might, they wouldn't be able to get enough traction to haul Vernon up. He probably weighed a hundred pounds more than the two of them combined.

Jonah stepped back, and Vernon propped his hands on his hips. "This is all your fault. You said it was going to be romantic. This is not romantic, and I am not having a *gute* time. You owe me an apology."

Jonah wasn't about to apologize for anything. Anna had tricked him into coming, and he'd done his best to make Martha Sue fall in love with Vernon. It wasn't his fault that Vernon was impossible to love.

"Don't get mad at Jonah," Martha Sue scolded. "If you hadn't eaten so much pie, you'd be more light on your feet."

Exactly what Jonah thought.

Vernon grunted. "The filling was runny, and the crust was overcooked. You should thank me for eating it."

Martha Sue cocked an eyebrow in his direction. "Maybe now isn't the best time to criticize my cooking."

Vernon suddenly looked a little concerned. "You wouldn't leave me down here?"

Martha Sue made a face and whispered, "It's tempting." She folded her arms, tapped her index finger on her chin, and made her voice louder. "I suppose not." She turned to Jonah. "You should probably go get your *dat*. And a rope."

Jonah grinned and nodded. "I'll go find him." He took two steps and turned back. "That pie was *appeditlich*. Don't let him upset you."

That made her smile. "*Denki*. I'm not upset. I'm irritated that Mammi is still trying to get me to marry someone who can't think about anyone but himself." She grimaced. "I'm sorry. Is that rude?"

"Maybe. But it's also true."

Jonah ran back to the top of Huckleberry Hill and found Dat stacking limbs from the pruned peach trees. Jonah quickly explained what had happened, which made Dat laugh right out loud. It was probably a sin to laugh at Vernon's misfortune, but it was kind of funny, and Jonah liked it when his *dat* laughed.

They found a long rope in the shed, and Dat and Jonah and the rope went back to the rocks where Martha Sue was waiting. She stood with her arms wrapped around herself, gazing down at Vernon who sat on the bench looking as mad as a bee with a boil. Jonah had never actually seen a bee with a boil, but it was an expression Dat used all the time.

Jonah didn't like it, but Dat always looked so happy when he saw Martha Sue. And Martha Sue always looked so happy to see him. Dat's grin was too big for his face. "How was the picnic?" he said.

Martha Sue scrunched her lips to one side of her face. "Delightful." She glanced at Jonah. "What's a better word?"

Jonah's lips curled upward. "Disaster."

Martha Sue giggled. "I don't think those are synonyms, and I didn't think it was a disaster. The food was *gute*, and the game was fun, but then it started raining. I'm sorry you had to interrupt limb stacking to help us out."

Dat's look was mushy. "I'm not."

Vernon stood up, and his scowl could have lit that

forsythia bush on fire. "Are you going to stand there talking even knowing your fellowman's life is in danger?"

Dat wiped the smile off his face. "*Cum*, Jonah. Let's tie the rope down there around that maple and then up here around this aspen and create sort of a railing that Vernon can hold to pull himself up the rocks."

"Okay," Jonah said, grabbing one end of the rope and hopping down the rocks to the bench area. Dat was so smart. He could figure anything out. Martha Sue was smart too, in a different way. She knew almost as many words as Jonah did, but she didn't act puffed up about it.

Jonah tied the rope around the maple tree, using one of the strong knots Dat had taught him to tie. Dat tied the other end, so the rope was taut enough to give Vernon some support. Then Dat skipped down the rocks and smiled at Vernon. "Okay. Grab hold of this rope and use it to pull yourself up the rocks. The rocks are slippery, so hold on tight."

"Did you use a clove hitch?" Vernon wanted to know.

"I don't know what Jonah used down here," Dat said, "but I used a tautline hitch up there so I could tighten the rope. You'll be nice and secure."

"I used two half hitches." It was a sin to be proud, but Jonah was quite pleased with himself for knowing how to tie a strong knot.

Dat nodded. "Two half hitches. Jonah knows his knots. You go first, Vernon. I'll be right behind you to help if you fall."

Vernon furrowed his brow. "When I go fishing, I make sure I can always get out of wherever I go in, but Anna and Jonah said it would be romantic. I shouldn't have believed them."

Dat looked around. "The yellow blossoms are pretty. I'd say this is most surely a romantic spot." His gaze flicked in Martha Sue's direction. "If you're with the right person." He cleared his throat and grinned at Jonah. "Maybe you should bring Lily here."

Jonah made a face. "Romance is stupid."

Dat shuffled behind Vernon as he grabbed the rope and step by step, climbed up the rocks. When all was said and done, it took him about one minute, because it wasn't all that hard. Jonah untied the rope at the bottom and climbed back up the rocks. Vernon didn't even wait. He was already halfway up the slope, huffing and puffing like an angry bear. If they wanted to, they could catch up with him in ten seconds.

Martha Sue gave Jonah a smile that warmed his insides. "You didn't have to help, but you stuck right by me. *Denki*."

Dat put a hand on Jonah's shoulder. "Jonah's a *gute* boy. As a reward, I'm going to buy enough wood to make a dozen birdhouses. We can spend all summer building them. Won't that be fun?"

Jonah thought he might have to pull all his hair out.

Chapter 10

Martha Sue strolled down the aisle at Lark's Country Store trying to decide what to make for dinner this week. Yost loved anything with cheese in it—except for maybe cheesy jalapeno banana bread. For sure and certain, he wasn't a picky eater. Still, she took great care to always make his favorite foods. She loved to see his face light up when she set dinner on the table.

She hadn't made spaghetti in a long time or lasagna, and Jonah liked both. Yost liked pot roast with carrots and potatoes. Jonah loved chicken broccoli casserole, even though he hated broccoli by itself. They both liked fish, especially when they had caught it themselves, but Jonah seemed to have lost his enthusiasm for fish ever since he'd met Vernon.

Martha Sue smiled to herself. The picnic hadn't been half bad. Making progress with Jonah was completely worth watching Vernon snarf down her pie and then listening to him complain about it. Jonah had liked the game, and then he'd helped Vernon up the rocks, even though he obviously didn't like Vernon. It was downright heartwarming.

Was Jonah starting to like her, or did he feel safe

because she'd told him she wasn't going to marry his *dat*? Was she deceiving Jonah by leaving space in her heart for Yost? She shook her head. She didn't want to think about that. She only wanted to think about the way Jonah had smiled at her when she'd given him the biggest piece of pie and the way he'd helped her with Vernon. Was Jonah's stony heart starting to crack?

She turned down the aisle where the pasta was and saw a tall figure reading the ingredients list on a bag of elbow macaroni. Her heart did three cartwheels. It wasn't fair, but Yost was getting more handsome every day. He had married his first wife at age twenty, so he was only thirty-five. He was tall and handsome, with dark hair and wintery blue eyes that danced like sunlight on a lake whenever he looked at her. Yost was naturally cheerful though reserved, but he'd been forced to be more social as Jonah had gotten older. When you had a thirteen-year-old son, you couldn't just disappear into your fields without associating with anyone. You had to talk to teachers and other parents and your son's friends. Martha Sue loved Yost's quiet, gentle ways, even though it meant Jonah hadn't always received the discipline he needed. Yost truly didn't like confrontation or conflict, especially with his son, and so sometimes Jonah got away with more than he should have. Driving Martha Sue away was a *gute* example.

Perhaps if Yost had been stricter with Jonah in the beginning, Jonah wouldn't have dared do what he'd done to Martha Sue. But Martha Sue had fallen in love with Yost for the very qualities that made him the *fater* he was. She wouldn't want him any other way, even if it meant losing him in the end. Yost was not a stern disciplinarian. Martha Sue wouldn't have loved him so much if he were. He had such a tender heart.

Yost looked up from his noodles and bloomed into a smile. *Ach*, that smile had the power to make her knees weak.

She folded her arms around the handle of her shopping basket and gave him a skeptical grin. "That looks like interesting reading."

He chuckled softly. "It surely is."

"They say you should always read the nutrition information."

He set the noodles back on the shelf and winked. "If you must know, I've been following you up and down the aisles, and I knew you'd come here next. I picked up this bag and started reading so you'd think we just ran into each other accidentally."

Her pulse was trying to break some sort of speed record. "You've been following me?"

Yost nodded. "You know I can't resist you. Anna told me you were coming to the store, so I saddled up Big Red and rode over here as fast as I could." Dawdi only had one buggy, so Yost often rode Dawdi's horse, Big Red, to the cheese factory for work. Apparently, he also rode Big Red to the store to chase after girls he hoped to marry.

Martha Sue couldn't keep a wide smile from her lips. She knew Yost loved her, but sometimes it was very nice to know how far he'd go to be with her. "You came all this way to see me?"

"*Ach*, *vell*, and to read all about noodle ingredients. If we're going to see each other behind Jonah's back, we can't be picky about where we meet."

Martha Sue's smile faltered, even though the affection

in Yost's eyes took her breath away. "I'm afraid Jonah is going to be wonderful mad when he finds out we've deceived him."

Yost dismissed her concern with a wave of his hand. "We haven't deceived him. We just haven't told him everything."

"I told him I wasn't going to marry you. He thinks I'm going to marry Vernon Schmucker."

Yost's lips curled upward. "I'm sorry to disappoint you, Martha Sue, but not even Jonah believes you're going to marry Vernon Schmucker."

She giggled at the dramatically tragic expression on his face. "I suppose only Mammi believes there's still a chance for me and Vernon."

"*Ach, vell*, Anna and Vernon." He took her shopping basket in one hand and laced his fingers with hers. Martha Sue melted like chocolate. Thank Derr Herr they were the only two people standing in the aisle. What gossip there would have been if someone had seen them holding hands in public. "I don't have any remorse about leaving Jonah in the dark. Haven't you enjoyed the peace of the last few weeks? Jonah hasn't pulled one trick, and he's stopped giving you the silent treatment."

She nodded. "He really is quite delightful when he's not pouting. He played a game with me and helped me get Vernon up the rocks. Two months ago, he would have stranded me there."

Yost raised her hand to his lips and kissed her knuckles. "Sometimes he remembers the manners I've taught him. Sometimes it seems he was raised by wild pigs. I'm *froh* he helped you."

"Me too."

"I know you say you're not going to marry Vernon Schmucker, but I'm so jealous of him I could spit, even though jealousy is a sin."

She drew back in surprise. "No need to be jealous."

"I'm jealous that every minute he spends with you is a minute I'm not spending with you. I want to be with you every minute of every day. I live a hundred yards from your doorstep, but it feels like a hundred miles. This separation is driving me insane."

The emotion on his face was heartbreaking. She laid her hand on his cheek. "Please don't go crazy," she whispered. Her lips twitched. "I'd rather not marry a crazy man."

"I'd rather not go crazy. Secret meetings at the market are the only thing keeping me afloat." He smiled in spite of himself. "The *gute* news is that *I* am slowly driving *Jonah* crazy. He's getting more and more annoyed. Lord willing, he'll soon be so sick of me, he'll beg you to marry me just to give him some peace."

She caressed his cheek with her thumb. He drew in a trembling breath. "I pray that happens. I pray that Gotte's will is done, and that we will have a happy ending."

"We will," he said, wrapping his hand around her wrist. "Otherwise you will have to put me in an institution."

An older Amish woman came around the corner, and Yost and Martha Sue pulled away from each other as if a stiff wind had separated them. Yost turned and examined a package of macaroni and cheese. Martha Sue peered at the jars of spaghetti sauce. The woman grabbed a package of egg noodles from the shelf and passed between Yost and Martha Sue. "'Idle hands are the devil's playground,'" she mumbled as she passed.

Martha Sue clapped her hand over her mouth so as not to laugh out loud. Yost's eyes flashed with amusement, but he didn't make a sound until after the woman had disappeared around the corner.

He cupped his hand around Martha Sue's elbow. "Let's go out behind the store and do some kissing."

"What?" Martha Sue squeaked.

"She already assumes the worst. I think we should prove her right."

Martha Sue laughed. "You said you don't kiss unless it's absolutely necessary." She nibbled on her fingernail and gave him an innocent look. "Besides, I'll get in trouble with my *mamm*."

"I feel like a naughty teenager." Yost glanced to his right and to his left, set the shopping basket on the floor, and gathered Martha Sue into his arms. "This time, it's absolutely necessary." She protested that they'd get caught for sure and certain. He pulled her close and kissed her until fireworks went off in her head.

He finally let go, even though she didn't want him to. "What do you think you are doing?" she scolded in mock indignation.

He laughed, and it sounded like pure happiness. "You won't go out back with me. I had to seize the opportunity."

"You're going to give the next shopper a heart attack with your shocking behavior."

"I am not. It's not like they haven't seen it before."

"Not in public!" Martha Sue protested, trying to act mad, even though the kiss had been the best thing that had happened to her all week.

"*Ach, vell*, nobody in Bonduel knows us very well.

We're out-of-towners and can't be expected to behave ourselves."

They separated again when a man with a gray beard and a cream-colored apron came shuffling down the aisle. He narrowed his eyes and headed straight for Yost. "I've had a complaint of some goings-on in aisle six." He pointed to the sign at the end of the row. "This is aisle six. May I ask if you've seen any goings-on?"

Yost pressed his lips firmly together. He was obviously trying very hard not to smile. "*Ach*, I apologize. I'm afraid we frightened a woman who just wanted to get some noodles. We're sorry."

"I don't like to hear of goings-on in my store."

Yost nodded. "I don't blame you. We'll pay for our things and get out of your hair."

"Do it quickly," the man said. "You're chasing away customers."

Yost pressed his lips together and nodded again, as if very concerned that he was chasing customers away. The man turned around and trudged down the aisle. Yost grinned. "Now I really do feel like a teenager. I've never been kicked out of a store before."

"You only have yourself to blame."

"Is it bad that I'm kind of proud of stirring up a little trouble? I was always so well-behaved as a youth. I didn't even go to movies during *rumschpringe*."

"You've never been to a movie?"

"Not once," Yost said.

Martha Sue let her mouth fall open in mock disbelief. "Yost Beiler, you don't know what you've been missing."

His eyes sparkled with amusement. "Probably not a lot."

"As soon as we get back to Charm, we're going straight to Matthew Peachey's house to watch a Disney movie. He has a TV."

Yost furrowed his brow. "He does not. He's Amish."

Martha Sue cracked a smile. "*Ach*, it's in his basement, and he goes down there almost every night with the blinds closed and watches TV. We can see the light from our window."

"How do you know it's a TV?"

Martha Sue felt her face get warm. She couldn't keep a smile from creeping onto her lips. "*Ach*, I sneaked over there one night and peeked into the crack between the blinds and the windowsill. He's got a TV. He was watching football."

Yost laughed. "I can't believe it. Matthew Peachey."

"*Ach*, he's old and lonely. I don't begrudge him a little pleasure in his older years. But I bet he'd let us borrow his basement for one evening."

"What Disney movie would we watch? I've only heard of *Cinderella* and *Snow White*."

Martha Sue winced. "Neither of those. They both have wicked stepmothers in them."

Yost's smile wilted. "You are not the wicked stepmother type, Martha Sue."

"I don't want to be."

He curled his fingers around her upper arm. "You aren't. I fell in love with your *gute* heart and your *gute* cooking."

She grunted. "Mostly my cooking."

He scrunched his lips together and looked at the

ceiling. "Probably eighty percent of my love is for your cooking."

She cuffed him on the shoulder. "The way you eat, it's more like ninety."

He suddenly got a misty look in his eyes. "You said, '*As soon as* we get back to Charm.' You're thinking very seriously about us together, aren't you?"

She lowered her eyes and nodded. "I think about it all the time."

"So do I," he whispered.

The man in the cream-colored apron stuck his head around the far corner of the aisle and frowned. Yost jumped as if he'd been pinched. "*Ach*. We better go."

"You'd better go. I still have a whole week's worth of groceries to buy."

He held out his hand and glanced down the aisle. "Give me half your list, and I'll help you finish."

"I don't have a list. I just think about what to cook while I shop."

He cocked an eyebrow. "That sounds very inefficient."

She pulled the basket from his grasp. "I get ideas while I look."

"Well, we're about to get kicked out of the store. You need to think fast."

Martha Sue laughed, then directed Yost to get milk, cheese, broccoli, and a few other staples from the produce aisle. She got ingredients for spaghetti, lasagna, and Yankee Bean Soup and chocolate and coconut for a German Chocolate Cake. She only passed the cream-colored apron man once, and he didn't give her a dirty look. He could probably tell she was trying to hurry, plus she was about to spend a lot of money.

Yost got the wrong kind of cheese, so he had to go back, but they finally finished and left the store with nine bags of groceries. Yost helped Martha Sue load everything into the buggy, making sure the bags were arranged neatly and securely on the floor. He was always careful that way.

Yost stood very close while he said goodbye. "This was fun. We should do it again."

Martha Sue took a few seconds to breathe in his manly, attractive smell. He smelled like leather and fresh air. "I don't think they'll let us back in the store."

He arched an eyebrow. "We can sneak in when they're not looking."

She laughed and shoved him away from her. She couldn't think straight when he was that close, and a few people in the parking lot were staring. She batted her eyelashes and tucked her chin. "You never know. I might be out on the porch swing tonight watching the stars come out. Maybe we'll run into each other then."

His smile was brighter than the sun. "Maybe we will. You never know. Bonduel is a small place."

Chapter 11

Lily Yoder was a *gute* hitter, even though she was only a sixth grader. She almost always got on base and sometimes she even got to second if Reuben was playing shortstop. She was the first batter of the game today. She picked up the bat, tapped her foot with it, and stepped up to home plate, which was a square piece of plywood from Lily's barn.

"You can do it, Lily," Jonah shouted.

She turned and smiled at him and almost knocked him over. He smiled back and did his best not to stare. Even though Lily was a girl, she was his best friend, even better than Ben and Paul. She was wonderful pretty and fun to be with, and Jonah didn't know how he'd gotten so lucky. Even though her *dawdi* was paying her a dollar a week to be nice to Jonah, Jonah kind of didn't think she was doing it for the money. Since Dat wouldn't let Jonah go anywhere without him, Lily came to his house a lot, and for sure and certain she didn't need to do that to earn her money.

Since they were playing in Lily's backyard, she and Ruth Glick were the captains, and Lily had chosen Jonah first. She didn't have to do that to earn her dollar.

Ruth was pitching, because she was an eighth grader and always had to be the pitcher, but mostly nobody minded because she was pretty *gute* and tall so she could get the hits that sailed over the shorter boys' heads.

Lily swung the bat and missed by a mile. Ruth was fast.

"Keep your eye on it," Jonah said.

She turned and smiled at him again. He felt like laughing for joy. He was just in that kind of mood today. Dat had agreed to let Jonah play softball after school for the first time, and Jonah was so happy, he thought he might float off the ground. Dat said he had some things he needed to get done in the barn, and Jonah didn't even care what those things were. As long as Dat let him alone, it didn't matter.

Lily hit the second pitch down the third base line and got to first before the ball did. First base was an embroidered pillow from Lily's house that said, "Let your light so shine." Jonah wasn't sure if Lily's *mamm* would be mad about her pillow being used as a base, but he wasn't about to interrupt the game by asking.

Jonah picked up the bat and pointed to Lily. "Get ready to run. I'll hit you home."

"Boo," Danny Sensenig called from left field. Danny was one of the younger kids, only ten years old, but he always tagged along with his older *bruder* Perry. Danny was a *gute* player, even if he was a little whiney sometimes.

Maybe Jonah shouldn't have acted so cocky and proud, but it was just the kind of mood he was in. He set his feet and lifted the bat. Ruth pitched something right in the strike zone, but Jonah never liked hitting the first pitch.

"Come on!" Ruth yelled. "That was a *gute* one."

Jonah dug his foot into the grass and gripped the bat tighter. Another decent pitch came his way. Jonah swung this time. He hit the ball hard, and it sailed into left field. Jonah dropped the bat, ran like the wind to first base, and turned to go to second. His heart lurched as he saw Lily run past second base and into the out-field. "Lily, go to third, go to third!" he yelled.

But Lily didn't turn. She and all the outfielders and the shortstop and basically everybody else ran toward Danny, who was lying on the ground clutching his leg and screaming like he was about to die. It didn't seem right to run the bases when no one was trying to get him out, so Jonah changed course and ran into left field with everybody else.

He and Lily got to Danny at the same time. "Are you okay?" Lily asked, which was kind of a *dumm* question because Danny was screaming and writhing in pain.

"It's broken," Danny moaned. "It's broken."

"Move your hands," Perry shouted, "and let us look."

Danny's face was already wet with tears. "*Nae, nae,* it's broken. Don't touch it."

Perry yanked on Danny's arm, and Danny screamed in agony.

Lily practically shoved Perry out of the way and knelt next to Danny. "Don't be such a baby about it. Let us look."

No matter how much pain he was in, no boy liked to be called a baby, especially by a girl. Whimpering softly, Danny let go of his leg and sank slowly to the ground until he was lying on his back. Jonah grimaced. Danny's hand was smeared with blood.

Ruth caught her breath. "Danny . . ."

Lily narrowed her eyes at Ruth and hissed. Ruth shut her mouth. Paul tried to get a closer look. Lily told him to back up. Perry, Ben, and Lorene gasped, and Gary looked as if he was going to pass out. Jonah felt a little dizzy and a little sick to his stomach. Lily stopped all the panicked reactions with one glare. She may have been bossy, but she was also the only one who was acting calm at the sight of blood.

She patted Danny on the shoulder. "It's going to be okay. Take some deep breaths and close your eyes." She looked up at Perry. "Go get my *mamm*."

Perry took off like a shot with Ben and Paul close behind.

Blood soaked Danny's pant leg. He noticed. "Is it bleeding? Is that blood?" His voice was high-pitched and desperate.

Lily pressed firmly on Danny's shoulder to keep him from trying to sit up. Then she leaned over, carefully lifted the bottom of his pant leg, and looked underneath. She turned a darker shade of pink and pressed on Danny's shoulder again. "Don't make such a fuss. There is a little blood, but you're going to be fine. I scraped my knee in the last game, and it bled through three Band-Aids."

"You're being so brave," Ruth said.

Lily gave Ruth another warning look. You didn't tell someone they were being brave unless they had something they needed to be brave about. Lily was trying to reassure Danny, not frighten him.

Maybe Jonah could help. "It was a *gute* hit. I wanted a home run." He did his best to act annoyed.

Danny draped his arm over his eyes. "*Ach*, I would have caught it, but then I stepped in a hole, and I heard my leg snap."

"You almost caught it," Lily said. "You're one of the best outfielders in the school."

Danny gave Lily a half smile. "Even though I'm only ten."

Lily's *mamm* came running out of the house with Perry, Ben, and Paul on her heels. "*Ach*, Danny, what has happened?"

"He's okay, Mamm," Lily said. She stood, turned her back on Danny, and whispered, "I think he broke his leg real bad. The bone is sticking through the skin."

Lily must have gotten her sensibleness from her *mamm*. *Sensibleness* meant that you didn't scream and panic and tear your hair out when something bad happened. Her *mamm* knelt next to Danny and laid a hand on his chest. "I'm going to take a look at your leg, but I'll do my best not to bump or move it." She lifted Danny's pant leg and cooed softly. "I'm so sorry, Danny. It looks like it hurts." She peered at Paul and pointed in the direction of the road that ran in front of their house. "Will you go to the neighbors across the road there and ask them to call an ambulance? We need to get Danny to the doctor."

Paul nodded and ran in the direction of the house. Ben followed him. They were two of the fastest runners in school.

"An ambulance!" Danny squeaked. He tried to sit up, gasped in pain, and sank back to the ground.

Unlike Lily, her *mamm* was also soft and gentle and sweet, like a *mater* should be. She stroked Danny's arm and patted his cheek. She took a dish towel out of her pocket and pressed it gently to his forehead. Then she whispered some soft words into his ear.

Jonah's heart clenched. Was this what it was like to have a *mamm*? Someone who would sponge off his forehead and say sweet things to him when he had a bad day? He suddenly ached to go back to Huckleberry Hill and get a hug from Dat.

Lily's *mamm* looked at Perry. "Run home and tell Sam what's happened. Do you think he could find a driver to meet us at the hospital?"

Perry's face puckered as if he were going to cry. "I don't want to leave Danny."

"Go get Sam and come with him to the hospital. Danny is going to need Sam and your *mamm*, and you need to explain to them what happened."

Perry, with tears streaming down his face, nodded and took off across the back pasture.

"Am I going to die?" Danny moaned.

Jonah frowned. No one called an ambulance unless someone was going to die.

"Of course not," Lily's *mamm* said. "We need to take you to the doctor for an X-ray, and the ambulance driver knows how to move people who are hurt without making them hurt worse."

Danny seemed to feel better about that. It was because Lily's *mamm* talked as if there was nothing to worry about, as if Danny didn't have anything more than a scratch. Jonah thought it might be nice to have someone talk to him like that when he was scared or sick—*ach*, *vell*, that was what his *dat* was for, and Dat was pretty *gute* at making him feel better about things.

It didn't take long for the ambulance to get there, and the sirens weren't even going when they pulled up. All the kids watched as they loaded Danny into the ambulance. Lily's *mamm* got in the ambulance with Danny. He had someone to take care of him until they got to the hospital.

No one wanted to play softball after that. Most of the team was gone anyway.

Jonah and Lily stood together and watched the ambulance pull away. Jonah realized he was shivering, and it wasn't even cold out. "I guess I'm going to have to finish the bread and make dinner," Lily said, as if her *mamm* rode in ambulances all the time. "Do you want to come in and knead bread with me?"

"*Nae*," Jonah said. "I gotta get home." Jonah needed to see Dat, and he suddenly felt terrible for ever being annoyed that Dat wanted to spend so much time together. Dat loved him. Dat would always protect him and take care of him and put a cool washrag on his forehead when he had a fever. But Jonah wouldn't ever tell Lily that. She'd say he was acting like a baby.

Lily frowned at him. "Danny is going to be okay."

Jonah slid his hands in his pockets. "I know. I'm just mad it ruined my home run."

Which wasn't true but was a lot better than saying, "I'm upset about Danny, and I sort of feel like crying."

Lily stared at him, a mixture of puzzlement and

disgust on her face. So what if she thought he was a *dumm* boy? At least she didn't think he was a baby.

Jonah felt a little better after he jogged all the way to the base of Huckleberry Hill. He took the hill slower, strolling while tossing rocks at the trees and keeping an eye out for lizards and squirrels. Martha Sue was making lasagna for dinner, and Jonah's stomach growled just thinking about it. If Jonah broke his leg, would Martha Sue care? She'd probably make him three different pies and a huge cake with cream filling and chocolate frosting.

Martha Sue seemed to be making a lot of desserts lately. She'd made a cake for Jonah after Vernon ate the first one. Then she'd made doughnut knots in honor of the knot Jonah tied around that tree to save Vernon. Yesterday she'd made an apple pudding cake. She said it was because she needed to use up all of last fall's apples, but Jonah knew it was because he adored the cream sauce that went on the top.

Jonah was starting to like Martha Sue almost more than he liked his *dat*, mostly because Dat made a nuisance of himself and wouldn't let Jonah have a minute's peace. Martha Sue wasn't annoying or irritating, and she often distracted Dat long enough for Jonah and Lily to run into the woods unnoticed.

A lump settled in Jonah's stomach when he thought of Danny lying on the ground and Lily's *mamm* rubbing his hand and kissing his forehead. Jonah hadn't been very nice to Martha Sue. The tricks he'd pulled had been necessary, but he still felt bad for pulling them. He was wonderful *froh* that Martha Sue didn't hate him— at least he didn't think she hated him. Would she make all those cakes for someone she hated? Would she ride in the ambulance with him if he ever got hurt while playing softball?

Jonah got to the top of Huckleberry Hill much earlier than anyone was expecting him. He strolled into the barn and to the back room. Nobody was there. Dat was home from the cheese factory because the buggy and both horses were in the barn. Jonah had decided to go look in the house when he heard soft voices coming from behind the barn.

He looked out the window and just about fell over. Dat and Martha Sue sat on the ground with their backs against the big maple tree that grew not two hundred feet from the barn. They were just sitting there staring at each other and smiling like two cats. Jonah's heart did a backflip. Dat had hold of Martha Sue's hand with her arm tucked under his. The Interloper held a cookie in her free hand. She lifted it to Dat's mouth, and he took a bite. She was feeding him? She set her cookie in her lap and brushed some crumbs off Dat's lips with her fingers, then she leaned close to Dat and gave him a kiss. Right on the lips! Dat didn't try to push her away. He didn't even try to dodge her lips. He just let her do it as if he wanted her to kiss him.

It felt like a punch to the gut. He was going to throw up. How could he have been so stupid? Dat and Martha Sue were *not* just friends. They were sneaking behind Jonah's back. They were tricking him, and he hadn't even suspected.

Martha Sue had positively assured him that she wasn't going to marry his *dat*; he had believed her. She'd lied to him. She'd made him cakes and cookies and lasagna so he wouldn't suspect, but all this time she'd just been pretending to like him. She'd pretended to like Vernon Schmucker just to trick Jonah. He could have kicked himself for believing that one. No girl could possibly like Vernon Schmucker enough to want to marry him.

Martha Sue had tricked Dat too. Jonah and Dat had been perfectly happy with just each other before Martha Sue had come along. She wanted a husband to take care of her so she didn't have to live with her parents anymore. She'd kick Jonah out of the house as soon as she and Dat were married.

Jonah sat down on the bed and doubled over with pain. Dat had tricked him, Martha Sue had lied to him, and Vernon had eaten his cake. There wasn't anybody in the whole world who loved him. He felt so lonely, he wanted to cry.

Jonah sat up straight and wiped the moisture from his eyes. He was thirteen years old, and he was not a baby. He needed his *dat*. He needed to save his family. It was time to get his *dat* back. It was time to grow up and be a man. It was time to get rid of the Interloper once and for all.

Chapter 12

Martha Sue finished wiping the kitchen counters, dread growing in her heart like a fungus. Something was very wrong, and no matter how many times Yost and Mammi reassured her, she couldn't feel easy. Of course, Yost and Mammi were reassuring her about two different things, but neither of them made her feel better.

Mammi thought Martha Sue's discomfort was because Vernon hadn't come to dinner for two weeks, but Martha Sue couldn't feel anything but relief about that. Vernon had made himself more than unpleasant, and Martha Sue wanted nothing more to do with him. Mammi still felt bad that none of the matches she'd planned for Vernon had worked out. She seemed determined to have Vernon Schmucker in the family, but if Vernon actually managed to marry one of Martha Sue's relatives, Martha Sue might have to declare herself an orphan.

Christmas and Thanksgiving with Vernon in attendance would be unbearable.

Martha Sue was more worried about Jonah, and Yost was no less reassuring about Jonah than Anna was about Vernon.

But Martha Sue wasn't naïve, and she wasn't blind, and Jonah was up to something. She'd made lasagna last week for dinner, and Jonah had refused to set foot in the house. Yost said it was because Jonah was upset about Danny Sensenig's accident. He had made up a plate for Jonah and taken it to him to eat in his room. But the next day, the same thing had happened. Jonah had refused to come in for breakfast, and Yost had let him eat in his room. Lunch was at school, but Jonah had missed dinner too.

Almost a week of no Jonah at meals and Martha Sue realized that Jonah was back to giving her the silent treatment. She wracked her brain trying to figure out why, but she couldn't come up with anything. The romantic picnic had turned out well for both of them. It seemed she and Jonah were making strides in their relationship until recently. She sighed. After the silent treatment came honey in her apron pocket and buckets of water to the face.

Martha Sue hung the towel on the hook and took a scouring pad from the drawer. She sprinkled the stainless-steel sink with cleanser and scrubbed it until she could almost see her reflection in it. Hard work kept her mind off her heartache, because, oh, how she wanted to cry! She was more in love with Yost than ever, and he was happier and more hopeful than she had ever seen him.

But if Jonah wouldn't accept her, what could she do? If she broke up with Yost yet again, he would be devastated. She feared he'd never recover. She couldn't bear the thought, not for herself or for Yost. She'd been so happy, and now she was standing on a cliff looking down at the swirling waters of despair. She'd been foolish to let him talk her into trying again. It would only make the inevitable separation more painful than either of them could possibly imagine.

Yost, of course, refused to see it. Jonah, he said, had been badly shaken up by Danny's accident, and he was coping with it the only way he knew how. Yost's disbelief would only make things harder in the end.

Mammi came into the kitchen with some squares of knitted yarn in her hand. "*Ach*, Martha Sue, that sink has never looked so shiny."

"*Denki*," Martha Sue said. "It feels *gute* to clean something so thoroughly."

Mammi's eyes sparkled. "I don't mean to offend you, but you're usually quite messy. You clean when you're frustrated or upset, I've noticed."

Martha Sue gave Mammi a sad smile. "Do I? I suppose I like to keep my hands busy."

Mammi patted Martha Sue on the cheek. "Don't you worry. I just know Vernon is going to come around and see you for the *wunderbarr* girl you are. It's my fault he hasn't come back, and I'm sorry for that, but I really thought he'd enjoy the forsythia bush."

"It's not your fault, Mammi. How could you have known Vernon would get stuck at the picnic spot? Those rocks aren't that hard to climb."

Mammi shook her head. "I can see why he was irritated, but he's too kind to hold a grudge."

Martha Sue didn't believe that for a minute, but it made Mammi feel better, so she didn't say anything. "Mammi, I'm not interested in marrying him. Not one little bit." She slumped her shoulders. "If I don't marry Yost, I won't marry anybody."

"This makes it all the more disappointing that Vernon didn't take advantage of the romantic picnic. We could have had a wedding in October, for sure and certain. But surely there is someone else if Vernon decides to dump you."

"Dump me? What kind of a word is that?"

"*Ach*, it just means that he'll lose interest in you and date someone else. We have to prepare ourselves for the possibility that it might happen."

"It has already happened, because I'm dumping Vernon."

Mammi frowned. "Well, okay, then, if you want to give up on him that easily."

"I do," Martha Sue said. She would never get her *mammi* to see reason, but it was always worth a try. She bent over and kissed Mammi on the forehead. "I'm going out to take the clothes off the line. It's a warm day. They should be dry."

Mammi set her yarn on the counter. "I'll come with you, and we can talk about all the single men in the neighborhood who are over thirty." She drew her brows together. "There aren't that many, but we can weigh the strengths and weaknesses of each, and then you can choose."

Martha Sue pursed her lips to keep them from twitching in exasperated amusement. "How many single men are there, Mammi?"

Mammi looked at the ceiling as if counting to a very high number. "Besides Vernon, two. And one of them is sixty-three. He's a young sixty-three, with very nice teeth. I like a man with *gute* teeth."

Martha Sue gave her *mammi* a hug. "Sixty-three is too old, Mammi. Don't even try." She grabbed the laundry basket, and she and Mammi went out the front door and around to the side of the house to the clothesline. Martha Sue stopped short and gasped. A ten-foot round mud puddle sat underneath the clothesline as if it had rained very hard that morning, and every piece of clothing Martha Sue had carefully washed and hung had been torn from the line and thrown in the water. Her heart sank like a stone in a deep lake. She had no doubt who had ruined her laundry and no idea what to do about it.

"*Ach*," Mammi murmured. "That little pill."

Martha Sue marched toward the mud puddle, but before she got there, her foot snagged on something, and she barely regained her balance. She could have fallen flat on her face! A fishing line had been strung between two trees in her path. If she hadn't been so light on her feet, she would have fallen. She gasped. "Mammi, stop!"

But it was too late. Mammi's foot caught on the line as she stepped forward. She fell hard to the ground before Martha Sue could catch her.

Martha Sue dropped her basket and knelt next to Mammi, who was lying on her stomach, her eyes open, her cheek pressed against the dirt. "Are you all right? *Ach*, Mammi, I'm so sorry."

Mammi grimaced in pain. "Well, stuff and nonsense. That sly little hooligan."

"Can you get up?"

"Help me roll onto my back," Mammi said, hissing between her teeth. "I've got a mouthful of dirt."

Martha Sue nudged Mammi onto her back and then grabbed her left hand and helped her sit up. Her black apron was smeared with mud and dirt, and little pieces of gravel were embedded in one side of her face. Martha Sue took one of Yost's shiny white handkerchiefs out of her pocket and gently wiped the dirt from Mammi's cheek.

Mammi made a face and wrapped her fingers around her right wrist. "*Ach*, Martha Sue, I think I've broken something."

Martha Sue's heart stopped. "Broken what?"

"My arm or my elbow. Or maybe my wrist. My fingers are tingling, and my arm feels like a cow kicked it. I haven't been kicked by a cow for a wonderful long time, but I remember."

"I'm so sorry," Martha Sue said, sorry for many things, not the least of which was how devastated Yost was going to be. "I hate to leave you, Mammi, but I need to go find Dawdi. We're taking you to the hospital."

"*Ach*, I don't need to go to the hospital. Just give me an aspirin and a mustard plaster, and I'll be fine."

Martha Sue shook her head. "I'm taking you to the hospital."

"But we can't just leave the laundry in the mud."

"*Jah*, we can. Jonah can pick it up and rewash it when he gets home from school."

Mammi frowned. "I try never to speak ill of anyone, but that boy has stretched my patience to the limit. What will Yost say?"

Martha Sue's eyes filled with tears. "There's nothing he can say that will make this better, I'm afraid."

Mammi sighed, and that small movement sent pain traveling across her face. "Vernon Schmucker doesn't look quite so bad now, does he?" Mammi was always looking on the bright side.

Jonah trudged up Huckleberry Hill, his steps getting slower and slower the closer he got to the top. He was going to get in trouble, no doubt about it, but that wasn't why he was so reluctant to make it to the top of the hill. About halfway through the day, right in the middle of his arithmetic lesson, an emotion that felt like regret started growling in his stomach. *Regret* meant that maybe he shouldn't have made that puddle, thrown all of Martha Sue's laundry in the mud, and then tied that fishing line between the trees so she'd trip. It was a mean trick, especially since Martha Sue made cakes and pies for him and had given him a whole book of cross-word puzzles. There would be no dessert for him tonight. Dat would make him rewash all the clothes, and he'd probably have to go to bed before it got dark outside.

Then again, he had to do something big to get rid of Martha Sue for *gute*, and getting the laundry dirty and making her trip was hopefully big enough.

What made it worse was that Lily Yoder had decided to be a pest and invite herself to dinner. She chatted about softball and Danny Sensenig as she walked beside him up the hill, not knowing that Jonah didn't want her anywhere near Huckleberry Hill tonight. He didn't want her to know what he'd done to Martha Sue.

He wasn't sure why he didn't want Lily to know. Was he ashamed? He kicked a pebble at his feet. Of course he wasn't ashamed. He was clever and sneaky, and when Lily found out what he'd done, she would probably be impressed that her best friend was so smart. Maybe she'd give him a kiss for caring so much about keeping his family together.

Give him a kiss? Jonah frowned. How had that thought gotten into his head? He didn't want a kiss from Lily. The thought was disgusting. He studied her out of the corner of his eye. Maybe he wouldn't mind a kiss on the cheek. Her lips looked wonderful soft, and her cheeks looked even softer. Maybe she would let him kiss her on the cheek when she realized what a sharp boy he was.

"Danny had to get a metal pole stuck up his leg," Lily said, twisting a leaf in her hand as she hiked up the hill.

"He did not," Jonah said. "They don't do stuff like that."

Lily propped her hand on her hip and glared at him. "How do you know? You don't know anything, it seems like. He had to get surgery, and they used screws and pins. His *bruder* Wally got his leg cut off after an accident years ago, but they didn't have to cut Danny's leg off."

"Wally did *not* get his leg cut off," Jonah said, though he wasn't sure about that. He'd never looked very hard at Wally's legs before.

"Did so. You don't know anything, it seems like."

Jonah stopped walking and made a face at Lily. "I

know lots of stuff. Why don't you just go home if you're going to be all stuck up."

Lily acted as if he'd insulted her whole family. "I'm not stuck up. And why are you so grumpy? You hit a triple at recess."

Jonah wasn't going to tell her the real reason for his bad mood, because he wasn't in a bad mood. He was as happy as a clam that Martha Sue was as good as gone from his life. If Lily didn't approve of what he'd done, well, then maybe she wasn't as *gute* a friend as he thought she was. Friends were supposed to stand up for each other. Who wanted a girl as a friend anyway?

When they were almost to the top, Dat rode up behind them in the buggy. He stopped and leaned his head out the window, a big smile on his face, as if he was so happy he could sing or dance or laugh out loud without warning. Jonah tried to swallow past the lump in his throat. Dat wouldn't be so happy when he found out what Jonah had done, even though it was for his own good and to save the family. "*Hallo*, Lily and Jonah. Climb in. I'll take you the rest of the way." They jumped into the buggy, and Dat prodded the horse forward. "Are you staying for dinner, Lily?"

Lily nodded. "*Jah*. Martha Sue invited me. She says Jonah needs to cheer up, and she's making tarts with raspberry filling."

Tarts with raspberry filling? Jonah loved tarts with raspberry filling. Would Martha Sue be too mad about the laundry to let him have one? He should have waited until next week to sabotage the laundry.

"Jonah does need some cheering up," Dat said. "He's been glum ever since Danny broke his leg."

Nae, he'd been glum ever since he'd seen Dat and Martha Sue kissing behind the barn. Jonah gave his *dat* an irritated scowl. "I'm not a baby."

"*Nae*, you're not. It must have been scary seeing Danny in the ambulance. Of course you were upset about it."

Lily sighed. "I wasn't scared, but some of the other kids were."

Jonah hadn't been scared, but he'd been . . . uneasy. And when he'd needed some comfort from Dat, Dat had been too busy kissing Martha Sue to even care. Jonah was *froh* he'd played that trick. He wanted his *dat* back. Dat shouldn't be paying attention to anyone but Jonah.

They got to the top of the hill and drove past the house. His heart sank. A basket full of wet, muddy clothes sat under the clothesline next to Jonah's home-made mud puddle, which was quite a bit smaller than when he'd filled it this morning. Wasn't it just like Martha Sue to leave the clothes for him to wash again? If she thought he'd lift a finger to help her, she was wrong. Let her wash her own clothes and leave his *dat* alone.

Dat didn't even look in the direction of the clothesline as he guided the horse to the barn, but he'd find out soon enough. Martha Sue would make sure Dat knew all about what Jonah had done. She was nothing but a tattletale. Dat would be mad, but eventually he'd come to see that Jonah had done it for the *gute* of the family. Jonah wasn't looking forward to Dat's anger, but better to be yelled at for a few minutes than to have an evil stepmother for the rest of his life.

Still, if he just disappeared for an hour or so, it would

give Dat a chance to calm down before meting out a punishment he'd regret later. Jonah jumped out before the buggy came to a full stop. "Come on, Lily," he said, with a little too much urgency in his voice. "Let's go to the climbing tree."

"Not so fast," Dat said, before Jonah could run out of earshot. "Help me unhitch the horse. And I need you to brush him down."

"Aw, Dat, Lily came to play. She doesn't want to wait around while I do my chores."

Lily was no help at all. "I don't mind. I can help you."

Jonah glanced toward the house and started un-hitching the horse as if the buggy were on fire. He growled at Lily, who was petting Big Red on the nose as if she had all the time in the world. "If you're going to help, help."

She shot him a look that would have scared a bear. "Okay, okay. You don't have to get huffy about it."

Dat chuckled. "He seems to be huffy a lot these days."

Jonah closed his mouth and suffered in silence. He was only huffy because his *dat* would rather kiss Martha Sue than pay attention to his own son. Jonah had every right to be huffy.

Lily ran her hands down Big Red's neck and cooed soft words to him while Jonah unhitched him from the buggy all by himself. Dat was also just standing there with his hand propped against the wheel, as if watching Jonah do all the work was the most interesting thing he'd ever done.

A car crawled slowly up the hill, and Jonah recognized one of the *Englisch* drivers that Anna and Felty sometimes hired to take them to Walmart in Shawano. Anna sat in the front seat of the car, and two people sat in the back, but Jonah couldn't see who they were.

The car pulled in front of the house, and Felty and Martha Sue got out of the back seat. Jonah ducked his head, grabbed Big Red's reins, and led him to the stall. As soon as he watered and brushed the horse, he'd sneak out the back. Lily quickly followed Jonah with a look of deep curiosity on her face. *Ach, vell*, it was either curiosity or suspicion. Lily was no dummy. She knew he was tense about something.

Dat called a greeting to Martha Sue, and his footsteps got softer as he left the barn. Jonah could hear Dat, Felty, and Martha Sue talking to each other, but he couldn't hear what they were saying no matter how hard he strained to listen. He heard the car drive off, the gravel crunching beneath the tires.

Lily shut the stall door behind her and grabbed the hose to fill Big Red's trough, watching Jonah out of the corner of her eye. She picked up a curry comb and started brushing Big Red's neck. "What's wrong with you?" she hissed.

Jonah tried to act more confident than he felt, reminding himself that Lily was going to be impressed at how clever he was. But maybe she didn't have to find out what he'd done. They still had time to escape. "Nothing," he said. "Hurry up. I want to go climb trees."

Lily narrowed her eyes. "You do not want to climb trees, Jonah Beiler. You're in trouble, aren't you? You've done something bad that your *dat* doesn't know about yet."

"It wasn't bad. I had to save my family."

Her eyes were mere slits on her face. "If it wasn't bad, why are you hiding in this stall like a baby?"

"I'm not a baby. You just say that to get people to do what you want."

Lily lifted her chin. "I do not. I know a baby when I see one."

"You don't know anything," he finally said, because she'd never understand how much Jonah suffered. She didn't know what it felt like to lose your *mamm*. She didn't know what it felt like to worry about losing your *dat* too. She'd never see how hard Jonah worked to keep his family together and to keep interlopers out. He'd already lost one parent. He wouldn't lose another one, no matter what he had to do to make sure it didn't happen.

"I know a lot of things, Jonah Beiler. You've done something bad, and you're pretending it wasn't bad because you're ashamed. You're being a baby."

Jonah threw his curry comb to the ground. "Don't accuse me of stuff you don't even know. You're the worst friend anyone ever had."

Lily puckered her lips as if she'd eaten a lemon. "*I'm* the worst friend?" She huffed out a breath. "This isn't worth a dollar a week. This isn't even worth three dollars a week." She laced her fingers together. "I suppose I could still be your friend for five dollars a week, but only because you're *gute* at softball."

"I wouldn't be your friend even if someone paid me a hundred dollars a week."

Lily's eyes got as round and as big as dinner plates. "Well, I wouldn't be your friend for a thousand dollars a week, so there."

"Jonah?" Dat roared from outside. "Come out here." A short pause. "Please."

Jonah's heart sank to his toes. He had been so busy arguing with Lily that he'd momentarily forgotten the bigger trouble on the other side of the stall door. And the "please" didn't fool him. Dat didn't sound like he was going to be polite. "I can't come, Dat," he called half-heartedly. "I'm busy brushing the horse."

Lily stuck out her tongue at Jonah, opened the stall door, and leaned her head out. "I can finish the horse."

Jonah stuck his tongue out at her, though it was usually something sixth graders did, not seventh graders.

"Come here, Jonah," Dat called again.

Jonah slunk out of the stall, squinted into the bright light outside of the barn, and shuffled toward Dat, Martha Sue, Felty, and Anna, who were all standing in front of the house staring in his direction as if he was wearing a flower in his hair.

He heard the stall door shut and glanced behind him. Lily was following him. "You said you'd finish brushing Big Red."

She sighed and gave him her most irritated frown. "I'm mad at you, but you need a friend right now. 'A friend in need is a friend indeed.'"

Jonah wasn't sure what that meant, but a spot right in the center of his chest suddenly felt warm and sticky. Lily wasn't being nice because of the dollar her *dawdi* was paying her. She really was a true friend, even if she was *dumm* and bossy and called him a baby. She grabbed his hand and squeezed it, and that warm, sticky feeling spread all the way up his neck.

Dat looked about as angry as anyone could look

without falling over dead from a heart attack. Martha Sue's lips were pressed together in a hard line as if she was going to cry at any moment, as if she was hurt that Jonah would trick her like that. A sharp, cold pin pricked Jonah's heart. Martha Sue had made him nine cakes, and he'd thrown her laundry in the mud. He was a terrible person, even though he did what had to be done.

Martha Sue looked past Jonah and smiled sadly at Lily. "*Hallo*, Lily. Nice to see you."

Lily planted herself next to Jonah as if she was a fence post and he was the fence. "Whatever he did, he's real sorry. Sometimes he acts like a baby even though he's thirteen, almost fourteen."

"I do not," Jonah said, even though the way everyone was looking at him made him want to bawl.

"Jonah, what do you have to say to Martha Sue and Anna?" Dat said, his voice dangerously soft and steady.

The lump in Jonah's throat nearly choked him, so he covered up his shame by acting as if he didn't care. "It's just some laundry. Can't anybody take a joke?"

Martha Sue's eyes flashed with something like raw, painful anger, and the expression stole Jonah's breath. "Playing tricks on me is one thing."

Dat held up his hand. "Playing tricks on you is not acceptable."

Martha Sue sighed as if she didn't want to hurt Dat's feelings. "I know, Yost, but this is worse." She flashed Jonah a stern gaze. "Playing tricks on me is one thing. I'm young. I was able to keep my balance."

Anna lifted her arm. It was wrapped below the elbow in a bright pink cast. Jonah's chest tightened. "People are always saying I'm old, but I'm only eighty-five. I'm still spry as a chicken. I'm not going to die anytime soon. Although I don't wonder but Jonah put me halfway in my grave this morning."

Jonah couldn't speak. He couldn't even swallow. He'd broken Anna's arm?

Lily's mouth fell open. "What did you do?" She looked at Martha Sue. "What did he do?"

Martha Sue seemed sadder and sadder every minute. "He dug a shallow hole, filled it with water, and threw all the clean laundry into the mud. Then he strung some fishing wire across the path so I would trip. I tripped, but Mammi fell. She went down hard and broke her wrist."

Anna nodded, not looking near as upset as Martha Sue did. "It didn't hurt as bad as childbirth, but it hurt worse than when I had that wart burned off my finger."

Felty put his arm around Anna. Jonah's mouth went dry at the look of disappointment on his face. "I'm not one to hold a grudge, Jonah," he said. "I still like you and think you're a *gute* boy. You're angry and foolish, but foolishness is no excuse for bad behavior, especially behavior that ends up hurting someone. I can't allow you in our house until you make amends for how you've treated my sweetheart."

"I wouldn't have allowed him in your house anyway," Dat said. "He needs to learn there are consequences to his actions."

Martha Sue squared her shoulders and looked Dat straight in the eye. "There *are* consequences, Yost."

Dat shook his head. "*Nae*, Martha Sue. We can work this out."

A tear rolled down Martha Sue's cheek. "I know you wanted it to be different. So did I. I desperately wanted you to be happy, but I only gave you false hope. I knew deep down that we were in an impossible situation." She took a shuddering breath. "It's my fault Mammi got hurt. I should have put a stop to this weeks ago."

"It's not your fault," Anna said. "It's mine, for not being as light on my feet as I used to be."

Dat, Martha Sue, and Felty all spoke at the same time. "It's not your fault," they said in unison. *Unison* meant that they all agreed that Jonah was a very bad boy.

Anna shrugged. "All I know is that my arm hurts and I need to go lie down. And I need to speak to Vernon Schmucker immediately. Felty, can you fetch him here for me?"

"*Cum*, Annie-banannie. We can talk about Vernon later." Felty tucked Anna's *gute* arm under his and led her up the porch steps and into the house.

Martha Sue gazed at Dat and gave him the most miserable look Jonah had ever seen. "I'm so, so sorry, Yost. I'm so sorry."

Dat sucked in a breath. "Don't say it. Please don't say it."

Martha Sue's voice trembled. "It's time for you and Jonah to go back to Ohio before anybody else gets hurt. I've got my grandparents' safety to think about. It's not going to work, and it's time we both accepted it."

Dat grabbed both of Martha Sue's hands. "Please don't say that. We can work this out. I know we can."

Martha Sue glanced at Jonah but quickly turned away, as if she couldn't stand to look at him. "You need to go, Yost. As soon as you can make arrangements."

Guilt settled like a stone in Jonah's gut. Martha Sue stood there with tears running down her face as if every *gute* thing in the world had died. Dat looked hollow, like all the happiness had been sucked out of his life. And then there was Lily, who stood with her hands propped on her hips and her lips pressed into a hard line, glaring at Jonah as if she was trying to peel the skin off his face with her thoughts.

Jonah should have been ecstatic. He had succeeded in making Martha Sue cry, which he'd never been able to do before, and he'd saved his family, just like he'd set out to do. But all he felt was empty and numb and . . . ashamed. Deeply, completely ashamed. Where was the joy or even the relief he thought he'd feel?

Dat didn't say another word. Didn't scold Jonah or beg Martha Sue for another chance. He kept his eyes to the ground as he turned around and trudged into the barn. Martha Sue watched him go, wiped her eyes, and slipped into the house where Jonah wasn't allowed anymore.

Lily twirled her finger around one of her *kapp* strings, staring at him as if she didn't even know him. "I didn't think you could be so mean."

"But did you think I could be so smart?" he said weakly. It was a *dumm* question. Nobody thought he was clever, not even Jonah himself.

"Congratulations," she said, folding her arms and giving him one of her "looks." "Martha Sue won't be your stepmother."

"*Denki*," he said, pretending that Lily was truly

happy for him and that she'd been convinced of his cleverness.

"Don't say *denki*, Jonah Beiler. You are mean and selfish, and it wonders me why you have any friends, even dollar-a-week friends."

For all her big talk about being a friend indeed, Lily wasn't making him feel any better. "You don't have to be my friend. Go and bother somebody else."

Unfortunately, she wasn't finished. "You made your *dat* cry. I made my *mamm* cry once, but nobody makes their *dat* cry."

"I said, go and bother somebody else."

"I'm not going anywhere. 'A friend in need is a friend indeed.'"

"You're not being a *gute* friend. You should say nice things to me and make me feel *gute* about myself."

Lily grunted her disapproval. "Don't be stupid. A *gute* friend tells people when they are acting *dumm* and mean, and you are both." She pointed at the road that wound down the hill. "If I weren't a true friend, I would march right down that hill and never come back."

Jonah shut his mouth. He believed her. He had done something vile and nasty, even if it was to save his family—and he was starting to doubt that. Dat was so hurt, he might never talk to Jonah again.

To his surprise, Lily linked her elbow around his and tugged him toward the barn. "You're so embarrassed right now, you can't even admit you're wrong." Instead of pulling him inside the barn, she put her finger to her lips and led him around to the back under the window. "Look inside, Jonah," she whispered. "What's your *dat* doing?"

Jonah didn't need to look to know what Dat was doing. The window was partway open, and ragged, gut-wrenching sobs were coming from the room he shared with his *dat*. Jonah felt like his heart was being ripped out of his chest. He sneaked closer to the window and peeked around the edge. His *dat* sat on his bed, his face buried in his hands, his shoulders slumped, crying like Jonah had only seen once before.

After Mamm died, Dat had sat on the sofa for hours every day, sometimes sobbing, sometimes deathly quiet just staring at the calendar on the wall watching the days go by without him. Jonah had seen Dat's pain and promised himself he would never let his *dat* be sad again. Sometime over the years, Jonah had forgotten his promise. When had his love for his *dat* changed to selfishness, to demanding that Dat be the one to make Jonah happy instead of the other way around? Had he destroyed his family instead of keeping it together?

"You need to stop being selfish," Lily whispered.

They stepped around the corner of the barn, and Jonah hung his head. The despair threatened to bury him. "But if my *dat* marries Martha Sue, he'll forget all about me. He might even make me go live with my grandparents. Then I'll be an orphan."

Lily's expression softened. "You're afraid your *dat* won't care about you anymore?"

He sniffed back some tears and nodded.

Lily draped her arm around his shoulders. "Your *dat* would never do that, Jonah. He's real nice, and he loves you. My *mamm* says love is like water in the ocean. It doesn't matter how much we give away, there's still plenty left for everyone. Your *dat* has more than enough love for you and Martha Sue at the same time."

"How can you be sure?"

"My *mamm* loves my *dat*, but she still loves me and my *bruderen* and *schwesteren*."

"But Martha Sue isn't my real *mamm*. It's different with a stepmother."

Lily frowned. "Jonah, Martha Sue has always been wonderful nice to you."

"She's just pretending so I'll let her marry Dat."

Lily sighed. "She doesn't seem like someone who pretends stuff. She makes you special cakes and all your favorite foods. She sews on your buttons and fixes your pants. Nobody pays her to be nice to you like my *dawdi* pays me. She tried to save your cake from Vernon. It had your name on it."

One corner of Jonah's mouth curled upward. "She was pretty mad at him."

"She's not pretending. And you've got to stop being so afraid."

He opened his mouth to protest that he wasn't afraid of anything, but Lily was too smart to believe it. "I'm not a baby," he finally said.

"Everybody is afraid of something. It doesn't mean you're a baby."

They both jumped when Martha Sue appeared around the corner of the barn holding a plate covered with a paper napkin. She didn't smile, but there was a kindly look on her face, as if she was one of the saints giving aid to weary travelers. Her eyes were puffy, but Jonah didn't want to think about her crying. He already felt bad enough. "I didn't want you to miss out on my raspberry tarts. They turned out very well."

Lily looked at Jonah and lifted her eyebrows as if to say, "I told you so." She took the plate from Martha Sue. "That's wonderful nice of you, even though Jonah broke Anna's arm."

"We all need forgiveness for our sins," Martha Sue said, still with that magnanimous look on her face. *Magnanimous* meant she was being nice because it was her duty as a Christian. She nodded at Jonah. "Will you be sure your *dat* gets one?"

"For sure and certain we will," Lily said. Martha Sue disappeared around the corner of the barn, and Lily kicked Jonah in the shin.

"Ouch! What did you do that for?"

"That's not someone who's pretending."

"She's nice," Jonah admitted.

"She's more than nice. I would have brought you Brussels sprouts."

Jonah drew in a mouthful of air, even though it hurt to breathe. "I really messed up, didn't I?"

"Really bad. Your *dat* wants to marry Martha Sue, and you just ruined it for him. He'll be mad at you for the rest of his life."

Sometimes Lily was too honest. She might have been a friend indeed, but she was also a friend who didn't know when to quit talking.

"You need to fix this, Jonah, because on top of everything else, if you move back to Ohio, I may never see you again."

The truth hit Jonah like a pile of bricks. He wasn't clever. He was as *dumm* as a sack of potatoes. In his haste to get rid of Martha Sue, he hadn't stopped to consider that he might lose Dat *and* Lily. Dat would definitely be mad at him for the rest of his life, and Lily wasn't going to move to Ohio for a dollar a week. She was a girl, but she was also his best friend, and he didn't know what he'd do without her. "How can I fix this?"

Lily shook her head and shrugged.

Suddenly she couldn't think of anything to say? *And* she'd kicked him. She was the worst friend in the world. "I don't know what to do."

"You think you're so smart, but you don't even know how to get yourself out of this mess."

Yep, the worst friend in the world. "Will you help me?"

Lily nodded and smiled. "That's what friends are for. Let's take a raspberry tart to your *dat* to soften him up. Then you can apologize."

"I don't know what to say."

"Let me do the talking. You'll just mess it up."

Jonah scowled. Lily was pretty bossy for a sixth grader.

And pretty *wunderbarr* too.

Chapter 13

Martha Sue stomped into the house with her basket of eggs and nearly broke the whole lot when she slammed the basket on the table. "Mammi, Yost won't leave. Why doesn't Dawdi make him leave?"

Mammi sat at the kitchen table trying her best to knit with one broken arm. "*Ach*, Martha Sue dear, I don't ask your *dawdi* his reasons for anything. That man does exactly what he wants."

Martha Sue stared at Mammi in disbelief. "That's not true. He always does exactly what *you* want."

Mammi drew her brows together. "I suppose you're right. Isn't it *wunderbarr*?" She went back to her knitting as if the conversation was over.

Martha Sue huffed out a breath. "You've got to tell Dawdi to make Yost leave. I can't stand to have him here any longer."

"We can't make him leave, dear. He leased out his Ohio farm to an *Englischer*, and the cheese factory is his only source of income. We feel sorry for him, so we're letting him stay."

"But don't you feel sorry for me? Your own grand-daughter?"

"Of course I feel sorry for you," Mammi said. "That's why I've invited Vernon Schmucker for dinner tonight. I'm sure he'll be able to cheer you up."

Martha Sue would have laughed hysterically if she weren't on the verge of tears every minute of every day. She tried to keep the irritation out of her voice. "I've dumped Vernon, remember?"

Mammi nodded and put two more stitches in her blanket. "You did, but then Jonah broke my wrist, and you got unengaged to Yost, and I just couldn't let you sit around here all day and pine for a lost cause. Vernon will at least take your mind off Yost."

Nothing could take Martha Sue's mind off Yost, but Vernon would definitely be a distraction, however unwelcome. Maybe if Martha Sue spent more time with Vernon, Yost would get discouraged and leave Wisconsin. But then she'd have an overeager Vernon to deal with, and she just didn't have the energy for it. "I'd move back to Ohio tomorrow if you didn't need my help." That would solve the Yost problem and the Vernon problem.

"You most definitely can't leave. I've at least six weeks in this cast. I'm completely helpless. And after the cast comes off, I have all that physical therapy and Christmas cooking to do."

"Christmas cooking? Mammi, it's May."

Mammi concentrated very hard on her knitting and didn't make eye contact with Martha Sue. "By the time I'm well enough for you to leave, it will be Christmas again."

Martha Sue wasn't *dumm*. Mammi was just saying that to convince Martha Sue to stay longer. But for what reason? She sighed. "Mammi, I've made up my mind. I am not going to marry Yost."

"Of course not. You're going to marry Vernon or someone else more deserving."

"If Dawdi told Yost to move out, he'd do it. I'm only thinking of your protection, Mammi. Jonah broke your arm."

"Jonah did not break my arm. He set the trap, but I wasn't paying attention and fell. He's very sorry for what he did, as he's already told you."

Martha Sue pressed her lips together. Yesterday, Jonah and Lily had missed school to rewash all the clothes, hang them to dry, and set them neatly in the laundry basket. She wasn't sure how Lily had gotten permission to miss school, but she'd been by Jonah's side all day, not only helping him with the laundry, but sweeping the sidewalk while he mowed the lawn, cleaning out the chicken coop, and even chopping wood for the well-stocked woodpile. After all that, Lily had knocked on the front door and asked Martha Sue and Mammi to come outside and sit on the porch swing.

After they had sat down, Jonah had appeared from hiding and extended the most heartfelt apology Martha Sue had ever heard. He'd cried and fretted and acted as if he meant it. He'd begged Martha Sue not to send him away and to give him and his *dat* another chance. *Isn't there anything I can do to make you love me?* he had asked.

He'd made such a fuss that Mammi had patted him on the hand and given him a kiss on the cheek and told him that he was going to turn out to be a fine man even if right now he was a pill. Jonah had ended his little speech by giving Martha Sue a bird's nest he'd found in the woods and Mammi a pot holder that looked suspiciously like one from the drawer in the kitchen.

Martha Sue hadn't been untouched by the gesture. Jonah had seemed sincere, and Lily had been so eager. But she wouldn't give Jonah the reassurance he seemed to desperately want. She simply couldn't bear to open her heart ever again. It was already covered with scars. If she gave him another chance, Jonah *would* disappoint her, and she *would* have to break things off with Yost. She couldn't bear to see that look in his eyes ever again. As it was, her heart would never be whole, and she had to protect herself more than ever.

Mammi held up the two-foot string of yarn she'd just knitted. "Isn't this a pretty color? I'm making a blanket for Lily. She's been so kind to Jonah, and he really needs friends right now."

Martha Sue's heart hurt for Jonah, for Yost, and for herself. "Mammi, I'm not trying to be cruel or vindictive."

"Of course not, dear. You don't have a mean bone in your body."

"But I need to be practical, like I have from the very beginning. That's why I moved to Wisconsin. It would have been a very tidy breakup if Dawdi hadn't let Yost move up here."

Mammi sighed. "Nothing is as neat and tidy as we want it to be. Life is one big mess. You can find the fun rolling around in the mud or be mad that you're getting dirty. It's up to you."

"I just want to be happy, Mammi. I wish I could forget Yost and go back to the way I was before I met him."

"You can't gather up the feathers once you've scattered them. And you can't unlearn lessons once you've been taught them. Believe me, you wouldn't want to. Some of life's lessons are hard, but they come with wisdom attached. I wouldn't give back that wisdom for anything."

"But I don't like being sad all the time."

Mammi reached across the table and wrapped her fingers around Martha Sue's wrist. "I don't either. But being happy or sad is your own choice. No one else can choose it for you."

Martha Sue couldn't keep her lips from curling upward. "I hate it when you say something sensible."

Mammi giggled. "*Ach, vell*, then it's a *gute* thing it doesn't happen very often."

"It happens all the time!"

Mammi pulled more slack from the yarn ball sitting on the table. "I want to help you along, Martha Sue. I really do. That's why Vernon is coming over. I think he'll give you some clarity."

Martha Sue cradled her forehead in her hands. "I don't know what clarity means, but can you treat it with antibiotics?"

"You should ask Jonah to look it up in his thesaurus." Mammi's eyes twinkled. "Try not to worry about Vernon or Yost or my broken wrist. I have a plan that will fix everything." She pulled at the yarn on one of her needles. "Well, almost everything. You would be happier if you forgave Jonah."

"*Ach*, I've forgiven him. I just don't trust him."

The line between Mammi's eyes etched deeper into her face. "It's not about trust. You don't love Jonah. Not one little bit."

Martha Sue drew in a breath then disintegrated into a puddle of tears. She didn't know if they were tears of shame that Mammi had guessed what a horrible person she was or tears of utter relief that someone finally knew her secret. "I used to love him—at least I thought I did. But then he started being naughty, and I just quit trying. Isn't it supposed to be easy to love a child? Marrying Yost wouldn't be fair to Jonah. I can't be his *mater*. I can't stand him."

Mammi nodded as if she knew every secret Martha Sue didn't want to tell. "It's understandable. He's made himself very unlovable."

"Do *you* love him? He broke your arm."

Mammi pushed her glasses up her nose. "I like him just fine, and I'd be so happy if he became my great-grandson. Who doesn't want more great-grandchildren? But he was trying to break your arm, not mine. Of course it's harder for you. Those feelings are normal, especially because of the way Jonah has treated you. I'll tell you a secret. Every *mater* has days where she doesn't like her own children. When your *fater* turned thirteen, he was so annoying that I thought about giving him to a pack of wolves to raise. I didn't especially like him until he turned eighteen. But that didn't make me a bad *mater*."

Martha Sue laughed through her tears. "That's a horrible thing to say about my *dat*."

"It's the truth. Peter was a trial. I try never to run from the truth or pretend it doesn't exist. If you run from it, the truth will eventually catch up with you. If you pretend it doesn't exist, it will just make you miserable."

Martha Sue let out a breath she didn't even know she'd been holding. "I don't have to pretend anymore. What's done is done. I don't have to try to love him."

"Uh-huh," Mammi said. "Love is hard work, for sure and certain."

"Love isn't work. It should be easy, like falling."

"*Ach*, falling in love is easy. Staying in love is the hard work. You'll find that out when you're married." Mammi studied Martha Sue's face. "Love takes work, but even more than that, love takes courage. It's not more love you need, Martha Sue, it's courage."

That didn't make sense. "The courageous choice is to let Yost go."

Mammi's piercing blue eyes bored a hole into Martha Sue's confidence. "Of course it isn't, dear. The deeper the love, the deeper the possibility of pain. Running from love to avoid pain is like running from the wind. It will catch up with you eventually, even when you think you've outrun it."

Martha Sue's throat tightened. "But, Mammi, I can't bear to be hurt again."

Mammi nodded wisely. "Do you know who you're named after?"

Martha Sue swallowed hard. "Aendi Martha Sue. Your daughter."

"*Jah*. She died when she was just eight years old."

"I know."

"There was so much pain at her death that I thought I'd been swallowed into a black hole. There was no light, no joy, nothing but raw pain. But if I'd never been her mother, I never would have felt that despair. I wouldn't trade one day I had with Martha Sue even though there was a mountain of pain at the end of it. To avoid pain is to avoid life, and that's no life at all."

Martha Sue held her breath. What did Mammi mean by that? She felt that she might be on the verge of an important discovery, but she couldn't decipher what.

Mammi was quiet for a very long time, the only sound between them the click of her knitting needles against each other. "True love will always leave a mark. Just look at Jesus."

Chapter 14

Jonah and Lily crept behind the big maple, and Jonah read the note again. "'Come to the shed at four. Make sure no one sees you.'"

Lily pointed to the old shed that held all of Felty's tools. "Is that it?"

"*Jah*," Jonah whispered.

"Who do you think sent you that note?"

Jonah glanced at the paper he'd found on his bed after school. "I don't know. Do you think it's a murderer or something?"

Lily frowned. "Not likely. But just in case, I'm coming with you. I know how to scream really loud."

"What if they want me to come alone?"

"Then they should have said that. They can't get mad at you for not following directions."

Jonah led the way as they ran full speed toward the shed. He pulled the door open, and he and Lily ducked inside. It took a second for his eyes to adjust to the dark, but he could see Anna clearly enough standing against the far wall holding a dim flashlight up to her face. She looked kind of spooky.

She pressed her index finger to her lips. "Shh. Be very quiet. We don't want Martha Sue to find us in here."

Jonah's heart raced even though it hadn't been a robber waiting for them in the dark. "What's going on?"

Anna held up her hand. "Wait a minute."

They stood in awkward silence, Jonah and Lily occasionally glancing at each other, unsure what exactly they were waiting for. After what seemed like half an hour, the door opened, and Felty stepped into the shed holding a note much like the one Jonah had received. Felty looked a little surprised when he saw who was in the shed with him. "Annie-banannie, why did you send me this note?" He scooted around Jonah and Lily and sidled next to Anna.

Anna shushed Felty just as she'd shushed Lily and Jonah. "Wait a minute."

Lily shuffled her feet and giggled. Jonah didn't know what to do except follow Anna's directions and wait.

There wasn't a lot of room in there. Felty could have stretched out his arms and touched either side of the shed at the same time. There were now four bodies and several tools crammed into the small space, and it smelled like mold.

In another minute, the shed door opened again, and Dat came in, looking just as surprised as everybody else.

Anna waved him in urgently. "*Cum reu, cum reu.* Shut the door. We don't want anyone to see us."

Dat didn't ask questions, just shut the door and crowded into the shed, stepping on Jonah's foot and knocking his knee against the push lawn mower. "*Ach,*" Dat grunted.

Felty put his arm around Anna, probably to make a little extra room for everybody else. If Martha Sue was invited to this secret meeting, she wouldn't be able to fit. "Annie," Felty said, "why are we standing in this stinky toolshed? The outdoors is so much roomier, and we're less likely to get eaten by spiders."

Lily caught her breath. "Will we get eaten by spiders? I don't think my *mamm* would be very happy about that."

"Now, Felty," Anna said. "Don't scare *die kinner*."

"I'm not trying to scare them. I'm just telling you the facts."

Anna shined the flashlight in Felty's face. It was very dim. "I don't want Martha Sue to catch us, and the spiders are more afraid of you than you are of them."

"I love you, Annie, but why couldn't we have had this meeting in the house like regular people?"

Anna looked shocked. "Felty, if Martha Sue found out, it would ruin everything. Besides, you won't allow Jonah in the house, and this meeting is about him." She reached out and patted Jonah's cheek. "Jonah needs our help, and we've got to be sneaky."

Jonah's heart sank. "I'm not going to be sneaky ever again. I broke your wrist being sneaky."

Anna swatted that thought away with her bright pink cast. "I broke my own wrist. You shouldn't have done what you did, but you feel sorry, and that's the end of it. Felty has even decided to let you back in the house."

Felty's eyebrows scooted up his forehead. "I have?"

Anna patted Felty on the stomach. "*Ach*, Felty, you can't hold a grudge forever."

"It's been two days."

Anna nodded. "Long enough."

"That's . . . nice of you," Jonah said, not sure if he should take Anna's word for it. It would be wise to wait for Felty to invite him into the house.

"Besides, Felty dear, you told me just last night that you are sick and tired of Vernon Schmucker."

"I *am* sick and tired of Vernon Schmucker," Felty said. "But that doesn't have anything to do with Jonah in my house."

Anna eyed Felty as if it should be obvious to him. "I'm going to keep inviting Vernon until Martha Sue agrees to marry Yost."

Dat leaned forward. "What do you mean, Anna?" Jonah had never heard such hope in Dat's voice before.

"Martha Sue needs to see the differences so she can make an informed decision."

Felty chuckled. "Martha Sue is well aware of the differences between Vernon and Yost."

Anna sighed. "You don't have to be so contrary, Felty. It will help move things along quicker if Vernon drives her crazy."

"That doesn't seem very nice," Lily said.

Anna waved the flashlight around, sending weak light beams pinging off the walls of the shed. "Don't worry. It's for the greater good."

Jonah frowned. That was what Anna had told him when Vernon ate his cake. It wasn't a *gute* thing.

Lily bumped Jonah's elbow when she folded her arms. "Why are we here?"

Anna smiled at Lily. "*Denki* for asking. It's hard to have a secret meeting when people keep distracting me.

Like I said before, we are here to help Jonah. And Yost. They both need our help."

"I'd appreciate any help I can get," Dat said.

Anna put the flashlight right under her chin and shined it upward. "I've talked Martha Sue into staying at least until I get my cast off, but that doesn't give us much time. Yost, do you want to marry Martha Sue?"

"More than anything."

Anna looked at Jonah. "Jonah, do you want your *dat* to be happy?"

"Of course I do. I already apologized. I was wrong about everything, and I want him to marry Martha Sue."

Lily poked him in the ribs. "I told him he was being a baby and that Martha Sue would not be a wicked stepmother."

"So now we need to convince Martha Sue to marry your *dat*."

Jonah heaved a sigh. "I already asked her to give Dat another chance. I don't think she wants to."

"*Nae*, she doesn't," Anna said. "She doesn't trust you. You two were getting along so well, and then you played that laundry trick. She doesn't want to reach out her hand only to get bitten again. She'd rather be alone for the rest of her life."

"Is she afraid of dogs?" Lily asked.

Jonah nodded. "She got bit once and had to get a rabies shot." Dat hung his head, as if bearing the weight of the world. Jonah felt the shame all over again. "I'm sorry, Dat. I didn't mean to . . ."

Dat sighed. "What's done is done, Jonah. You've apologized to all of us. But Anna is right. Martha Sue doesn't trust you. And after how you've treated her, I don't think she likes you all that much."

Lily shook her head. "Oh, she likes him. She gave him a whole plate of raspberry tarts the day Anna broke her wrist. She wouldn't have done that if she hated him."

That didn't make Jonah feel any better. "She was just doing her Christian duty. We're supposed to love our enemies."

"You're not her enemy," Dat said.

"*Jah*, I am. I despitefully used her and Anna."

Anna pointed the flashlight at Jonah. "I do not have any enemies, and neither does Martha Sue, but she's hurting, and you're the one who needs to make her see."

Jonah lowered his eyes. "Make her see what? I usually make things worse."

Lily poked him again. "Don't say that. Everything is better since you moved here."

A ribbon of warmth trickled down Jonah's spine. Lily liked him. Lily believed in him. Lily was the best friend anyone could ask for, even if she was bossy and nosey and talked too much. "I want to fix things between Martha Sue and my *dat*, but what can I do?"

Felty glanced at Anna and furrowed his brow. "You don't have to fix things between Martha Sue and your *dat*. You need to fix them between Martha Sue and you."

"You don't need to fix things," Anna said. "You need to help her *see*."

"What do you mean, *help her see*?" Jonah said.

Felty drew his brows together. "*Jah*, Annie-banannie. What do you mean by that?"

Anna frowned. "If none of you can see it, I'm not going to explain it to you. Just trust me. I have a plan, and we're all going to help Jonah."

Jonah looked around him at the smiling faces in the shed. The sight should have bolstered his courage. *Bolstered* meant he should be feeling a lot more confident than he was. "I don't even know what you want me to do."

Anna didn't lose her sweet but devious smile. "I have a plan."

Chapter 15

Martha Sue knew what Jonah was doing, and it made her sad that he was trying so hard. Jonah wasn't the only one. Yost, Dawdi, Lily, and especially Mammi were conspiring against her, and she wanted to cry and laugh and pull her hair out all at the same time.

Jonah, with Lily's help, had taken on so many chores, he barely had time to eat meals. He gathered the eggs, milked the cow, washed breakfast and dinner dishes, made his own lunch in the mornings, and mopped the kitchen floor once a week. He asked Mammi to teach him how to knit, probably so he could spend more time in the house around Martha Sue. He complimented Martha Sue on her cooking, her laundry hanging, her weeding. And he brought her a crossword puzzle from the local newspaper every week. How could she resist that? Lily was often his helper, cheerfully assisting Jonah to make a *gute* impression on Martha Sue.

It seemed to be Dawdi's job to point out Jonah's *gute* qualities, how smart he was, how kind, how enthusiastic. Yost mostly just looked longingly in her direction whenever they were near or flashed that smile that always made her knees weak. Mammi seemed to be working against everybody else, as she invited Vernon over for dinner almost every night, except when Dawdi asked her not to, and sometimes even then.

Martha Sue loved that Yost loved her enough to persist. She appreciated that Jonah was trying to make amends for his atrocious behavior. She felt grateful that Mammi and Dawdi desperately wanted her to be happy, but she was going to disappoint all of them because Jonah was bound to disappoint her. She hated the thought of disappointing anyone, but she had to guard her heart and her sanity. Lord willing, Yost and Jonah would come to understand.

Mammi never would. Someday she'd probably be looking for a husband for Martha Sue from her seat in heaven.

Hearing a buggy come up the hill, Martha Sue looked out the window and groaned right out loud.

"Is something wrong?" Mammi asked from her perch on the sofa.

"Vernon is here, and it's two hours before dinnertime. What am I supposed to do with him for two hours?"

Mammi paused her knitting and bloomed into a smile. "He said he wanted to ask you a very important question, so I told him to come early so the two of you would have some time alone."

Martha Sue's heart stopped. "*Ach*, Mammi, you didn't! We're both going to be terribly embarrassed when I tell him I won't marry him."

Mammi didn't seem ruffled in the least. "What makes you think he's going to ask you to marry him? He might just want to ask you to make him a pecan pie."

"I've made him half a dozen pecan pies. I'm done making pecan pies."

"The peaches will be on soon enough."

This was Martha Sue's own fault. After she realized Yost wasn't going to move back to Ohio, she'd welcomed Vernon's presence on Huckleberry Hill. He loved to talk, he loved to eat, and he was a *gute* buffer between Martha Sue and Yost. Martha Sue didn't have to work at ignoring Yost when Vernon was around because Vernon monopolized every conversation and all the food at any given meal. She had even made all of Vernon's favorite foods so he'd come to dinner more often. Now she wished she hadn't been so dedicated to avoiding Yost. Vernon had gotten the wrong idea.

Jonah and Lily burst into the kitchen, each carrying a half a bucket of milk. They weren't quite strong enough to carry a full bucket so after they milked, they divided the milk into two pails so they wouldn't spill any on the way from the barn. "We finished milking the cow," Jonah said, smiling at Martha Sue.

Lily set her pail on the table. "Jonah already strained it and everything."

"That's wonderful nice of you, Jonah," Martha Sue said. Would Jonah come to resent all the work he was doing for Martha Sue's sake?

Jonah set down his pail and brushed his hands on his pants. "We'll help if you want to make cheese."

"*Denki*, but I'll have to make cheese in the morning while you're at school."

Jonah's expression fell, and Martha Sue felt guilty for not dropping everything and making cheese right then and there. But she still had to get dinner ready *and* deal with Vernon Schmucker. She wouldn't have time to make cheese.

"We could help you cook dinner," Lily said.

"Um, okay. That would be nice."

Jonah and Lily both beamed like kerosene lanterns. "What can we do?" Lily said.

"You can start by peeling and grating carrots for the salad."

Mammi looked up from her knitting. "Are you making green Jell-O with carrots and hot dogs? That's my favorite."

"*Nae*, Mammi. I'm just making a carrot raisin salad."

Mammi smiled. "I love raisins."

Yes, she did. That was why Martha Sue tried to make at least one dish a day with raisins in it.

Lily and Jonah went to the kitchen, pulled the bag of carrots from the fridge, and started peeling eagerly. Jonah was a little slow, but he was just learning how to peel a vegetable without taking his skin with it. "Guess what, Martha Sue. I saw Tennessee today. I can't wait to tell Felty."

Dawdi and Jonah had started playing the license plate game about three weeks ago, and their enthusiasm for it was quite endearing. Martha Sue watched out the window as Vernon clomped up the porch steps. "How many license plates have you found yet?"

Jonah slid the peeler across a carrot. "Tennessee makes eighteen. We might go into Shawano next week to see how many more we can find. Felty says it's tourist season at the lake. Do you want to come?"

"Um, sure," Martha Sue said, because she didn't want

to disappoint Jonah. He'd be disappointed enough when Martha Sue didn't marry his *dat*.

The expected knock came at the door. Martha Sue wiped her hands and opened it. Vernon stood on the doorstep with an unruly bouquet of wildflowers. Martha Sue wasn't all that impressed. The flowers looked suspiciously like the wild roses that grew on a bush at the bottom of Huckleberry Hill. He held out his hand. "I brought pretty flowers for a pretty girl. And a *gute* cook."

Martha Sue didn't want to take them. Even that small gesture would encourage Vernon to do what he'd come here to do. "*Denki*, Vernon." She reluctantly took the roses, only because they were going to die if they didn't get in some water immediately. "You're early," she said, stating the obvious.

Vernon wiggled his eyebrows as if he had a *wunderbarr* secret to share with her. "I am early. Very early. It wonders me if we could take a private walk—but not a long walk because I don't want to be sweaty for dinner. Anna says you're making *yummasetti*." More eyebrow wiggling. "How nice of you to make my favorite casserole today of all days."

Martha Sue clenched her teeth, filled a glass, and slid the roses into the water. They were wild, so they'd be dead within a couple of hours. "I don't know if I can go on a walk. I need to finish dinner."

"It won't be long. I'll get out of breath if it's long."

"I'll finish dinner," Mammi said.

Jonah and Lily nodded to each other and set down their carrots and peelers. "We want to come."

Vernon forced a smile, which made him look consti-
pated. "I'm sorry. No children allowed."

"Aw," Lily groaned. "We want to come. We've been
doing chores all day."

Jonah rinsed his hands under the faucet. "We can
show you our special spot."

Vernon didn't even try to maintain his smile. "The
last time you showed me a special spot, I almost died."

Martha Sue raised an eyebrow. "What a great idea.
Let's all go together."

Lily and Jonah jumped up and down and cheered as
if a walk with Vernon Schmucker was the best thing that
would happen to them all year.

Mammi hissed to get Martha Sue's attention. "Vernon
wants to have a private talk with you."

Martha Sue wasn't about to bar *die kinner* from
coming with them. She'd rather not be anywhere alone
with Vernon, and she refused to let him propose to her
today. She just wasn't up to it. She pretended not to
understand what Mammi meant. "It will be fun. I've
always wanted to see Lily and Jonah's special spot."

"Can we take Sparky?" Lily asked.

Mammi's little white dog raised her head from the rug.

Mammi slumped her shoulders in dejection. "I sup-
pose, but it will be too crowded for any private talks.
Just make sure you brush all the cockleburs from
Sparky's coat before she comes back into the house."

To make sure there were no further protests, Martha
Sue opened the door and walked out onto the porch.
Jonah and Lily followed close behind, acting more
excited than they had reason to be. Vernon came last,

shooting dirty looks at Jonah and Lily. If they noticed, they didn't seem to care.

Martha Sue skipped down the steps. Even though it was overcast, it was a beautiful day. She wouldn't let Vernon ruin a perfectly *gute* walk. "Okay, Jonah, Lily. Show the way."

Jonah pointed down the main path that wound farther into the woods. "*Cum*. It's this direction."

The slope on this side of the hill was gentle, but if they went too far, Vernon wouldn't be able to get back. Martha Sue whispered, "A hundred feet is all Vernon will be able to do."

Jonah shrugged. "We'll go slow."

Even walking like snails, Martha Sue and Jonah were soon way ahead of Vernon and Lily and Sparky, who was faithfully sticking with the stragglers. Martha Sue kept glancing back at her companions. Lily seemed content to stick with Vernon, chattering by his side while he trained his gaze on Martha Sue and moped like a two-year-old.

Jonah grinned like a cat with a canary in his mouth. "Vernon wants to ask you to marry him, doesn't he?"

Martha Sue was so surprised, she laughed out loud. "What makes you think so?"

"He's showing all the signs. Sweating, staring, sulking. *Sulking* means he's really mad that me and Lily came along because he wants to be alone with you."

"I don't want to be alone with him."

"We know. That's why we offered to come along."

A spot right in the middle of Martha Sue's chest felt warm and tingly. She tried to ignore it. "*Denki*. I appreciate you watching out for me."

"I'm sorry about the time I rigged that bucket to dump water on your head. I know how you hate water. It must have really scared you."

Martha Sue fingered the small scar on her eyebrow where the bucket had conked her on the head. "The bucket was worse than the water."

"I'm sorry."

"It's okay, Jonah. I've forgiven you."

He slid his hands in his pockets. "But you don't trust me."

"Who told you that?"

"Anna. She says I need to make you trust me, but I don't know what I can do. You still won't look at me."

Martha Sue drew her brows together. "That's not true. I look at you all the time. I'm looking at you now."

"But you don't really look at me like you used to. You never look in my eyes because you don't like me."

Jonah was too perceptive by half. "I suppose I don't want you to think we're making a connection. I don't want you to hope for something that isn't going to happen."

"It could happen," Jonah said. "If I'm *gute* enough. That's why I've got to make you like me, or you won't marry my *dat*, and he won't love me anymore."

Martha Sue stopped walking and placed her hand on Jonah's shoulder. She looked him straight in the eye, even though she'd been avoiding it. "Jonah, how many times do I have to tell you, your *dat* will never stop loving you no matter what you do."

Jonah kicked at a rock in the path. "I know, I guess. But he'll never be happy again if you don't marry him.

I want him to be happy, and it will be my fault if he isn't."

"Don't blame yourself. Some things just weren't meant to be."

"I'm almost fourteen. I'll be out of the house before you know it. Can't you just put up with me for a few more years, even if you don't like me? Dat is despondent without you. *Despondent* is like he's lost in the woods all by himself and the wolves are circling because they want to eat him. Because of me."

He looked so sad that Martha Sue couldn't leave it at that. "I know you're trying very hard. It's sweet."

He looked at her sideways. "Am I smothering you? Because I don't want to smother you. For a while there, my *dat* was smothering me. He wouldn't even let me go play softball after school. Then he threatened to quit his job and bother me all summer."

Martha Sue laughed. "I'm sure you're glad he didn't do that."

"I sure am."

Vernon and Lily finally caught up with them, Vernon looking as if he'd eaten a whole lemon, Lily still talking like a blue jay, Sparky still waddling happily alongside. "I don't care how special this special place is," Vernon said. "I refuse to go any farther. Martha Sue, I want to talk to you. Alone."

Lily gazed at Vernon and batted her eyelashes. "But you wouldn't leave us little kids out here in the woods by ourselves, would you?"

Vernon had run out of patience. "You know the way back."

"But what if you get stuck again?" Jonah asked. "We should be here to help you."

A clap of thunder startled all of them. Martha Sue hadn't noticed how dark the sky had become. A light rain pitter-pattered on the trees overhead. Vernon shielded his eyes and looked up. Then without a word, he turned around and trotted back up the path, faster than Martha Sue had ever seen him move. Martha Sue, Jonah, and Lily gazed at each other in surprise then started to laugh. Vernon was a fast walker when he wanted to be.

In an instant, the rain turned to a downpour. Sparky looked at the sky and whined. Martha Sue put her arms around both of the children and nudged them up the path toward the house. They hadn't gone twenty yards when Yost met them with a big yellow umbrella. He put his arms around Martha Sue and Jonah, and Martha Sue held on to Lily so they could all squeeze under the umbrella. Martha Sue didn't mind one little bit. It felt so *gute* to be close to Yost, even though she had no intention of marrying him. "I saw you go down the path," he said, chuckling. "Then I saw Vernon come back."

"He abandoned us," Jonah said, looking quite happy about it.

"Well, I won't abandon you," Yost said, giving Martha Sue a look that warmed her all the way to her toes.

Lily grinned. "You came to find us." She eyed Jonah then shoved him with the palm of her hand. They broke free from under the umbrella and raced up the path with Sparky chasing them all the way.

"You're going to get wet," Martha Sue called.

Lily turned and ran backward a few steps. "We don't care. Have fun without us."

Yost tightened his arm around Martha Sue. "How could we possibly have fun without you?" he yelled. They were already so far away, they probably hadn't heard him.

Martha Sue giggled, lowered her eyes, and kept walking, savoring the sound of plump raindrops against the umbrella, the smell of strong soap and leather that always hung about Yost, and the comfort of his arm around her, like her missing puzzle piece.

Today, she wouldn't fight it.

It would end all too soon.

Chapter 16

Martha Sue pulled the buggy into the camping spot near the lake and gave Jonah a weak smile. "This will be fun," she said, which was probably the biggest lie she'd ever told in her life.

Mammi, who sat between Martha Sue and Jonah, looked like she was the only one who believed it. "*Jah*, it will be so much fun. Vernon has been eager to take you fishing ever since he met you. He's hoping to impress you with his fishing skills. I hear he's quite a *gute* fisherman." She gave Martha Sue a playful, knowing look. "What girl doesn't want a husband who can bring home dinner every night?"

"My *dat* is a better fisherman than Vernon," Jonah said. "Before we came to Wisconsin, we used to catch trout on the river, and Martha Sue cooked it for us. She's a real *gute* fish fryer. She puts these special spices on it, wraps it in tinfoil, and fries it in a pan. It's *appeditlich*."

Martha Sue smiled. Watching Yost and Jonah enjoy her cooking was a fond memory.

Mammi's lips formed into an O. "You'll have to give

me your recipe. I'm always looking for new ways to cook fish."

That was probably a *gute* idea. Mammi's old ways of cooking fish proved inedible.

Vernon had invited Martha Sue to go fishing, no doubt to attempt another proposal. Mammi was probably right that Vernon wanted to impress Martha Sue with his skills as a fisherman, but he also wanted to get her alone without Lily and Jonah so he could profess his undying love. Martha Sue cringed. She didn't love Vernon. She could barely stand him. But it was also plain that Vernon didn't love her. He was too concerned about himself and his own comfort to love another person. Why did he want to get married? Maybe he was tired of his *mamm*'s cooking. Maybe Martha Sue made a better pecan pie. Maybe the bishop was pressuring him to find a mate. Whatever the reason, Vernon wanted a *fraa*, and Martha Sue was a convenient choice, even though she had no interest in fishing. Vernon obviously thought she'd say yes without a moment's hesitation. In his mind, she was desperate for a man to save her from being an old *maedel*. He didn't realize there were worse things than being single. Being married to Vernon for one.

Thank Derr Herr Lily and Jonah were pesky when it came to Vernon. Jonah had overheard Vernon invite Martha Sue to go fishing, and Jonah had invited himself to come along and teach Martha Sue how to fish. Martha Sue had agreed to go only to make Jonah happy. He was trying so hard to win her approval, and she just didn't have the heart to squash his hopes and dreams. Vernon had protested that children were not allowed on fishing trips because they were loud and scared away the fish. But Vernon was no match for Jonah's cleverness. Jonah had bragged that he could catch more fish and bigger fish than Vernon, and Vernon had taken the challenge.

Mammi had volunteered to come with them, probably so she could orchestrate some time for Vernon and Martha Sue to be alone, but Martha Sue wasn't going to let that happen. And from the look on Jonah's face, he wasn't going to let that happen either.

They got out of the buggy and carried their picnic basket and fishing pole to the picnic table. Vernon stood at the shore with his back to them, already fishing. He turned and motioned for Martha Sue to come to him but quickly turned back to his pole as if he would miss a fish if he looked away for one second.

Martha Sue didn't want to go near him, but she was feeling charitable so she trudged down the slope and stood next to him. "You need something?"

Vernon frowned. "Please talk softly," he whispered. "I just wanted to make sure you didn't bring anything crunchy in that picnic. You'll scare away the fish."

Martha Sue stifled a smile. "Nothing too crunchy."

"*Gute,*" he said.

Nothing crunchy like carrots or popcorn, but she had brought Nacho Cheese Doritos, potato chips, and cheese puffs because those were Jonah's favorites. If the fish were scared off, Martha Sue wouldn't feel one minute of remorse. Then Vernon wouldn't catch any, and a little humility would do him *gute.*

Martha Sue left Vernon to his important work and spread a red-and-white checkered tablecloth on the table. Mammi set out the sandwiches with the small bags of chips and a bag of cookies. She waved Jonah over to the table. "Jonah, *cum*. Have a sandwich before you teach Martha Sue how to fish."

Jonah eyed the sandwiches. "Tuna fish?"

"*Jah*," Martha Sue said. "With dill pickles."

Jonah's face lit up. "I love tuna fish with dill pickles."

Even though Martha Sue had given up on any relationship with Jonah, it did her heart good to see how happy a tuna fish and pickle sandwich made him. She still cared about his feelings.

Mammi called to Vernon. "*Cum*, and get a sandwich, Vernon. There's plenty of time to fish."

Vernon turned and frowned, obviously not happy that Mammi had yelled loud enough for the fish to hear. It seemed he liked fishing even more than he liked eating—but just barely. He motioned for Martha Sue to come to him. She wasn't going to play that game again. She pretended not to see. After motioning three times, he finally gave up and raised his voice. "Could you hand me a sandwich, Martha Sue? I don't want to interrupt my rhythm." He glanced at Jonah. "I've already caught one fish."

Jonah folded his arms and smirked. It was just as Martha Sue had suspected. Jonah didn't care about beating Vernon in a fishing contest.

Martha Sue set napkins on the table and ignored Vernon completely. Mammi grabbed half a sandwich off the plate and took it to Vernon as he concentrated on his rhythm.

Mammi sat next to Jonah, and Martha Sue sat opposite them at the table. They said prayers and dug into the food. Martha Sue glanced behind her, leaned forward, and whispered to Jonah, "At least he won't hog all the Doritos."

Jonah scrunched his lips to one side of his face. "My *dat* never hogs the Doritos."

Martha Sue laughed. "He doesn't like Doritos."

"He wouldn't hog them, even if he did. And he would never steal someone's cake."

That was true enough. Yost was unselfish to a fault. Martha Sue studied Jonah's face. He looked so much like his *dat*, she almost couldn't stand it. She wished she didn't love Yost so much.

Mammi opened the bag of cheese puffs. "I'm sorry Vernon ate your cake, Jonah, but it was for the greater good."

Martha Sue grunted her disapproval. "Vernon needs to learn some manners."

"Which you can teach him after you're married," Mammi said.

Martha Sue smiled at Jonah and sighed. "For sure and certain, Mammi. After we're married."

Mammi thought she was serious. "I'm *froh* you agree. Every man needs a few repairs before he gets married."

Jonah nodded. "For sure and certain, Vernon needs lots of repairs. My *dat* doesn't need any repairs. I like him the way he is, except maybe that he tries too hard."

"I like him just the way he is too," Mammi said. "What about you, Martha Sue? Do you like Yost just the way he is?"

Martha Sue propped her chin in her hand and looked very hard at her sandwich. "It's not my job to change anybody but myself."

Jonah seemed suddenly irritated. "Can't you even acknowledge that my *dat* is kind and loyal? *Acknowledge* means that you can admit that Dat would make a much better husband than Vernon Schmucker. At least Dat doesn't steal people's special cakes."

Jonah's *dat* wasn't the problem, as Jonah very well knew. "I can acknowledge all of that, Jonah. For sure and certain, your *dat* is the best kind of man." She didn't want to make Jonah feel any worse than he already felt, so she changed the subject. "Do you think trout or bass are better for frying?"

Mammi always had an opinion about food, so she immediately took up the subject of oysters and seafood and why raisins made everything taste better.

After they ate, Martha Sue and Mammi cleaned up while Jonah inspected his fishing pole. "Martha Sue, why don't you watch me fish? Then you can use one of Vernon's extra fishing poles and try it yourself."

Martha Sue nodded, not especially excited about fishing, but willing to let Jonah show her. Jonah stood on the shore about ten feet from Vernon, and Martha Sue stood next to Jonah, doing her best to show some interest. Jonah cast his line into the water and reeled it back in, explaining to Martha Sue that she needed to keep it moving so the fish thought the lure was actually alive.

She watched and nodded. "It's less disgusting when you don't use real worms. Your *dat* likes real worms."

Jonah grinned. "Me and Dat would get up early in the morning and dig for worms in the garden. I used to sell nightcrawlers to fishermen who were heading out to Lake Buckhorn. Worms catch the fish better, but they're messy and sometimes you run out." He reeled in his hook. "Vernon, Martha Sue is ready to try to fish. Can she use one of your poles?"

Vernon didn't even so much as glance in their direction, but his ruddy cheeks turned even redder. "She can't use my fishing poles. They're expensive."

Jonah frowned. "You have three of them. Let Martha Sue use one."

Vernon shook his head. "She'll have to borrow yours. This pole cost me four hundred dollars."

Martha Sue turned her head so Vernon wouldn't see her face, scrunched her lips together, and raised her eyebrows. Jonah returned her expression with a sneer of his own. "Okay, Martha Sue. You can use mine."

"Are you sure?"

He handed his pole to her. "I trust you. Hold it like I showed you." He nudged her fingers until she was holding it the right way. "Now let out the line and toss it into the water." She did as he directed. "Okay. Now pull it back and forth across the water slowly. *Nae*, even slower. You want the fish to catch it."

Jonah sat next to Martha Sue on the shore giving instructions while she did her best with the fishing pole. Vernon changed poles twice within ten minutes, probably to prove to Martha Sue and Jonah that he needed all his poles and shouldn't have been expected to share one with the girl he was going to propose to.

After about half an hour, Martha Sue was bored and annoyed with the whole thing. Vernon didn't talk to her because he didn't want to scare the fish away, and his silence was the only *gute* thing about fishing. Vernon only spoke when he caught another fish, taunting Jonah that he was winning the fishing contest, even though Jonah wasn't fishing. Jonah didn't seem to care about the fishing contest, but he seemed increasingly irritated that Vernon was so smug about it, especially when there were plenty of fishing poles to go around.

Suddenly, Martha Sue's line went taut. Her gaze flew to Jonah's face. "Have I . . . have I caught one?"

Jonah leaped to his feet. "Okay, reel it in but not too fast or you'll lose it."

She yanked up on the pole.

"*Nae, nae.* Gently. It's going to get away."

Martha Sue's heart galloped like a horse. "You take it. You know how to reel one in, don't you?"

"*Ach, vell, jah,* but it's your catch."

"I want you to finish it for me. You're the expert."

Jonah carefully, breathlessly, took the pole from Martha Sue. "It's wonderful nice of you to let me reel in the fish. It's the best part of fishing."

Vernon was suddenly right at Jonah's side with one hand on the reel. "Let me finish it up. It's too big for you."

"I can do it," Jonah said, his tongue stuck out in concentration, his eyes glued to the water. "Let go."

Vernon tightened his grip on Jonah's pole. "I'm the better fisherman. You don't want Martha Sue's first fish to get away."

"Vernon," Martha Sue scolded. "Let go. It's Jonah's pole. I asked him to do it."

"Stop it, Vernon!" Jonah yelled.

Vernon wouldn't let go, and Jonah couldn't begin to yank free because Vernon was six inches taller and at least two hundred pounds heavier. Martha Sue rushed to the other side of Vernon and tried to pry his hand off

Jonah's pole. Vernon didn't exactly shove Martha Sue away, but it wasn't a gentle nudge either. She stumbled, caught her foot on a stone, and fell backward into the water. She gasped as she went under, memories of her near-drowning experience rendering her helpless in the cold lake. The water wasn't deep, but she had gone in *hinnerdale* first, and her feet couldn't find purchase on the bottom.

After less than a second, Jonah jumped in the water and sloshed toward her. He grabbed her hand and firmly pulled her up so she could find her footing. She stood up in the chest-deep water, coughing and spitting, more angry than hurt or frightened. She glared at Vernon, who was holding tightly, possessively to Jonah's pole, fighting to reel in that fish. Grasping Jonah's hand, she slogged her way onto the shore. Their teeth were chattering by the time they got out of the water.

"Oh, dear!" Mammi said. She grabbed a handful of napkins from the picnic table and started dabbing at Martha's Sue's dress. It didn't help, but Mammi liked thinking she was useful.

"I got it!" Vernon yelled, as a three-foot fish came out of the water dangling from Jonah's hook. "Get the net! Get the net!"

Jonah didn't move. Martha Sue didn't move. Vernon had stolen Jonah's fish. He could get his own net.

Still struggling with the fish, Vernon turned his head, and the look on his face was priceless. Vernon obviously couldn't believe that they weren't rushing to help him get the fish in the net. His surprise turned to panic as the fish thrashed around just above the surface of the water. "Help me, somebody," he called, but Jonah seemed content to watch Vernon dance, Martha Sue was busy wringing water from the hem of her dress, and Mammi was trying to dry Martha Sue with a napkin.

Vernon shuffled along the shore toward his tackle box. His net was propped against it. When he got close, he released one hand from Jonah's fishing pole, reached out for his net, and fell to his knees. He somehow managed to pick up the net and keep hold of the pole. In one swift movement, he caught the fish in the net and stood up. It was quite a feat for someone who couldn't walk all the way up Huckleberry Hill without four stops to catch his breath.

"I got it!" Vernon yelled, doing a little jig as the fish flopped around trying to escape from the net. "I got it!" He turned and gave Jonah a triumphant smile. Jonah folded his arms and glared. Martha Sue pretended Vernon was invisible because she was too mad to acknowledge his presence.

Mammi marched up to Vernon, propped her hand on her hip, and gave Vernon the evil eye. Even though Mammi was a short little thing, Vernon cowered as if she were six feet tall with broad shoulders and wearing an eye patch. "Vernon Schmucker," Mammi said, her face as dark as a gathering thunderstorm, "you pushed my granddaughter into the water. What do you have to say for yourself?"

Vernon backed away from Mammi and tried to smile. "Look, Anna." He held out his net to show her. "If it hadn't been for me, Martha Sue never would have caught such a fine largemouth."

"Give me that fish." Vernon tried to avoid her, but Mammi snatched the net from him with her *gute* hand.

"Jonah and Martha Sue were doing just fine before you came along." She marched back up the bank, faster than Martha Sue had ever seen her move before, and handed the net to Jonah. "Here you go. This is your catch. Vernon doesn't deserve it."

Vernon followed Mammi up the bank, protesting all the way. "I do so deserve it. I did most of the work."

Mammi gave the net to Jonah, who held it and eyed the huge fish, still wriggling but running out of energy. "It's the biggest fish I ever caught, but I didn't really catch it because Vernon is so selfish."

Vernon puffed out his chest. "I'm not selfish. I'm the only one who could have reeled in that fish."

Jonah shoved the net into Vernon's chest. "You've ruined it. I don't want it."

Martha Sue was still dripping like a leaky faucet, still mad as a wet hen, still shivering like a cold puppy. "Are you sure, Jonah? You deserve that fish."

Jonah shook his head. "You deserve it more than I do. You hooked it."

She waved away his praise. "I don't want it. Vernon ruined it for me too."

Vernon lifted the fish so that it was close to his eye. "My *mamm* will be *froh* to see this. She's always so proud when I come home with a catch."

Shivering violently, Martha Sue gave Jonah a look of disgust, and Jonah nodded back at her.

Mammi put her arm around Martha Sue and nudged her toward the buggy. "Let's get you out of these wet clothes before you catch cold." She turned and pointed at Vernon with her glob of soggy napkins. "You've got a lot of apologizing to do if you want Martha Sue to marry you."

Martha Sue and Mammi climbed in the buggy. "I'm not going to marry him, Mammi."

Mammi sat up straighter. "Not until he apologizes."

Jonah jumped in the buggy with his fist wrapped around his pole. "Vernon Schmucker is a menace. *Menace* means that nobody wants him around because he ruins people's lives."

"And he ruins perfectly lovely fishing trips," Mammi said.

Jonah's lips curled upward. "I didn't know you could get mad like that, Anna. You seem like such a sweet old lady."

"First of all, I am not old. Second of all, I am a sweet *middle-aged* lady. But don't try to hurt my family or I'll turn into a bear."

Martha Sue jiggled the reins and got the horse going. "Can't you see, Mammi? A man who pushes people into the water won't make a very *gute* husband."

Mammi took a deep breath and seemed to cheer up immediately. "I suppose it wouldn't have worked out. Vernon doesn't like my cheesy raisin and bacon asparagus casserole, and he refuses to try my jalapeno banana bread. I'm not especially fond of picky eaters." Her eyes twinkled merrily, as if she'd suddenly forgotten all about Vernon Schmucker. "What about that sixty-three-year-old? The one with nice teeth."

Chapter 17

Martha Sue set the plates on the table and glanced out the window, her chest tightening as she scanned the empty yard. Jonah and Lily were out exploring the hill as they often did on these warm early summer days. Mammi and Dawdi had hired a driver to take them to Greenwood to visit Aendi Ruth Ann and Onkel Matthias, and they would be back tomorrow. Yost had gone straight from work at the cheese factory to help a team of Amish *faters* put a new roof on the schoolhouse, and he wouldn't be back until after dark. Martha Sue and Jonah were eating dinner together tonight, just the two of them, and Martha Sue was more than a little unsettled about it. Maybe she should invite Lily to join them.

Jonah was trying so hard to make her like him, but in the end, they'd both end up heartbroken and disappointed.

She couldn't deny that she was softening toward Jonah, but she'd opened herself to him before, and he'd left scars in a dozen corners of her heart. But scars or no scars, she'd truly be hard-hearted not to appreciate what he'd done for her three days ago.

Jonah had abandoned his giant largemouth bass to pull Martha Sue out of the lake. She hadn't been in danger of drowning. The water had only come up to her chest, but she'd panicked when she hadn't been able to get her footing, and Jonah must have seen the look on her face. He could have let her flail about—she would have eventually found the bottom—but instead, he gave up his battle with Vernon and the fishing pole to help her. Vernon, who supposedly wanted to marry her, was more concerned about taking the credit for that fish. Vernon's behavior hadn't surprised her in the least, but Jonah's behavior had. He'd been extraordinarily unselfish, lost his fish, and gotten wet in the bargain.

The most touching part was that Jonah didn't like water either. His jumping in to help her wasn't some manipulation to show her what a *gute* boy he was. It had obviously been a natural instinct, and the thought warmed Martha Sue's heart, even though it still felt as hard as a stone in her chest. Jonah was like his *dat* that way. So kind, thinking of others over himself.

She folded two napkins and set them under the forks at each plate. Then she went to the fridge and pulled out one of her finest creations: a Jell-O salad in the shape of a fish. She'd created it with five different colors of gelatin, layering them in a rainbow pattern, one on top of the other. It had taken her all day to layer each flavor, let it set, and do the next layer. The colors were quite beautiful, and it looked delicious. She'd done it in memory of the fish Jonah had lost. Lord willing, Jonah was going to get a big laugh out of it. She set it in the center of the table, where Jonah would see it the minute he walked in the house.

She frowned. There was always the same battle in her head. If she did nice things for Jonah, would she get his hopes up? Or was it crueler to ignore him so he lost hope altogether? She didn't want to think about that today. Her first instinct was to be kind, and for sure and certain, it was what Jesus would want her to do.

Something thumped against the window, and she looked up to see Lily standing there with her hands cupped around her eyes looking into the kitchen. When Lily saw Martha Sue, she knocked on the glass and motioned for Martha Sue to come outside.

Martha Sue glanced at her Jell-O fish before walking out onto the porch. Jonah was going to love it, but she'd feel more comfortable if Lily ate dinner with them. Jonah and Lily stood next to the porch swing with their hands behind their backs. Lily was grinning, but Jonah was dead serious, as if the weight of the world was on his shoulders. It made her feel bad that he wasn't sure of her, but there was nothing she could do. She *wasn't* sure of him, so they were at a standstill.

Lily beamed from ear to ear. "Jonah has something to give you." She nudged him with her elbow.

"I just . . . I just wanted to . . ." Jonah pulled his thesaurus from behind his back. His hands shook as he held it out to Martha Sue. "I want you to have this. You won't have to ask me about words anymore, and it will help you do crossword puzzles."

Martha Sue's heart pushed against her rib cage as she reached out and took the book. She thumbed through the pages. Someone had written notes in the margins and drawn little flowers and hearts in the corners around the page numbers. It was like a piece of art. "*Ach*, Jonah, this is . . . this is so sweet, but I can't take your thesaurus. You love this book. It belonged to your *mater*."

Lily seemed cheerful enough for all three of them. "Now it will belong to his new *mater*."

Jonah glanced at the book, the uncertainty flashing in his eyes. "I want you to have it."

Martha Sue couldn't speak past the lump in her throat. This thesaurus was Jonah's most valued possession. That he would even consider giving it to her made her heart crack in ten different places. She sat down on the porch swing and pulled Jonah and Lily to sit on either side of her. "*Ach*, Jonah, this book is a piece of your *mater*. I can't take it."

Lily's smile faltered. "But Jonah wants to give you something to show you how sorry he is and how much he wants you to marry his *dat*."

Martha Sue patted Jonah on the leg. "I know, but just being willing to give it to me is enough."

"You don't want it?" Jonah said. She knew what he must be thinking—that rejecting the gift was the same as rejecting him.

"*Ach*, I want it. I need it, and I didn't even know I needed a thesaurus until I met you. But it wouldn't be right to take your *mamm*'s thesaurus. I want you to keep it."

Jonah let out a breath as if he'd been holding it for a long time. "Are you sure?"

"I'm sure."

"But . . ." Lily scrunched her lips together.

Martha Sue put her arm around Lily. "It's the best, most *wunderbarr* gift anyone has ever wanted to give me. *Denki* for being so thoughtful."

Jonah didn't look happy. Should she have accepted the gift? She didn't know anything about anything anymore.

Lily sighed. "*Ach, vell*, okay." She stood, took Jonah's hand, and pulled him from the swing. "Let's go to the old hollow tree. We can read your thesaurus and look for ladybugs."

"Do you want to stay for dinner, Lily?"

Lily shrugged. "I guess. What are you having?"

"It's a surprise."

Lily grinned. "I like surprises."

Martha Sue smiled at Jonah, who was clutching his thesaurus like a long-lost friend. "Be back in twenty minutes, and bring your thesaurus. I have a new game we can play."

Jonah seemed to perk up. "Okay. I'll let you go first."

He and Lily ran down the porch steps and into the woods. Martha Sue pressed her lips together and watched them go. *Ach*, she was touched that Jonah would offer her his thesaurus, but she also felt terrible that he was willing to give up his thesaurus in hopes he could win her love. She'd made him believe he had to earn her love, and she felt as low as the dirt at her feet.

Martha Sue went into the house and sat at the table. She stared at the Jell-O rainbow fish. Was she trying to win Jonah's love just like he was trying to win hers? Did Jonah feel as hopeless as she did?

Sighing, she went to the fridge and pulled out the pizza dough. She rolled out one round, spread the pizza sauce and cheese, and dotted the pizza with pepperoni. Jonah's favorite.

The *clip-clop* of horse's hooves and the grinding of

buggy wheels took her to the window. Her heart leaped at the thought that maybe Yost was home early. The four of them could have dinner together, like maybe a real family that loved each other. She tried to push that thought out of her mind. Hope was a dangerous thing.

Her stomach turned when she saw Vernon Schmucker coming up the road. *Ach!* What was he doing here? Had he come to apologize? Not likely. Did he still think she'd say yes to a proposal? Well, he'd be surprised, wouldn't he?

Maybe it was a *gute* thing Vernon was here. It would take her mind off the confusion with Jonah, and she would be able to have the conversation she should have had with him weeks ago. Martha Sue wasn't looking forward to it. As difficult as he was, Vernon still had feelings, and he was going to be wounded—how deeply wounded, Martha Sue didn't know, but his pain would be her fault.

She watched from the window as he walked up the steps carrying a bouquet of yellow cornflowers in his fist. Martha Sue *had* to get rid of him, if only to save the hill from being stripped of all its wildflowers. He looked like a man about to make a marriage proposal, confident, determined, and arrogant. Martha Sue squared her shoulders. She could be confident too and just as determined—determined to send Vernon off kindly but firmly, making it clear she never wanted to see him again.

How hard could that be?

He knocked on the door, and she wasted no time opening it. No use delaying the unpleasant conversation for another second, and if she got rid of him quickly, maybe he'd be gone before Jonah and Lily came back for dinner. "*Hallo*, Vernon. *Vie gehts*?"

Vernon sort of pushed his way into the house without being invited. "Where's Jonah?"

Jonah? What did he want with Jonah? Martha Sue reluctantly shut the door behind him. Even though she hoped his visit would be short, she'd rather not leave the door open for flies. "Outside playing in the woods."

Vernon pushed the flowers in her direction. "Anna said you'd be alone today and that I should come over."

Martha Sue gritted her teeth. Dear, dear Mammi. Then again, this was exactly the conversation the two of them needed to have. Maybe Mammi had done her a favor. She filled a vase with water and deposited the flowers with little hope they'd survive for more than a few hours. That was the problem with wildflowers. They were better enjoyed in the meadow and by the side of the road because their beauty was fleeting when cut off from their roots. "I'm *froh* you've come, Vernon. We need to talk."

"For sure and certain we do." He glanced at the Jell-O fish on the table. "Did you make that?"

Martha Sue scooted over so she was between Vernon and his view of the fish. "It's for Jonah."

Vernon puckered his lips. "I guess you know what I've come to say."

"I suppose I do, and I just want to . . ."

Vernon took a step to his right. "Is that fish made out of Jell-O?"

"It's for Jonah," she said again.

"Then I guess you know what I've come to say."

Now they were going in circles. "Vernon, I don't know what you expect . . ."

"My *mamm* says you need to make a choice."

"About what?"

Vernon kept his eye on the Jell-O. "That Jonah boy has been wonderful rude to me, and if you want me to marry you, you need to stand up for me and tell Jonah to treat me better." Sweat beaded on his lip, and he folded his arms and stuck out his chin. "If we get married, you can't be friends with him anymore. Which will it be? Him or me? You have to choose."

It was all Martha Sue could do to keep from laughing. She bit down hard on her tongue and pressed her lips together so she wouldn't smile. Vernon was *not* going to be crushed. His *mamm* might even be more disappointed than he was going to be. Martha Sue should have known all along that he was just in it for the food. "That's too bad, Vernon, but I'm going to have to choose Jonah."

He wilted like a dandelion in the hot sun, furrowing his brow and shuffling his feet. "I didn't really mean that. I still want to marry you, even if you stay friends with Jonah. My *mamm* is just overprotective."

"Well, Vernon, words are like feathers. Once you've scattered them, they're impossible to pick up. I'm afraid it's too late to take back your words now."

"Not too late. I changed my mind. Jonah is a nice boy. I'd go fishing with him anytime." He looked at the Jell-O again. "I know how bad you want a husband. I'm just trying to do my duty as a Christian by marrying you."

If Vernon wasn't out of the house in one minute,

Martha Sue was going to say something she would deeply regret. "I'm sorry if I've caused any confusion, Vernon, but I will never want a husband *that* badly."

His mouth fell open. "You'd rather be an old *maedel*?"

"Oh, *jah*. Much rather." She didn't want to hurt Vernon's feelings, but she had to be blunt, and Vernon didn't seem to have many feelings to hurt. She made a show of studying Mammi's clock. "Look! It's time for you to leave." She opened the door and motioned for him to go, but Vernon had never been especially quick.

"Don't you like fish? I could bring you fish every day. I like it fried with a little salt and pepper. With onions and butter too."

"I don't want to marry you, Vernon, no matter how many times you ask or how many fish you offer."

"Why not?"

She pressed her palm to his elbow and nudged him toward the open door. "May the *gute* Lord bless you in finding a *fraa*, but it will not be me. And don't come back, even if my *mammi* invites you. I won't change my mind."

Unfortunately, trying to "nudge" Vernon to do anything was almost impossible. He stared dumbly at her then at the Jell-O fish on the table. Then back at her again. "Are you going to eat that rainbow fish all by yourself?"

"Jonah and I are going to eat it, but thanks for asking. *Sei gute*, Vernon. For sure and certain we'll see you at church."

"I won the fishing contest. I should get at least half that rainbow fish."

"Please go now, Vernon."

"I can take it home on a paper plate. Have you got a paper plate?"

"No paper plates."

He frowned. "Can I borrow a plate? I'll bring it back, washed and everything."

Martha Sue growled softly. She marched into the kitchen, taking the rainbow fish with her so Vernon wouldn't be tempted to taste it. She put the fish back in the fridge and pulled out one of Mammi's famous raisin bran muffins. She marched back to Vernon and handed him the muffin. "Here. This will keep you regular."

Vernon looked deeply disappointed as he took the muffin. He obviously didn't appreciate how well that muffin would clear him out. But he still didn't go. Martha Sue finally took both hands and shoved him out the door. She tried to do it nicely, but since he hadn't taken the sixty hints she'd already given him, she had to be a little forceful. He pried his gaze from the fridge, turned, and tromped down the steps. Thank Derr Herr Martha Sue hadn't made a pecan pie. She would have had to wrench Vernon out of the house with a crowbar. He stopped at the bottom of the steps and looked at her as if she'd betrayed him and his *mamm*. Maybe he was still thinking about that fish. Maybe he was thinking about muffins and regularity.

Martha Sue didn't want to find out. "The fish is not for you, Vernon. They sell little Jell-O cups at Lark's Country Store. Go buy a case." She was tempted to slam the door, but who knew what windows she might break in her anger? She shut the door calmly and rationally and with barely a sound. She went to the sink and got herself a glass of water and drank the whole thing before she heard Vernon's buggy go down the hill.

She looked out the window to make sure he was gone, bloomed into a smile, and pumped her fist in the air in a silent cheer. If she never saw Vernon Schmucker again, it would be too soon.

Martha Sue really looked at the clock. She needed to get the pizza in the oven soon. *Die kinner* would be back any minute.

Martha Sue jumped as the door flew open and Lily rushed into the room. Her head covering was missing, and strands of her golden hair floated around her head like an unruly halo. She was breathing heavily as if she'd run a long way, and her brows were pulled so tight on her forehead, they were almost touching. "Martha Sue, you need to come. Jonah is stuck."

Chapter 18

Martha Sue followed as Lily stormed down the path and into the woods. "I told him not to climb in there, but he thinks he's too smart to listen to a sixth grader, even though I'm almost in seventh grade and he's only eleven months older than I am."

Martha Sue felt a little silly, but she carried a crosscut saw because Lily said she was going to need one to cut Jonah out of the tree, even though Martha Sue doubted her ability to cut anything with a saw. Martha Sue walked fast to keep up with Lily, who seemed more angry than anything else. Surely Lily would be panicked if Jonah was in any real danger, wouldn't she?

Martha Sue's dread grew the farther they tramped into the woods. Where was Jonah, and if he was really stuck, how would she be able to help him? The path took them on a gentle downward slope toward the wild huckleberry patch. If they walked long enough and followed the stream, they'd make it down the hill to the pasture and farm that used to belong to Mammi's *dat*. "Are we close?" she said, stepping over a fallen log in the path.

Then she heard it. The cry of a wounded animal, long and high-pitched and wretched. But it wasn't an animal. It was Jonah, and he sounded terrified. Lily ran toward the sound, and Martha Sue followed her, her chest tightening with every breath she sucked in. They came to a small bend in the path, and Lily plunged into the bushes to her right. A branch scratched Martha Sue's cheek as she followed Lily, but she barely felt it. She had to get to Jonah.

They came to a narrow clearing surrounded by huge aspen trees and sumac bushes. Martha Sue caught her breath. It looked as if Jonah sat in the cleft of a tree about three feet in diameter with two main branches sticking out to either side of the trunk. His arms were wrapped around the left trunk, hugging it for dear life. Except he wasn't sitting on the fork of the trunk. His body was down inside it, sunk up to the waist as if the tree had swallowed his lower half. His hat was nowhere to be seen, and his hair looked like a bird had tried to make a nest in it. His face was shiny with tears, and angry red welts marred one side of his face, as if he'd dragged his cheek down the rough bark of the tree.

"Martha Sue, help me," he howled. "I'm sinking. I can't hold on."

Martha Sue dropped the saw and ran to Jonah. On her tiptoes, she grabbed onto his upper arm with both hands and squeezed tight. "I've got you," she said, but there was no way she would be able to hold his body weight if he sank farther into the tree.

"Help me. I'm going to die."

Martha Sue cupped one hand around the back of

Jonah's neck. "You're not going to die. I'm right here. I won't let you die."

Jonah looked into her eyes, and the fear she saw was so thick, she could have cut it with a knife. "I'm so sorry for what I did. Please don't let me die."

She planted a firm kiss on Jonah's cheek, even though he was almost in eighth grade. "I will not let you die. I don't care what you did. I *will not* leave you." She looked into his eyes. "Do you understand?"

He nodded, whimpering softly.

She pulled away slightly, still holding on to his arm. "Do you have a foothold, or are you dangling?"

"My right foot is on a piece of wood, but it slips off if I put much weight on it. My left foot is dangling. I'm going to fall deeper into the tree."

"I told him not to climb in there," Lily said.

"Maybe I can pull you out. If I get above you where this branch levels out, I might be able to hoist you up."

Jonah looked up. "I tried to pull myself out. I don't think you're strong enough. I'd be pretty much dead-weight."

Martha Sue had never wished for anything more than she wished for a rope right at this minute. "If we had a rope, we could do something like what we did with Vernon." She smiled, hoping Jonah would share in her joke.

His lips twitched. "Do you know how to tie any knots?"

"*Nae*, but you could show me."

"My *dat* always says you never know when you're going to need a clove hitch."

Jonah's *dat*. The thought of Yost stole Martha Sue's breath. "I could run back to the house and get a rope."

Jonah's breathing got shallow. "Don't leave me."

Martha Sue glanced behind her at Lily, who had her arms folded across her chest as if supervising the task of freeing Jonah from the tree. "Lily, could you go back to the house and find a rope?"

Lily nodded. "For sure and certain I could, if you tell me where it is."

Martha Sue pressed her lips together. Even with a rope, she might not be strong enough to pull Jonah out. It was a fifteen-minute walk to the house and another fifteen minutes back. Half an hour was a long time to wait for a rope that might not even help them. "Lily, I'm going to need you to be very brave."

Lily smirked as if Martha Sue had insulted her. "I'm always brave. You don't have to talk to me like I'm a baby."

At least Lily wasn't lacking in confidence. "Okay, then. I need you to go find help. Anna and Felty's nearest neighbors live in the redbrick house just down the other side of Huckleberry Hill. They moved in about a year ago."

"I know their house. It's the one with the mailbox that looks like a football helmet."

The Kirklands loved the Green Bay Packers, a football team that Martha Sue knew absolutely nothing about. "They're *Englischers* so they have a phone. Go ask them to call the police and the fire department."

"The police?" Jonah said, a tinge of panic in his voice. "Am I going to die?"

Lily frowned. "You're not going to die. Plenty of

people have to call the police. Like when they need to get their cat out of a tree."

Martha Sue tried to smile reassuringly. "That's right. You're like a big cat stuck in a tree."

Jonah frowned. "I'm definitely stuck."

"I don't think that's a *gute* idea," Lily said. "Going to the neighbors will take a long time. You should try pulling him out with a rope first."

Martha Sue eyed Jonah. "If you go get the rope, that will take fifteen minutes there and fifteen minutes back. And then it might not even work, especially since he seems to be wedged in there wonderful tight. If we can't get him out with the rope, we will have wasted a lot of time and you'll still have to go get help from the neighbors."

Lily tapped her finger to her chin. "I guess that makes sense. But if the rope works, it would save a lot of time."

"I don't think I'll be able to pull Jonah out." She turned to Jonah. "What do you think? This is your decision, because you're the one who's stuck."

Jonah was silent for a few seconds, his eyebrows slowly inching to the middle of his forehead. "Will the police get mad at me?"

"I can't imagine that they would."

Jonah caught his bottom lip between his teeth. "Lily should go get help. I think trying to pull me out with a rope will just be a waste of time."

Martha Sue pinned her gaze on Lily. "Can you be brave?"

This time, Lily groaned out loud. "I'll be in seventh

grade come September. If I haven't learned how to be brave by now, I never will."

"Okay then. Have the police meet you at the bottom of the hill, then you'll have to show them where we are. Can you do that?"

"Of course I can do that. Mamm says I've got a *gute* head on my shoulders."

"Go as fast as you can, but be careful. I don't want you to trip and hurt yourself."

Lily nodded gravely. "If I fall, Jonah will be stuck here forever."

That wasn't anywhere near likely, but at least Lily took her job seriously. "That's right. So be careful."

Lily took off through the bushes like a shot.

Martha Sue gave Jonah's arm a squeeze. "How blessed you are to have a friend like Lily."

"She's okay. She talks too much, and sometimes she gets bossy, but I like her. She's one of the best softball players."

"If I let go, can you hold on for a few minutes?"

"Don't leave me."

"I won't, but even though Lily went to get help, I think we can still try a few things to get you out of there."

"Like what?"

"Well, I'm not really a tree climber, but if I can brace myself on that branch above you, I can maybe pull you up and out."

"You can't," Jonah said. "I'm stuck pretty *gute*, and you're not strong enough."

"Both true, but it's worth a try."

"Okay. It's better than sinking into this tree."

Martha Sue took off her apron and draped it over a branch. "Not as *gute* as a rope, but it might come in handy." She found the biggest rock she'd be able to move. Grunting, she pushed it to the base of the tree. It gave her an extra foot of height, which wasn't much, but standing on it, she was able to hoist herself up on the branch behind Jonah. The bark snagged her stockings and scratched her legs, and she got a sliver in her finger, but she was able to stand up and step around the tree until she stood above Jonah on the branch he was holding on to. She lay down on her stomach so she was facing Jonah and then stretched out her arms. "If you grab my hands, maybe I can pull you up."

Jonah didn't look convinced, but he wrapped his hands around her wrists, and she did the same to him. "I will try to help you with my legs," he said, "but I think they're going to be useless. *Useless* means I can't even move them."

"Okay. One. Two. Three." Martha Sue pulled and strained with all her might. Jonah's face turned red, but she couldn't get enough leverage to even budge him.

"You have a scratch on your cheek," he said, after she'd let go of his hands and he'd wrapped them around the branch again.

"You have about five hundred scratches on your cheek."

He winced. "I know. My face slid down the branch with me. It slowed me down a little, but it sure stings."

"It looks like it hurts." Martha Sue reached out, grabbed her apron, and hung it over a smaller branch just over Jonah's head. "Can you reach both ends of that apron? Maybe you can hold on to it to pull yourself up while I also try to lift." Jonah wrapped his hands around both ends of the apron. Martha Sue grabbed Jonah's upper arms just below his armpits. "One, two, three," she said. She lifted with all her might, as bumps in the branch dug into her ribs and stomach.

Jonah pulled hard on the apron. There was a breathless moment when it felt like maybe he was moving, but then they heard a loud rip, and Martha Sue's apron tore in half and Jonah's arms fell, a piece of Martha Sue's apron in each hand. He grabbed on to the branch again to keep from slipping farther into the trunk.

Martha Sue groaned. "I wish I'd been wearing my canvas apron. It would have held."

Jonah panted for air. "We should have had Lily bring the rope. I think I could pull myself out with one."

"*Ach*, maybe."

A tear trickled down his cheek. "You shouldn't have let me make the decision. I'm too *dumm*."

Martha Sue took half of her apron and dabbed at his face. "Of course you're not. You do crossword puzzles. You know how to read a thesaurus. You play clever tricks."

"I dropped my thesaurus inside the trunk."

"We'll find it. Don't worry." She gave him a half smile. "When you use your brain to help people, you are one of the smartest boys I know. You made Dawdi that grabber so he doesn't have to bend down to pick things up. You're very smart. Don't worry about the rope. You made the decision I would have made. A rope might not have worked either. No use crying over spilled milk."

His lips curled upward. "That's what I told my *dat* about moving us up here—mostly because he said he felt guilty about it and was thinking of missing an entire summer of work to be with me."

"And you didn't want that?"

"*Nae*. He would have driven me crazy."

Martha Sue cracked a smile. "I think that was his plan."

Jonah's eyes went wide. "He was tricking me?"

"He thought you'd get tired of him and not mind if he spent more time with me."

Her honesty didn't seem to make him mad. "It would have worked." He lowered his eyes. "I was real upset the day Danny broke his leg." He glanced up at Martha Sue. "Don't tell Lily. She'll call me a baby."

"I won't tell anyone, but there's no shame in being upset or sad or lonely. Those are just feelings. Everybody has them, even Lily."

He sighed. "I ran most of the way home because I needed Dat. I knew he wouldn't call me a baby. But when I saw you and Dat kissing behind the barn, I thought you were trying to steal him from me. I got mad, and all I could think about was getting rid of you, once and for all."

"You saw us kissing?" Martha Sue was mortified. No wonder Jonah had played that laundry trick. "It's okay. You've already lost your *mamm*. You thought you were losing your *dat* too. And we shouldn't have been kissing."

"I was mad, but I understand." He leaned his head closer to her. "Sometimes I think about kissing . . . well . . . someone. It seems kind of fun."

Martha Sue's face got warm. "Very fun, but don't tell Mammi I said so. She'll be shocked."

Jonah lost his smile. "If I had really wanted my *dat* to stop giving me so much attention, I would have pretended I didn't see the kissing. Instead, I got angry and scared. I'm sorry about what I did."

"No more apologizing. I know you're sorry." She pushed herself up to a sitting position, braced herself on the branch, and jumped to the ground.

"Don't leave me," he squeaked, the panic back in his voice.

"I'm not leaving. I already said I won't leave you."

"I wouldn't blame you for leaving. I've been very bad."

"It doesn't matter how bad you've been." She pressed her lips together. "You say you got angry and scared when you saw me and your *dat* kissing. What were you scared of?"

"I don't know. I was just scared."

Mammi had accused Martha Sue of being scared. Was Jonah scared of the same thing Martha Sue was? Her heart beat faster as thoughts came crashing toward her. "Jonah, did you play all those tricks on me because you wanted me to leave? Or did you play all those tricks because you wanted to see if I'd stay?"

He frowned. "I don't know."

Martha Sue grabbed on to his upper arm again. The support she gave him wasn't much, but it was what Jonah needed. He needed to know she wouldn't leave him, not today, not tomorrow, not ever. For sure and certain, Jonah had played those tricks to test Martha Sue's courage and her love—to see if she had enough courage to love Jonah even when it felt impossible to love him. Whether he understood it or not, Jonah had been testing her, and she had failed miserably. She finally saw what Mammi was trying to tell her. Love took courage: courage to face inevitable sorrow, courage to endure the growing pains of starting a new family, courage to accept that getting close to another person might hurt, courage to give up your old life for something better.

A lump the size of a buggy lodged in Martha Sue's throat. Was she punishing Jonah? Was she punishing Yost? For what? Breaking her heart? She had pulled away from Jonah and Yost because she hadn't the courage to stay. No doubt it felt the same as a punishment to Jonah. Yost had never wanted anything but Martha Sue's happiness. Jonah had never wanted anything more than to be loved. He had put the strength of her love to the test, and she had failed. Was she punishing him for that? Jonah had already lost his *mater*. All the bad things he'd done to Martha Sue were out of fear. How could she condemn a scared little boy? His misbehavior was a sign he needed more love, not less.

Isn't there anything I can do to make you love me?

What had she done but let her fear keep her from loving Jonah the way she should have? Now Jonah was doing his best to be lovable, but no child, no person should ever have to prove his worth. Everyone was a child of Gotte. Everyone deserved love simply because Gotte loved everyone, no matter what they did. *Ach!* She had withheld her love, and now Jonah didn't think he deserved it, not even trusting her to stay by his side out here in the woods.

She closed her eyes for a second, took a deep, shuddering breath, and clasped Jonah's arm even tighter.

How could she have been so blind and so cruel? "I love you, Jonah."

She burst into tears, because suddenly, just like that, her words became true. She felt them all the way to her bones. They traveled through her veins. They echoed with every beat of her heart. She loved Jonah. She loved him with everything she had in her. She would do anything for this incorrigible, infuriating, devious boy, and she'd stand up to anyone who didn't believe her. Love always left a mark, sometimes a painful one, but what were scars but proof that you had actually lived?

New tears cascaded down Jonah's cheeks. "But you said you didn't like me."

Martha Sue sniffed and willed herself to stop crying. Jonah needed reassurance, not more distress. "I suppose I didn't really know what love looks like. Jesus loves you no matter what you do, and so do I." She rubbed her hand up and down on his arm. "Which means there's nothing you can do to get rid of me. I love you enough to stay."

To her surprise, he smiled. "I bet you love my *dat* more."

She put her thumb and index finger half an inch apart. "Maybe just a little."

Her pulse raced with new hopes and reclaimed happiness. Would Yost still want to marry her after how foolish she'd been? She would have to leave that in Gotte's hands.

Her arms were getting tired, and that couldn't have been anywhere near the discomfort that Jonah must have been feeling. How long had Lily been gone? It couldn't have been more than twenty minutes. She had to try something else, if only to keep Jonah's mind off being trapped. "What do you think? Should I try the saw?" She let go of Jonah and walked over to the place she'd left it.

Jonah bit down on his bottom lip. "Do you know how to use a saw? I don't want to get cut in half."

Martha Sue picked up the saw and showed it to Jonah. "I thought I could cut off the branch behind you first, then slice into the trunk lengthwise, like when you peel the frosting layer off a cake and leave the cake part inside. I'd cut the bark and leave your trousers intact."

"But what if you accidentally slice my leg?"

She shrugged. "You have an extra."

"Was that a joke?"

"*Jah*."

He made a face. "It wasn't very funny."

She giggled. "I thought it was." She eyed the branch. "At the very least, I should cut this branch. It's thick so it will take me a long time. Maybe they'll be here by the time I'm done. It will save them some time, maybe."

He thought about that for a minute then nodded. "Can you do it without cutting off your own hand?"

Martha Sue gave him a teasing smile. "Is that a joke?"

"*Nae*. You're *gute* with cakes, but I've never seen you use a saw. Maybe you're terrible."

Martha Sue dropped her jaw in mock indignation. "I'll have you know, I use my *dat*'s hedge trimmers all the time."

"Hedge trimmers? Those are for babies."

She mussed his hair, and he protested loudly, but it

was all for show. Hope and relief were written all over his face.

"I'm not nearly as strong as your *dat*, so the firemen might get here before I can cut through this, but it's better than waiting around doing nothing."

"*Jah*, Lily is a fast runner, but don't get her talking or she'll waste twenty minutes."

Martha Sue laughed. "Let's hope she chooses brevity."

Jonah shifted his arms farther around the branch. "'Brevity'? What does that mean?"

"It means not saying very much."

He snorted. "It would be the first time in her life."

Martha Sue picked a spot on the branch close to the trunk and started sawing. She was extra careful getting started because the back of Jonah's head was only a foot to her left. She made very slow progress. It was hard to saw something at eye level, and soon her arms screamed for her to stop. While she pushed and pulled the saw back and forth across the branch, she and Jonah played the letter game where one of them named a category and a letter and took turns trying to come up with something. Jonah was smart, and the game took his mind off being stuck in a tree.

After their fifth game where they traded names of foods that started with *F*, Martha Sue had to take a rest. "Just how did you get into this tree in the first place?"

"*Ach, vell*, we were looking for a secret hideout, and I thought this would be a *gute* place to hide. Lily told me not to try it, but I thought I'd be able to slip right into this rotted tree and slip right out."

"Oh, dear." Martha Sue started sawing again. "I would have done the same thing when I was a kid."

Jonah nodded. "You and I are a lot alike. We don't like water. We know lots of words, and we both love my *dat*."

Martha Sue's heart felt as if it was on fire, and she could barely speak. "For sure and certain." Yost was the best man she'd ever known. Jonah and Yost were her home. "I'm getting wood chips in your hair."

"My arms are falling asleep."

Martha Sue frowned. "Do you want me to quit cutting and come hold you up?"

"*Nae*. The faster you cut, the sooner I'll be out of here."

"*Denki* for your faith in my cutting abilities," Martha Sue said.

He turned his head and grinned at her. It was the most heartwarming look Martha Sue had ever seen. "I have faith in you."

Despite the pain, she cut faster. Finally the branch gave up. With a mighty crack, it split from the rotten trunk and tumbled to the ground. Martha Sue whooped in triumph, and Jonah smiled weakly. For sure and certain his strength was waning. Martha Sue studied the tree, knocking on the trunk to test its thickness. The saw would break before she got through all the layers of wood. "What would happen if you let go of the branch?"

"I'd sink into the tree."

"Maybe. Or maybe you're stuck so tight, you'd just stay where you are."

"But what if I sink? I'd be buried inside this tree. It would feel like being under water. I wouldn't be able to breathe."

Martha Sue shuddered. *Nae*, he couldn't do that. "We've got to prop you up then, because I don't want your arms to give out." She looked around and found a stick about the size and length of a cane. She laid it across the opening to one side of Jonah, wedging it into two jagged notches in the trunk. "Here, let go of the branch and rest your weight on this stick. That's right. With your armpits."

Jonah did as he was told and sighed. "That feels better."

She grimaced. "I'm afraid I can't cut you out. The trunk is too thick."

"It's okay. Lord willing, Lily is on her way . . . unless she's sitting in the *Englischers'* house eating cookies and visiting."

Suddenly, the sound of a very loud engine echoed through the trees. Martha Sue caught her breath. Someone was coming. She squealed in delight, grabbed Jonah's face in her hands, and kissed him on the forehead.

He growled. "Will you stop doing that? It's embarrassing."

She giggled at the look on his face. "Lord willing, that is the first of many more to come, young man. I love you. I plan on kissing you every night before bed."

He puckered like a sourpuss. "Save the kissing for my *dat*. He likes it."

A small ATV, like a motorcycle with four wheels, appeared, holding two riders. One was a firefighter or maybe a paramedic. The other was Lily, wearing a helmet about three times as big as her head. She sat behind the paramedic, clutching his thick coat as he barreled over the rocks and through the bushes. Lily sat up straight, said something to the paramedic, and pointed to Jonah, as if she thought she was in charge. She probably was. They wouldn't have been able to locate Jonah without Lily.

Lily jumped from the ATV, threw off her helmet, and ran into Martha Sue's arms. "I hurried real fast, and we didn't even have to walk. They parked their fire truck and trailer at the bottom of Huckleberry Hill, and we rode these special four-wheelers."

Another ATV carrying two more firefighters came into the small clearing. A black canvas bag sat on the back of the ATV. The men jumped off their vehicle and unzipped the bag. It was full of tools.

The paramedic who had been on Lily's ATV took off his helmet and marched straight to Jonah. "Are you Jonah?"

Jonah nodded.

"Well, I guess that's a dumb question since you're the only person I see stuck in a tree. My name is Drew. And that's Cooper and Calvin." Drew put his hand on top of the jagged trunk and tested its strength by giving it a firm tug. "It's pretty thick, but we're going to get you out of there as soon as we can. Okay, Jonah?"

Jonah nodded, quickly blinking back tears of relief.

Lily was obviously feeling sympathetic because she didn't even accuse Jonah of being a baby. "I had to show them the way. They said I was their best helper."

Drew said something into the walkie-talkie at his shoulder then looked at Jonah. "Are you injured? Does anything hurt or feel broken?"

"My stomach hurts," Jonah said. "And it feels like

there's a stick poking in my ribs. My shoe came off and fell into the tree. And my thesaurus. Can you get them?"

Drew gave Jonah then Martha Sue a reassuring smile. "Let's get you out first, then I'm pretty sure we'll be able to find your shoe and your dinosaur."

Jonah laughed. "No, it's a book. Not a dinosaur."

A look of mild confusion traveled across Drew's face. "Okay. First, I'm going to see how stuck you really are. Warn me if anything hurts." He slid his gloved hands underneath Jonah's armpits and gently tugged upward. Jonah didn't budge. "Hmm. I can see why you called us. Lily told us her best friend was in trouble, so we hurried extra fast. She showed us the way."

Lily beamed. "I got to ride on that four-wheeler and give him directions."

Martha Sue put her arm around Lily. "You did a wonderful *gute* job, Lily. *Denki.*"

"I told Jonah not to climb in there, but I couldn't just leave him, even if he was being *dumm.*"

Martha Sue wrapped her fingers around Jonah's arm as the three firefighters surrounded the tree and took the measure of the situation. "Miss, I'm going to need you to step away and give us some room," Drew said.

Martha Sue squeezed Jonah's arm. "I'll be right over here. If you need anything, just call my name. They're going to take *gute* care of you."

Jonah gave her a crooked, anxious grin. "At least they'll be faster with a saw."

"We're going to attach you to a harness," Drew said, "and try to pull you out. At the very least, it will hold you fast and give your arms a rest if we have to cut you out."

Jonah nodded. He was frightened, to be sure, but he had always loved figuring out how things work, and Martha Sue could see his eyes light up with curiosity.

Calvin, the shortest of the firefighters, grabbed a tangle of straps that looked like they were made of seat belt material. He and Drew worked to get Jonah fastened to the harness, but there wasn't even the tiniest of spaces to get the harness into the trunk and below Jonah's waist. "We're just going to secure this under your armpits for now."

"I'm going to get scabs under my arms," Jonah said.

The firemen attached another strap to the harness, draped it over a neighboring tree, and then connected it to three successive pulleys, more straps, and finally the ATV itself.

Drew grinned at Jonah. "Instead of towing a car out of the snow, we're pulling a boy out of a tree." He tested the strap around Jonah. "Okay, Jonah. We're going to pull the strap taut. Do you know what *taut* means?"

"It's going to get tight so I don't have to hold on so hard."

"Right. We've secured it so it won't squeeze too tight, but if you want to hold on to the strap above your head, that will probably be more comfortable. If at any time it feels too tight, yell or wave, and we'll loosen it."

Cooper, the firefighter with the wide grin, stood near the ATV. He pulled slightly on the strap, and all the straps between him and Jonah went tight.

Jonah got a huge grin on his face. "My arms were about to fall off."

Drew and Calvin studied Jonah and the tree and talked quietly between themselves.

Lily slipped her hand into Martha Sue's. "What do you think they are saying? Do you think they're giving up?"

Martha Sue stifled a smile. "They will never give up. Don't worry. They'll have Jonah out in no time."

Drew grabbed a thick tarp from the canvas bag. "Jonah, I think we can cut you out of there, but we want to make sure you're safe. I'm going to drape this tarp over your left side so you don't get hit by any wood chips or splinters."

Jonah looked a little less confident about that. "Do you have to cover my head?"

"We'll secure the tarp between you and us, so it will be more like a curtain than a blanket."

Still, he wouldn't be able to see what they were doing. Martha Sue stepped around to the other side of the tree and took Jonah's hand. "I'll stand here while they work." She motioned for Lily, who stepped gingerly around the firefighters to Martha Sue. "Lily, would you stand on the other side and tell me what they're doing so I can tell Jonah?"

Lily's eyes grew wide with her added responsibility. "Okay. I'll do my best."

Drew gave all of them, including Martha Sue, Lily, and Jonah, special glasses. "These will protect your eyes, in case."

Lily looked as if she might float off the ground when she put on her glasses. She was getting more and more important by the minute. She stood far to the side of the trunk so she had a view of what Drew and the others were doing but could also see Martha Sue. Lily gave Martha Sue the thumbs-up sign.

Martha Sue smiled at Jonah and smoothed his hair. "You're almost out."

"Just don't kiss me again."

"I guarantee that I'll kiss you at least one more time today."

He grimaced. "Don't do it."

"Okay," Lily said in her loud voice. "They've got a giant pair of scissors, and they're going to cut through the trunk. Well, I guess it's not a pair of scissors. It's some sort of cutting tool."

Jonah stiffened. "Tell them not to cut me."

Lily paused and drew her brows together. "You won't cut Jonah, will you?"

"We promise we won't," she heard Drew say. "We're just going to pull the trunk away."

Lily turned to Martha Sue. "They're just going to pull it away. Don't worry, Jonah. They promise they won't hurt you."

Jonah rolled his eyes. "*Jah.* I heard."

"They've got some special tools. Now the short one is pulling on the bark with some tweezers, but they're big tweezers."

Martha Sue heard Drew chuckle. "Calvin, you're the short one."

"I'm stronger than you and Cooper combined."

Lily kept talking, telling Martha Sue and Jonah what the firefighters were doing, but neither of them could really figure out what was going on behind the tarp because Lily didn't have the vocabulary to describe the tools or the work. But her calm, steady voice seemed to put Jonah at ease, and Martha Sue was *froh* Jonah had a friend who was bossy and talked too much.

Jonah gasped. "It's loose."

Lily clapped as the tarp came down, and Drew reached out with both hands and pulled Jonah out sideways. They had made a wide slit in the trunk, and getting him out was a matter of seconds. Drew carried Jonah to the ATV and set him down on the seat. It was a *gute* idea because Jonah was more than a little shaky.

Drew braced a hand on Jonah's shoulder. "You okay? How are you feeling?"

"Kind of weak, like maybe I won't be able to walk home."

A distant call echoed through the trees. "Jonah! Martha Sue!"

Martha Sue turned in the direction of the sound. "It's your *dat*, Jonah."

Lily nodded enthusiastically. "Mr. Kirkland said he'd go get your *dat* from the school, but he doesn't know where we are so he's just yelling people's names. I'll go find him." She took off through the bushes like a race-horse.

Cooper and Calvin took down the pulleys and straps while Drew checked Jonah for injuries. Once he was satisfied that Jonah wasn't seriously hurt, he gave him a bottle of water to drink. Cooper reached into the hollow trunk and pulled out Jonah's shoe and his thesaurus. Jonah looked almost as relieved at having his thesaurus back as he was about being out of that tree.

"This looks like a very important book," Drew said.

"It was my mother's," Jonah said, nearly losing his composure.

Lily came through the bushes holding Yost's hand and looking very pleased with herself. Martha Sue wanted to run into Yost's arms, but his first concern had to be for his son. He caught sight of Jonah, strode to the ATV, and knelt down on one knee. "Are you okay?" he said, wrapping his hands around Jonah's arms. "Mr. Kirkland said there was an accident, and I just about had a heart attack."

The "I'm about to cry" expression traveled across Jonah's face.

Martha Sue leaned over and gave him a huge, loud, smacking kiss on the cheek. "He's just fine. Aren't you, Jonah?"

Jonah made a gagging sound and swiped his hand across his cheek, but he didn't look like he wanted to cry anymore. He flashed her a grateful look. "She keeps doing that, Dat. Make her stop."

Surprise popped all over Yost's face, and he looked at Martha Sue with awe, as if she were a bright, shiny angel. He obviously sensed something was different, but she would have to explain things later. So much had happened in the last two hours that Martha Sue felt like a different person. Would Yost still want to marry her after all she'd put him through? *Ach*, how she ached for his love and regretted how selfishly she'd tossed it aside.

The firefighters stowed their gear while Jonah explained to his *dat* how he'd gotten in the tree and how he'd gotten out. Lily couldn't help but interject her opinion when she thought Jonah got the details wrong, and she couldn't help scolding Jonah again for climbing in that tree in the first place.

Yost listened to the whole story with rapt attention, occasionally glancing at Martha Sue when Lily or Jonah said her name. His looks couldn't have been more tender, which gave Martha Sue hope that maybe he'd already forgiven her.

Yost stood up and placed a hand on Lily's shoulder. "My son couldn't have a better friend. What would we have done if you hadn't led all of us here to help Jonah?"

Lily preened like a swan. "He's my best friend. I couldn't let him die."

Jonah took another swig of water. "For sure and certain you earned your dollar this week." Poor Jonah! That dollar had always been a sore spot with him.

Lily swatted Jonah on the arm. "*Ach*, Dawdi quit paying me weeks ago. He said he was paying me to do something I would have done anyway." She folded her arms. "I am your friend for free."

Jonah exploded into a smile. "Really?"

"*Jah*. I like you, even though you're *dumm* sometimes."

Jonah's face turned red. "You like me?"

Lily sighed. "We're best friends, aren't we?"

Drew finished putting his tools away, took off his gloves, and shook Yost's hand. "Are you Jonah's dad?"

"I am. Thank you for helping my son. I'm very grateful yet."

"We're always happy to help, and Jonah was very brave." Drew put his hand in his pocket and pulled out a green sucker. He handed it to Jonah. "Very brave."

Lily snatched the sucker away.

"Hey!" Jonah protested.

Lily held the sucker out of Jonah's reach. "You're too

old for suckers. Besides, I saved your life today, and I didn't get paid one dime, not even from my *dawdi*."

Jonah pressed his lips together and glared at Lily. "If I'm too old, you're too old."

"I am not. I'm in seventh grade almost. You're in eighth grade almost."

Drew laughed. "Well, I'd say an eighth-grade-almost boy deserves a sucker too." He pulled a red sucker out of the same pocket and handed it to Jonah. "You're never too old for a sucker."

Lily's mouth fell open, and she huffed out an indignant breath. "I want red."

Jonah tore open the sucker and popped it into his mouth before Lily had a chance to steal it.

Drew pointed to the tree, which looked like it had been through a very rough fight with a thunderstorm. Martha Sue had cut off the branch on the right, and the branch on the left leaned as if it might pull the trunk over with it. A tangle of smaller branches rose above the hollow trunk. "If I were you, I'd come out as soon as possible and cut that thing down. There are about ten ways to hurt yourself on that tree."

Yost nodded. "I'll bring a chain saw out here first thing in the morning."

Drew handed Lily's helmet to Jonah. "Put this on. We're going to give you a ride back to the house."

Lily's indignation grew more righteous. "That's *my* helmet. I want a ride."

Drew knelt down so he was roughly eye level with Lily. "We couldn't have done it without you, Lily, but look at Jonah. Do you think he should walk back?"

Lily's lips drooped into a frown. "I guess not. He

looks like he got in a fight. But why can't I ride too? There's room on the back for both of us."

"We don't want to risk you falling off," Drew said. "I know you're tired, but Jonah is your best friend. Right now, we should all be more concerned about him."

Lily scowled. "I told him not to climb in that tree."

Drew smiled at Jonah. "You should always listen to Lily. She's very smart."

Lily folded her arms smugly. "That's right. If you just do what I say, you'll be much better off."

Jonah looked too tired to argue, though Martha Sue could see the defiance flash in his eyes. He'd probably decided to argue about that another day.

Calvin and Cooper drove away first. Drew made sure Jonah was secure then followed his companions through the bushes and onto the overgrown path. Lily was still annoyed, so Martha Sue gave her a wink and took her hand. "You're going to have to lead the way. I have no idea how to get back to the house from here."

Lily seemed glad that she could be helpful again. "Okay. I don't want you to get lost. I'm *froh* Jonah and I have been exploring. We can find anything on this hill. Did you know there's a wild rose bush just down this way a little? It's about eight feet tall, and it's got thousands of little pink roses on it. That's where I want Jonah to ask me to marry him."

It was all Martha Sue could do to keep the surprised amusement from showing on her face. Lily might think Jonah was *dumm*, but apparently, she was also madly in love with him. Martha Sue looked back and grinned at Yost, who was quietly following them up the path. He smiled back at her and set her heart racing. How could a simple smile communicate that much love? *Ach*, maybe he still wanted to marry her. Maybe she should have Lily show her where the wild rose bush was so Yost could propose there.

Again.

And for the last time.

When they got to the house, the three firefighters were there waiting with Jonah, plus Mr. and Mrs. Kirkland, the *Englischers* who lived just down the hill from Mammi and Dawdi, Lily's parents, Uriah and Ruth Yoder, one of the ministers, the bishop, and the bishop's *fraa*. And surprisingly, Vernon Schmucker, who marched right up to Martha Sue.

Martha Sue eyed him suspiciously. "What are you doing here?"

Vernon did his best to smile. It was not a happy look. "I saw the fire truck at the bottom of the hill, and I was curious." He glanced behind him as if expecting someone to jump out of the bushes and attack him. "I'm glad Jonah is okay, but I have to be going now."

"Okay?" Martha Sue said, glad he wasn't planning to hang around and puzzled as to why he'd come up the hill again. She'd given him a firm send-off.

Jonah moved close to his *dat* and held on tight. Lily's *mamm* gave her *dochter* a big smile and an even bigger hug. The firefighters drove their ATVs down the hill, and Vernon followed close behind in his buggy. Together, Martha Sue and Jonah explained to everyone what had happened, with Lily correcting and adding facts as she saw fit. After all the fuss died down, everyone but Uriah, Ruth, and Lily went home. Lily's parents were pleased as punch that Lily had been such a *gute* helper. "She's always been my most sensible child," Ruth said.

Lily agreed. "It's because I don't cry, and I tell myself that everything is going to be okay. It saves a lot of stomachaches."

Martha Sue giggled. "*Jah*, it does."

Ruth wrapped her arm around Lily and tugged her close to her side. "We need to get home. I left Raymond to tend the soup, and I don't think that will go very well."

Martha Sue nodded. "Could Lily stay? I made pizza and a yummy surprise for dinner. We'd like her to be our special guest."

Ruth smiled. "That would be all right. At least Lily will get a *gute* dinner. Who knows what shape the soup will be in when we get back."

Martha Sue glanced at the sky. It was more than an hour past dinnertime, and she hadn't started the pizza yet. "We'll bring her home in the buggy so she doesn't have to walk in the dark."

Lily gave her *mamm* a hug, and Ruth and Uriah climbed into their buggy. Martha Sue, Yost, and *die kinner* stood close together and watched Lily's parents drive down the hill. A bright flash of light exploded in Martha Sue's head when Yost reached over and took her hand. Lily and Jonah had their backs turned and had no idea what was going on immediately behind them. Martha Sue met Yost's eye and caressed Yost's knuckle with her thumb. Lord willing, that told him everything he wanted to know.

Jonah must have had eyes in the back of his head. He

didn't even turn around. "Dat, you don't have to hold Martha Sue's hand in secret anymore."

Yost started in surprise, let go of Martha Sue's hand, and plastered an innocent expression on his face. "What are you talking about?"

Jonah cocked an eyebrow. Yost didn't fool him for one minute. "I don't mind if you hold Martha Sue's hand. She wants you to hold her hand. She wants to marry you."

Yost's eyes pooled with tears. "Is that true?"

Martha Sue felt her face get warm. "If you'll still have me."

Yost's eyes nearly popped out of his head. "If I'll still have you? What kind of insane thought is that? I'd marry you right now if the bishop were here."

"*Ach*," Lily said. "He just left. But I think he would have said *nae* because you have to invite lots of people and serve cake." She looked at Jonah. "I want pink cakes at my wedding."

Jonah obviously had no idea she was talking about his wedding too. "I want fireworks at my wedding. Big ones."

"I guess that would be okay," Lily said.

Yost slid his arms around Martha Sue and pulled her close, apparently not caring that the children were watching. "Will you marry me, Martha Sue?"

"Tell him," Jonah prodded.

The desire to have Yost propose to her next to the wild rose bush evaporated. She was so happy, she didn't care where he proposed, just that he did. Martha Sue snaked her arms around Yost's neck and kissed him on the mouth right in front of the children. There was no fear in her heart, only love. "I've never wanted anything more."

Lily jumped up and down and clapped. Jonah's smile was so wide, Martha Sue couldn't have peeled it off his face with a crowbar.

"Can I be a *newehocker*?" Lily asked.

Jonah smoothed his unruly hair out of his eyes. "You have to be older."

"I do not. My cousin Eva was an attendant when she was ten."

Martha Sue bent over to get closer to Lily. "I think you would make a wonderful *gute newehocker*."

Lily squealed and danced around Jonah as if she'd just beaten him in a race. Jonah stood with his arms folded, looking at Lily as if he was barely tolerating her. Martha Sue stifled a giggle. They made a *gute* couple.

"*Cum*," Martha Sue said. "Let's get that pizza in the oven."

"I'm so hungry, I could eat it all by myself," Jonah said.

Lily made a face. "That would be very rude." Thank Derr Herr Jonah had Lily. She would keep him on his toes, whether he wanted her to or not.

They walked up the porch steps. Yost opened the front door for Martha Sue and gave her an adoring smile. Martha Sue hadn't known she could be this happy. "I made you a surprise, Jonah."

"You did?"

"Vernon wanted to eat it, but I put my foot down."

"Do I need to be worried that you and Vernon are still seeing each other?" Yost asked with a teasing glint in his eye.

Martha Sue growled. "I told Vernon never to come here again, not even if Mammi invited him."

Yost laughed. "I was never worried about Vernon. I hoped your getting to know him would make you love me better."

Martha Sue's heart was so full, she could barely contain it. "I couldn't love you any better."

Yost kissed her, sorely testing Jonah's patience. "Okay, okay, Dat. We know you love Martha Sue. Please quit kissing her. I'm going to throw up."

Martha Sue preheated the oven then opened the fridge. "Look what I made for you, Jonah." Her heart lurched. Her beautiful fish-shaped Jell-O was gone! "Oh, no!"

Yost frowned. "What's the matter?"

In place of her Jell-O was a piece of notebook paper. Martha Sue took it out of the fridge. In scrawled, barely legible handwriting, it said, "You broke my heart. I deserve your fish. Vernon."

Martha Sue handed Yost the note, and they both laughed for a full minute.

Chapter 19

Martha Sue and Lily stood way back as Yost took the chain saw to the hollow tree. Jonah planted himself next to his *dat* with a pair of protective goggles over his eyes, but he wasn't really doing much more than watching Yost work on the tree. Martha Sue smiled to herself. Jonah wanted to feel important and needed. Yost had always been sensitive to that, even if Jonah wasn't of much help.

Lily leaned over and yelled in Martha Sue's ear, "He looks handsome in glasses, don't you think?"

Martha Sue smiled and nodded. Lily was talking about Jonah, but Martha Sue only had eyes for Yost. He was the kindest, handsomest man that ever was. And she was the happiest woman in the world.

Yost cut the remaining branches off first, and Martha Sue and Lily dragged them away from the base of the tree so Yost would have room to work on the trunk. Lily dragged a small branch out of the way into the thick undergrowth and looked down. "I found Jonah's hat!" She bent over and picked it up then held it high over her head and waved it around like a flag.

"How did it get over there?" Jonah said.

Lily grinned sheepishly and handed it to Jonah. "I might have kicked it out of the way when I ran for help."

Jonah laughed. "That's okay. You saved my life. And in the end, you found my hat."

Lily nodded. "That's right. Remember that the next time you want to do something stupid. You'll always be safer if you just listen to me and do what I say."

Jonah rolled his eyes. "You're so bossy."

"I am not. I'm smart and sensible. There's a difference."

Yost ended up taking down the trunk in sections. The wood was wonderful hard in some places, butter soft in others. Martha Sue, Jonah, and Lily stacked wood while Yost meticulously attacked the tree. Once the trunk was reduced to a stump, Yost cut what branches he could with the chain saw, and the others stacked them in the wheelbarrow from Dawdi's shed. Yost took off his hat and swiped his arm across his forehead. Sweat trickled down his neck and dripped off his hair. Martha Sue handed him a water bottle. "Drink. You don't want to get heat exhaustion."

Jonah smoothed his hand along the jagged stump of the old tree. "I'm sorry we had to cut you down, but we didn't want you swallowing any more people."

"Careful," Lily scolded. "You'll get slivers."

Before she'd even finished saying it, Jonah hissed and drew back his hand. He grimaced and studied his middle finger. "Ouch."

Lily sighed. "I told you so."

If only Jonah would listen to Lily more often.

Martha Sue held out her hand and motioned for Jonah. "Let me see."

Jonah gave Lily an arch look and stepped closer to Martha Sue. Martha Sue examined his finger. "We'll have to go back and get some tweezers. It's deep, and there's nothing sticking out I can grab on to."

Lily came closer. "Let me try."

Martha Sue couldn't keep her lips from curling upward. Lily was not lacking in confidence.

Jonah made a face. "If Martha Sue can't get it, you can't get it."

Lily took Jonah's hand in hers, drew her brows together, and poked at the skin around the sliver. Jonah pretended it didn't hurt, but Martha Sue could tell it was a little tender. "What do you think, Lily?" she said.

"Does Anna have a *gute* pair of tweezers? It's in there deep."

Under no circumstances would Martha Sue smile. "I think she does."

Jonah pulled his hand away. "I knew you wouldn't be able to get it."

Lily gave him the stink eye. "Just remember who saved your life."

Yost pushed the wheelbarrow up the path, but he obviously didn't go fast enough for Lily and Jonah. They ran ahead and were soon out of sight among the trees. Yost stopped walking, put the wheelbarrow down, and winked at Martha Sue. "I thought they'd never leave." He snaked his arms around her waist and pulled her close.

"You know, we might be old, but we can still get in trouble with the bishop."

"Our bishop is in Ohio. He has no idea. Anna and Felty's bishop doesn't even know my name."

"Of course he knows your name," Martha Sue said. "Vernon told him you're trying to steal his girlfriend."

Yost raised his eyebrows. "He did not."

"*Ach*, yes he did. But this was weeks ago, and Mammi told the bishop to mind his own business."

Yost's chin practically scraped the ground. "Your *mammi* told the bishop to mind his own business?"

Martha Sue giggled. "She's just a sweet old lady. What's the bishop going to do?"

Yost chuckled. "Mind his own business, I guess."

"At the time, she was still trying to get me to marry Vernon. She didn't want the bishop to ruin it."

"*Ach*, *vell*, somebody ruined it for Vernon. Whoever it was, I'm grateful." He pulled Martha Sue closer. "Why are we talking about the bishop when we should be kissing?"

"Because as much as I love you, I don't want to get in trouble with the bishop or Mammi or Jonah."

He slumped his shoulders in mock dejection. "So many ways to get in trouble. If you kiss me one more time, I will behave myself for at least an hour. How does that sound?"

"*Gute* enough. But hurry. *Die kinner* will get suspicious and come looking for us."

Yost smiled playfully and brought his lips down on hers in an unhurried, supremely gentle kiss that took her breath away and made her forget all about the bishop. It was hard to even remember her own name.

He pulled away, cleared his throat, and grabbed the wheelbarrow handles. "I probably better not do that again until we're married." Without another word, he took off down the path pushing the wheelbarrow at a dizzying speed. Martha Sue had to jog to keep up with him.

Jonah and Lily were sitting on the porch steps as Martha Sue and Yost came out of the woods. "What took you so long?" Jonah said, smiling as if he already knew the answer.

A car drove up the road with Mammi and Dawdi in the back seat. Mammi waved to Martha Sue as if she'd been gone for weeks instead of days. The car stopped in front of the house, Mammi and Dawdi got out, and Yost grabbed their suitcase from the trunk. The *Englisch* driver drove away, calling her goodbye to Mammi and Dawdi as she left.

Mammi hugged Martha Sue. "*Ach, du lieva*, we have so much to tell you."

"I have so much to tell you."

Jonah and Lily raced down the steps and into Dawdi's arms. "I saved Jonah's life," Lily said.

Jonah nodded. "I almost died."

Dawdi was sufficiently impressed. "Well, then, I must hear about this adventure."

Jonah looped his elbow around Dawdi's arm. "We were exploring the . . ."

Lily, it seemed, was determined to break the news first. "Jonah got stuck in the trunk of an old, rotten tree, and I got Martha Sue, and then I went and got the firemen, and they had to cut Jonah out of the tree. And Vernon stole our fish."

Mammi frowned. "I told him to come over and apologize. Did he not come over?"

Martha Sue took a deep breath and reminded herself that Vernon's last visit had been mostly a *gute* thing. "Not *that* fish, Mammi. I made fish-shaped Jell-O for Jonah yesterday, and Vernon stole it from the fridge."

Mammi's frown etched itself more deeply into her face. "I suppose you told him no when he proposed?"

"Mammi! You knew he was going to propose?"

Mammi shrugged, as if Vernon was not her responsibility anymore. "I thought it was worth one more try. I'm sorry to hear he took your fish. What flavor was it?"

Dawdi put his arm around Jonah. "So you almost died, and the firemen saved you."

"*Jah*," Jonah said.

"And they let us both ride on their four-wheeler, but I got to ride longer. Drew gave me a sucker."

"He gave me a sucker too," Jonah said with a hint of irritation in his voice. Was he annoyed that Lily had interrupted him again or annoyed that she had taken his sucker?

Mammi clapped her hands. "I'm *froh* you both got suckers. And I'm *froh* that Jonah did not die. You've had a very exciting few days."

"Very exciting," Lily said. "Did you know Jonah wants fireworks at his wedding?"

"Everybody should have fireworks at their wedding." Mammi's eyes twinkled. "Speaking of fireworks, today is about to get more exciting. I have a surprise."

"What surprise?" Lily said, looking at Mammi eagerly. Lily didn't know that Mammi's surprises were things like Vernon Schmucker and cheesy jalapeno banana bread.

"*Vell*, I had a feeling that Martha Sue would tell

Vernon no, so I found her another man. From Greenwood. He'll be here any minute." She furrowed her brow. "*Ach*, *vell*, *they* will be here any minute."

Martha Sue's heart did a somersault. "*Ach*, *nae*, Mammi, what have you done?"

"Well, I didn't know if you would prefer the *fater* or the son, so I invited them both."

A wave of nausea roiled through Martha Sue's stomach. "A *fater* and a son?"

"Gary is fifty, and Simeon is twenty-eight. I think they're both within your age range."

Martha Sue thought she might suffocate. "How did you talk them into coming all this way?"

Mammi looked surprised. "That was easy. I told them I have a beautiful granddaughter who is a wonderful *gute* cook and very light on her feet. I also gave each of them one of my knitted pot holders. My pot holders are guaranteed to make people fall in love."

Yost came to Martha Sue's rescue. "*Ach*, *vell*, Anna, I hate to disappoint Gary and Simeon, but Martha Sue is already engaged."

The look of confusion on Mammi's face was almost worth all the aggravation. "But I thought you told Vernon *nae*."

Yost laughed. It was a hearty, joyful, carefree sound. "*Ach*, Anna. Martha Sue has agreed to marry me. We are going to be married in September or earlier if we can hurry things along with the bishop."

Mammi was struck completely speechless, but her eyes twinkled as if this was what she had planned all along. Dawdi smiled, stepped forward, and shook Yost's hand. "Congratulations! I had a *gute* feeling about you two from the beginning."

"Even though Jonah almost ruined it," Lily said.

Dawdi tapped the brim of Jonah's hat. "I knew Jonah wasn't going to ruin it, but I was a little worried after the broken wrist."

"I wasn't worried at all," Mammi said. "I gave Yost the first pot holder. Their love was bound to happen." She smiled at Martha Sue, affection shining in her eyes. "Are you happy, my dear?"

Martha Sue's heart pounded. "Wildly happy, Mammi. Wildly happy."

Mammi's eyes sparkled. "I can't ask Gotte for anything more than that."

Jonah took Mammi's hand. "Dat is going to sell the farm in Ohio and buy one up here. He wants to raise soybeans and cows."

Mammi's eyes widened. "You're moving up here?"

Yost nodded. "I can work for Moses while raising a small herd of dairy cows. Martha Sue loves it here, and Jonah doesn't want to move."

"It's because his best friend lives here." Lily was already certain that Jonah's staying had been all her doing.

Mammi bloomed into a wide smile. "*Vell*, that is the best news I've heard since Christmas."

Yost turned to Dawdi. "It wonders me if we can stay in your barn until I sell our farm and buy a house here."

"You're welcome to stay as long as you want yet."

A white van lumbered up the hill. Mammi's brows inched closer together, and she nibbled on her bottom lip. "*Ach*, Simeon and Gary are going to be so disappointed."

Martha Sue had never been so happy to disappoint someone in her life. "I've made a green salad, a pasta salad, and a Jell-O salad." She narrowed her eyes in Mammi's direction. "As long as they are fully aware that I am getting married to Yost, they are welcome to stay for dinner."

Mammi gave Martha Sue that innocent look she'd seen dozens of times. "Of course, dear. I don't know why you're looking at me like that."

Gary, a thin, young-looking fifty-year-old, and Simeon, a younger version of Gary, stepped out of the van. They each grabbed a duffel bag out of the back, and the van drove away. Gary and Simeon greeted Mammi, shook hands with Dawdi, then stood awkwardly looking at Martha Sue and Yost. They *should* feel awkward, especially because Mammi had convinced two grown men to come to Bonduel to vie for the same woman. It was nauseatingly awkward.

Mammi smiled sweetly at Gary. "I have *gute* news and bad news." She motioned to Martha Sue. "My granddaughter recently got engaged to this nice young man."

Gary smiled wide and shook Yost's hand. "Congratulations. I'm happy for both of you."

Martha Sue wouldn't let herself be fooled by a genuine smile and good-natured handshake. If dealing with Vernon had taught her anything, it was that she had to be blunt or risk weeks of torment. "Just to be clear," she said. "I'm not going to marry either of you. I'm engaged to Yost."

Gary's smile faltered, and he eyed Martha Sue as if she might be a little crazy in the head. "Uh, okay."

Mammi suddenly seemed in a great hurry to get into the house. "*Cum*, Gary, Simeon, you must be thirsty after your trip."

"Wait a minute," Martha Sue said. She stepped right in front of Mammi, blocking her path to the house. She pointed at Gary. "Why did you come to Bonduel?"

Gary's concern for Martha Sue's sanity seemed to increase. "Anna invited us to stay here so we could do some fishing on Shawano Lake." His gaze flicked in Mammi's direction. "I hope that's okay."

Mammi gave Gary her best, fakest smile. "Of course that's okay. I thought you might like to set up a tent in the side yard. Lots of shade there."

Martha Sue felt her face get so warm it was practically on fire. "So, you didn't come all this way to meet me?"

Gary took a step backward, as if to put a little distance between himself and the crazy woman. "Um, we came to fish, but it was nice to meet you."

Mammi had brought them all this way to meet Martha Sue, but that was not why Gary and Simeon had actually come. Martha Sue wanted to find a hollow tree trunk and crawl inside.

Gary obviously wasn't the type who liked long, drawn-out silences. "Um, do you like to fish?"

Martha Sue glanced at Yost, who looked as if he would burst into laughter at any minute. "I hate to fish. Absolutely despise it."

Yost chuckled. "She's had a few bad experiences."

Gary took another step away from Martha Sue. "I'm sorry to hear that."

Too late, Martha Sue tried to seem like a normal person. "I hope you have a *wunderbarr* time fishing."

Gary seemed eager to get into the house. He leaned his whole body in that direction. "I'm sure we will."

An open-air buggy trundled up the hill, and Martha Sue groaned out loud wondering just how Vernon Schmucker had the nerve to show his face on Huckleberry Hill again. He stopped in front of the house, grabbed something silver from his buggy, and made a beeline for Martha Sue, who didn't know whether to charge at Vernon and scare him away or run for the woods where he wouldn't be able to catch her.

It took her a few seconds to realize that he was carrying the Jell-O fish mold in his hand. Sheer curiosity rooted her feet to the ground. He half floated, half tiptoed to where Martha Sue was standing. His eyes seemed sort of misty, and his lips were puckered into an amorous smile. He showed her the fish mold as if she hadn't seen it before. "Martha Sue," he panted, "this. Was. Delicious. The best thing I've ever tasted."

Martha Sue lifted her chin and glanced at Jonah, who was staring at Vernon with a mixture of curiosity and utter surprise on his face. "You stole that from my fridge," she said.

Vernon got down on one knee, set the mold on the ground, and took Martha Sue's hand in both of his. She hadn't thought he was capable of moving so fast.

"Vernon," Yost said. There was a warning in his voice but also a hint of amusement that made Martha Sue want to kiss the smug smile right off his face.

Vernon was not distracted. He gazed at Martha Sue as if she was the biggest largemouth bass in the world. "If you make me one of these Jell-O fish every day, I'll take you back. I'll forgive you for everything. We can be married as soon as the bishop gives permission."

Gary's gaze flitted from Martha Sue to Vernon to Yost. He paused for half a breath then turned and sprinted into the house.

Chapter 20

The September morning was cool but not chilly, with plenty of sunshine and blue sky. A perfect day for a wedding. Even the leaves on the trees seemed to be celebrating Martha Sue and Yost's special day. They were just starting to turn brilliant red.

Anna glanced out the window where several grandsons were setting up the large tent on the gravel right in front of the house. "Felty, isn't it *wunderbarr*? Our sixth wedding on Huckleberry Hill."

"Five *dochters* and Martha Sue. At least we should be pretty *gute* at it by now," Felty said.

"It's nice to have something to show for all the work we did getting Martha Sue and Yost together."

"A wedding and a broken wrist, Annie-banannie. We've got a lot to show for all our work. That's why I think we should take a break from matchmaking for a few years. Who knows what you or I will injure next?"

"Take a break? Felty, what are you thinking? I would never abandon our grandchildren like that." She pointed out the window to their grandson Nebo, who was helping to set up the tent. "Just look at poor Bo out there.

You can tell by his expression that he's wonderful lonely. He needs a *fraa*."

Felty squinted in Bo's direction. "He looks fine to me."

"That's because you're not as observant as I am, Felty dear. Bo puts on a happy face, but he's crying on the inside. You know, a life of quiet desperation and all that."

"I don't think so, Annie girl. Let's just stay out of it for once."

Anna refused to be that uncaring about Bo's future happiness, but it was Martha Sue's wedding day, and Anna wasn't going to be cross with Felty. He had been a great help in getting Martha Sue and Yost together, and Anna was always able to persuade him in the end.

Their *dochter* Frannie motioned to Felty. "Dat, can you make room in the fridge for Esther's Jell-O. I'm afraid we've run out of room."

Relatives and friends bustled around the kitchen, putting the finishing touches on the stuffing and the potatoes, slicing bread, and cutting vegetables onto plates. There was barely enough room for anyone to move, and barely enough quiet for Anna to hear herself think. She knew enough to sneak over to the stove and sprinkle a few raisins in the creamed celery while Frannie's back was turned.

Felty, bless his heart, tried his best to make room in the fridge for Esther's salad. Esther had dropped it off just a few minutes ago, and it was spectacular. Word had spread that the bride and groom liked Jell-O, and four of Anna's *dochters* had volunteered to make a Jell-O salad for the wedding dinner. Esther's Jell-O salad consisted of twelve thin layers of gelatin in a round, fluted mold. Diana's Jell-O was shaped like a star with blueberries and strawberries on top. Abigail's was a more traditional salad with bananas and whipped cream, and Frannie had topped her Jell-O with peach slices.

There were so many sweet, elegant Jell-O dishes, they didn't even need cake. But it was too late because Martha Sue, Mandy, and their *mamm*, Clara, had made and decorated fourteen cakes just yesterday. Martha Sue couldn't choose just one cake or one kind of decoration, so they'd made six different flavors with four different colors of icing. There was even a fish-shaped cake especially for Jonah.

Felty did his best with the Jell-O, but when he tried to close the fridge, it wouldn't shut. He glanced at Anna. "The fridge won't fit one more thing."

"What are we going to do? We don't want the Jell-O to melt before dinner."

Felty motioned for Lily. Lily, very eager to be helpful, set down the napkin she'd been folding and ran to Felty's side. "What do you need, Felty? Do you want me to give someone instructions? I'm wonderful *gute* at giving instructions."

"*Nae*," Felty said. "I want you to stand right here with your back against the fridge and hold the door closed."

Lily's smiled faded. "Forever?"

"Not forever. Just until I get back."

Lily scrunched her lips together. "How long will that be? I don't want to miss the wedding."

Felty was already halfway out the door. "Soon."

Lily frowned, folded her arms, and leaned against the fridge. "I can't wait very long for him. I've got to finish folding the napkins. Besides, I'm one of Martha Sue's *newehockers*, and they can't start the wedding without me."

Lily took her job as *newehocker* very seriously. She'd helped Martha Sue embroider flowers on five handkerchiefs for the attendants, insisted on choosing the cake flavors, and drew a "floor plan" of the tent for the wedding luncheon, which she gave to Martha Sue's *mater*, Clara. This morning, she had marched into the house and insisted that she would take charge of folding all the napkins, because the bride and groom deserved heart-shaped napkins at their wedding. Lily was a girl after Anna's own heart. Any job worth doing was worth doing well, whether in matchmaking or *newehocker*-ing. But Clara didn't share Anna's opinion. She gritted her teeth whenever she saw Lily coming and secretly made a floor plan of her own without consulting Lily.

Poor Clara didn't know that Lily was planning on marrying Clara's future step-grandson-in-law in about ten years—with fireworks. Maybe Anna wouldn't tell her until after the wedding.

To Lily's relief, Felty was soon back with a bungee cord, which he wrapped around the fridge door handle and hooked to the drawer pull on the drawer next to the fridge.

He patted Lily on the shoulder. "*Denki* for helping me out, Lily. You've saved the Jell-O."

Lily nodded. "I really don't know what you and Anna would do without me."

Deciding to check on the bride, Anna strolled down the hall to her bedroom where Mandy and Clara were helping Martha Sue get ready. Martha Sue turned when

Anna walked into the room. "*Ach*, Mammi, look at this beautiful apron Mamm sewed for me."

Clara beamed while Anna examined the stitches on Martha Sue's white wedding apron. "This is truly *wunderbarr*, Clara," Anna said. "You were always so *gute* with a sewing machine."

Clara's smile got even wider. "*Ach*, Anna, no better than anyone else." She smoothed her hand down Martha Sue's sleeve. "Martha Sue was just telling us about how Vernon Schmucker stole her fish-shaped Jell-O."

Martha Sue giggled. "It's why I wanted to serve Jell-O at my wedding. Jonah loves it, and I wanted him to know that there would always be plenty of Jell-O and love to go around."

"I know he appreciates it," Anna said. She held her tongue about the fridge problem. No bride should have to worry about fridge space on her wedding day. "Are you *froh* to finally be getting married?"

"*Jah*, it's definitely past time."

"Are you happy, my dear?"

Martha Sue's eyes pooled with tears. "*Ach*, Mammi. No one has ever been happier or more in love than I am right now. Yost is everything I ever wanted. Gotte is so *gute*." Felty definitely needed to see Martha Sue's expression at this very moment. He would never question Anna's judgment again. Martha Sue took both of Anna's hands. "If you hadn't been so persistent in getting Yost and me together, I don't think it ever would have happened. You even broke your wrist."

Anna lifted her hand and turned her arm so Martha Sue could get a *gute* look. "*Ach*, no permanent harm done, and it was all for the greater good."

Martha Sue pulled Anna in for a hug, even though she risked getting wrinkles in her beautiful new apron. "*Denki*, Mammi. This is the best day ever."

Now that Martha Sue was happily matched, it was time to move on to the next grandchild, whether Anna had Felty's approval or not. "Martha Sue, I am a little worried about your cousin Nebo."

Martha Sue furrowed her brow. "What's wrong?"

"Nothing is wrong except that he is a very lonely boy, and he needs my help finding a *fraa*. Have you coupled him up with someone for the wedding?"

Martha Sue's smile was sympathetic. "It's already been taken care of. Bo asked me to couple him up with one of the Coblenz twins. Ruth. She's a sweet girl, don't you think? No need to worry, Mammi. Bo is well on his way to finding a *gute fraa*."

Anna pressed her lips together. Martha Sue had been trying to do the right thing, but Bo's situation had now become dire. He had chosen the wrong twin.

Recipe

Martha Sue's Ten-Layer Gelatin Fish

6¼ cups boiling water, divided
5 3-ounce packages Jell-O gelatin,
    any 5 different colors/flavors
15 tablespoons sour cream

Spray fish mold with nonstick cooking spray.

Pour 1¼ cups boiling water into 1 pkg. gelatin in small bowl and stir for about 2 minutes until completely dissolved. Pour ¾ cup of the dissolved gelatin into 8-cup fish mold sprayed with cooking spray. Refrigerate about 15 minutes or until set but not firm. Refrigerate remaining gelatin in bowl for 5 minutes until slightly thickened. Gradually stir in 3 tablespoons of sour cream. Spoon sour cream mixture over gelatin in mold. Refrigerate about 15 minutes or until gelatin is set but not firm.

Repeat process with each remaining gelatin flavor. (Be sure to cool dissolved gelatin to room temperature before pouring into mold.) Refrigerate gelatin as directed to create a total of 10 alternating clear and creamy gelatin layers.

Refrigerate 2 hours or until firm. Unmold. Cut into 16 slices to serve. Store leftover gelatin in refrigerator.

Visit our website at
KensingtonBooks.com
to sign up for our newsletters, read
more from your favorite authors, see
books by series, view reading group
guides, and more!

Become a Part of Our
Between the Chapters Book Club
Community and Join the Conversation

Betweenthechapters.net

Submit your book review for a chance to win exclusive
Between the Chapters swag you can't get anywhere else!
https://www.kensingtonbooks.com/pages/review/